THE EMMA WILD MYSTERIES

Books 1-4

HARPER LIN

CONTENTS

BOOK 1: KILLER CHRISTMAS

BOOK 2: NEW YEAR'S SLAY

BOOK 3: DEATH OF A SNOWMAN

BOOK 4: VALENTINE'S VICTIM

BOOK 1: KILLER CHRISTMAS

CHAPTER 1

$\mathcal{I}$'ve had people faint in my presence before, but never had one to drop dead at my feet —literally. The girl I was chatting with at the cafe suddenly began to choke and shake. Her drink slipped from her hand and she collapsed onto the floor. Her body convulsed and her eyes rolled to the back of her head. The spilt hot chocolate made it look as if she were lying in a pool of brown blood.

I knew the drink had been poisoned. I knew it in my gut when I bent down to inspect her body and the drink on the floor. And I also knew that I was somehow responsible for what happened. She died because of me. But I didn't admit any of this to myself until later.

At the time, however, I only thought that perhaps it was a good idea to stay away from hot chocolate.

Maybe I should start at the beginning. Or should I say the end? A story can begin with heartbreak or end with one, but I was sure not willing to let both happen.

In my instance, the story began with heartbreak and I was not willing to let it end until a happy ending was reached.

My name is Emma Wild. Yup, that Emma Wild. The crooner with the two Grammy award-winning albums. Jazz, blue-eyed soul, alternative and main-stream pop are some of the ways they would try to categorize my music.

How would I categorize myself? An incurable romantic. And a singer.

I wasn't always that girl on MTV singing about heartbreak in a husky alto voice choked full of tears. I didn't always wear body-hugging dresses and my red hair in glamorous waves styled over one eye. I grew up in Hartfield, Ontario, a town about an hour and a half from Toronto. It was a charming town and my family still lived there, but at eighteen years old, I tailed on out of there, forgoing college to pursue my singing career. For two years, I busted my ass singing at every open mic in New York City. I knocked on every door and pushed demo tapes into the hands of anyone who was connected to anyone until finally somebody gave me a chance. Then it became a blur from there.

My record company was behind me every step of the way—at least in the looks department. I was a control freak in the studio, so I let them play with my hair and makeup and put me in designer clothes and on the cover of magazines while I picked which producers, musicians and video directors I wanted to work with.

Along with all that came the world tours—Paris, Tokyo, Melbourne, you name it. TV appearances, award shows, press conferences, and movie premieres consumed my years. A "thank you" and a smile here, a funny quip there, a twirl to show off who I was wearing—I could do all that stuff in my sleep. Literally. Sometimes I was so tired from all the work and travel that I would give an interview while I was half asleep. Still, I had fun with it; playing the fame game came pretty easily to me because I didn't take it seriously.

The only thing I took seriously was my work, the music. I'd been writing my own songs since I learned how to write my name. In high school, I played clarinet in the school band...nerd alert. I sang at every event where somebody allowed me to take hold of a mic. I'd even go to poetry slams and sing with a guitar instead.

During my childhood and teen years in Hartfield,

every winter I'd sing at the Christmas concert at the town square, and every summer I'd sing at the food festival. Then there was everything in between: talent shows, private parties, baseball games. Whoever needed a singer would only need to speed dial my mom.

So it didn't surprise my friends and family that I would make it big with all the ambition and the steely determination that I possessed. Due to my busy schedule, their relationship with me was pretty one-sided most of the time. Sure, I called them whenever I could, and I would fly them into New York, where I lived, but on a day-to-day basis they learned about what was happening in my life through the tabloids. Especially in recent years when I started dating someone more famous than I was.

In general, my private life was pretty tame up until I met him. All I did was work. I'd ignore all the stories in the papers, magazines and blogs written about me to keep my sanity and self-esteem intact.

After dating a few industry types, I'd sworn celebrities off, bored with their massive egos and self-entitlement. Then along came Nicolas Doyle. Yes, that Nick Doyle. The movie star who had a bad habit of dating supermodels until he met me. Me, a five foot two redhead with pale skin and freckles—a little ball of fire, as the journalists would sometimes call me. I didn't think I was his type; I wasn't under contract with Victoria's Secret as one of their Angels. But once Nick has his eyes set on something, or someone, he usually got what he wanted.

Soon I started showing up at his movie premieres, separately. We tried our best to keep our private lives private, but it didn't take long for the tabloids to put two and two together, and soon I was being photographed in my sweatpants during my daily morning runs in Central Park.

When I first ran into him at the Vanity Fair party, I was joking around with a bunch of joke writers. They were a pretty funny pack. They kept teasing me for how bad my jokes were and kept trying to make even worse jokes to one-up me. Nick joined in, seemingly out of nowhere, with an extra glass of champagne and a witty remark of his own (something about horse butts—don't ask), and I downed the glass to keep myself from shaking.

Back then, he wasn't Nick. He was the Nicolas Doyle that the public knew. The piercing blue eyes that burned through movie screens, the mischievous grin, the raw talent that allowed him to disappear into any role—I'd grown up with him from baby-faced TV star to strong-jawed leading man.

I was totally starstruck at first, but I fell in love with him after I knew him. I loved that he got involved with all sorts of causes. All the charity work that he did during his time off was not a publicity act,

I came to find out. It was what made him irresistible. Underneath all the Hollywood hoopla, he was a caring guy. When he had passion for something, he threw everything into it, whether it was acting, saving extinct pandas, or brightening up the lives of children born with cleft palates. So when he didn't want to get married after four years of being together, I knew that something was wrong.

When a guy could take or leave you, it wasn't a good sign. I'd been down that road before, got the T-shirt and didn't want to go back there again. It was in my best interest to move on, even if it was the hardest thing I had to do—maybe the second hardest.

I packed all my stuff from his New York penthouse and stayed holed up for a week in a hotel, churning out song after song on this little hotel notepad. I couldn't think about finding another apartment yet, but I knew I had to eventually. I didn't know if I even wanted to stay in the city, where I'd be constantly paranoid about running into him or his millionaire friends.

Luckily, Christmas was coming up and I had the excuse to go back to Canada to spend the holidays with my family for a while, so I booked the next flight to Toronto, then hired a driver to take me to my hometown.

It was in the car that I began to panic about

something else. I hadn't been back in Hartfield for at least two years.

It wasn't until I was getting close to the town when I remembered that I stayed away from Hartfield as much as I could for good reasons. One, to be exact. The cause of the first story of my life. The one that ended in heartbreak.

CHAPTER 2

I haven't celebrated Christmas in Hartfield for five years. Usually around this time, I'd be touring or doing promotional work somewhere in the world, or spending the holidays with Nick's family.

I never thought that staying away from Hartfield was a conscious decision, but now I saw that maybe it was. I had flown my family to Mount Tremblant in Quebec for most of those winters and we'd spent time together there. I'd meet them on neutral grounds some weekends, mostly in New York, where I lived and they never got tired of visiting. They would also fly to my concerts all the time, which could be in any part of the world.

Since Mirabelle got pregnant five months ago, it'd

been more of a challenge for her to travel in recent months, so I was eager to see her most of all.

I did love Hartfield at Christmas. It was so lovely during this time of year. The Christmas Market was probably all set up at the town square. Performers would sing, play music or put on shows most evenings. There would be a little more pep in the townspeople's steps, although the stray from their usual lax attitude could also be from the stress of shopping and finding the right gifts for their loved ones.

And of course, the best place in the world was sitting in front of the fireplace at my old house, nursing a cup of my dad's eggnog and chatting with my family. The lovely smell of something baking in the oven would waft in whenever somebody passed through the door from the kitchen to the living room, and Christmas muzak would set the mood from the vinyl player in the corner.

In a word, Hartfield was cozy this time of year.

All I had to do was put my sour memories in the gutter and focus on having a joyous time with my family.

But as I sat in the back of the car that was driving into Hartfield from the airport, I suddenly started to cry.

The stress was getting to me. It had been an emotional week. I'd been with Nick for so long and I was madly in love with him. I still was, but my pride gave me the strength to walk away. I knew if I didn't get out now, I'd be losing the best years of my life to someone with commitment phobia.

The driver was kind enough not to notice the sobbing, and even turned on the radio a little louder out of consideration.

After a few songs, one of mine came on. "Falling Into Pieces" was a smooth jazz song that I'd written last year about how much I loved Nick. That made me sob even harder. It really hurt to love a man who didn't return your love the way you wanted him to. But I was too stubborn to accept anything less. I'd written a handful of new songs about that recently.

When we reached Hartfield, my tears had more or less dried. I looked out the windows at the fresh white snow blanketing over the houses and the stores. Christmas decorations were everywhere, with lights strung up from lamppost to lamppost. The sight of my old hometown cheered me up; a smile began to crack on my face.

I instantly regretted being too chicken to come back every Christmas. This was the best place to be this time of year. Plus, nobody was here to hound me with questions about my personal life. No paparazzi here and the townspeople who did recognize me left me alone. This was Canada after all, where no one was overly impressed by anything. I was used to being mobbed by fans and paparazzi in big cities around the world. Getting your picture taken when you have no makeup on, wearing sweats, and just want a cup of coffee from down the block did very little for your self-esteem when you were torn to shreds on some gossip blog or Page Six the next day. Hartfield could've been my sanctuary.

When the driver pulled up in front of my parents' house, my breathing was no longer punctuated by uncontrollable sobbing. The driver helped me with my luggage and I slipped him a huge tip. Any acts of kindness from strangers were magnified tenfold and I was beyond grateful.

"Thank you so much, Carl," I said to the driver.

"You're welcome," he said with a wink. "Take care of yourself. Oh, and my wife is a big fan."

"Oh really? What's her name?"

"Sadie," he replied.

I reached into my purse and pulled out a copy of my third CD. It wasn't released yet, but I'd brought some extra copies for family and friends.

I signed it and gave it to Carl.

"Here."

A toothy grin appeared on his face and I couldn't help but smile back.

"Merry Christmas," he said.

"Merry Christmas!"

When he drove off, I took in the crisp air. But my moment of appreciation was cut short.

A woman stared at me from across the street. She looked like she was either squinting in my direction or giving me a dirty look. She was dressed in an oversized wool sweater, her strawberry blonde hair in a messy ponytail. She looked familiar.

"Emma Wild," she called.

At the sound of her shrill voice, I recognized her instantly. Kendra Kane. I'd call her my nemesis if the term didn't make me laugh. We were friends in grade school until her bossy nature conflicted with my independent one. She was the mean girl of the school. Maybe she was every girl's nemesis.

I couldn't stand the way she was always so competitive, trying to outdo me, or anyone really, every chance she got. I couldn't stand girls who brought other girls down to lift themselves up, and I largely ignored her from middle school on. That was when I started hanging out with Jennifer and Cassandra, who still remained my two BFFs, although they were both scattered around the country now.

Unlike most of the other girls who moved to big cities as soon as they graduated high school, Kendra was still around.

"Hi, Kendra," I said, putting on a smile. "Good to see you."

She only smirked in response. Nonetheless, she

crossed the street to where I was standing. I braced for the worst but hoped for the best. We were both pushing thirty, too old for any more teenage cattiness.

"Giving the fans what they want, I see?"

She must've seen me autograph the CD. There was a certain awkwardness about being famous that I didn't like to think about unless someone brought it to my attention.

"So, what have you been up to?" I asked. "It's been so long."

She waited before answering. Kendra had a habit of making me feel uneasy. She stared at me, but there was a blankness in her cool green eyes, a deadening chill that made me feel as if she wasn't all there. She had a way of exercising her power this way.

"A lot has happened," she said. "I got married and had a baby boy."

"That's great! What's your boy's name?"

"Blake, Junior."

I was genuinely happy for her. Maybe she had changed. People did grow up, after all.

"Wow. So you live across the street now?"

"Just recently. Couldn't pass up the opportunity."

"That's great. I didn't know that. It's a lovely house."

"Yeah, well, I'm sure you've been busy singing your songs."

She said it as if it were a dirty word. I couldn't let

her get to me and maintained the smile on my face. This was nothing. If I had a dime every time I smiled pleasantly at someone who was mean to me...

"Yup," I replied, smile still plastered on my face. "My third album's coming out, so I'm happy about that."

"Congratulations," she said flatly. "I'll be sure to buy a copy."

"No need." I reached into my bag.

When I handed my CD to her, she shook her head.

"I want to buy it," she said. "You know, to support you. Maybe you should give this to Sterling. I'm sure he'll appreciate it."

At the sound of his name, my smile faltered. My cheeks burned and suddenly I wanted to throw my CD at her face. She always knew which buttons to push. Kendra smirked again just as my mom opened the door.

"Emma!" Mom said. "Hello, Kendra."

Kendra gave a half-hearted wave.

"Lovely catching up," she said before she walked back home.

Mom ran down and hugged me so tightly that I couldn't breathe.

"Hey, kiddo." Dad helped me with my suitcase.

"Kendra lives across the street now?" I said when we were inside.

"Don't sound too excited," Dad said.

I supposed there was a groan in my voice.

"The poor girl's been through a lot," Mom said. "She needs your support."

"I very much doubt that," I said. "But what do you mean?"

"Her husband Blake died last summer."

"Died? She didn't mention that."

"Yes. She was head over heels in love with him, but one day she came home and found him dead."

"How?"

"We don't know the details," said Mom. "But I did hear from somebody in my knitting circle that he had a stroke or something."

"God, I didn't know."

I felt bad now for wanting to throw that CD in her face. She had her reasons for being a miserable person. She wasn't angry at me. She was angry about life.

"Poor thing," Mom continued. "She'd been a single mother raising that little boy of hers. They lived in a house down on Lakeshire, but after the funeral, she sold the house and moved here when Margot passed away. It's closer to the elementary school, and I'm sure she didn't want to live in a house full of memories of her husband."

"She didn't want anybody at the funeral," Dad added. "I don't even think she held a funeral."

"I should do something nice for her," I said. "Maybe we can invite her over for dinner one day."

"It's hard to reach out to her," Dad said. "She's closed off, doesn't like to talk to people and never wants to go to any social gatherings. Neighbors keep trying to go to her house and offering her all kinds of food and advice, but she's not having it. The death is still fresh, so I think she's still grieving."

"I just can't imagine what she's going through," I said.

I supposed everyone had personal tragedies. Mine suddenly didn't feel so life shattering.

CHAPTER 3

There was something utterly bizarre about being back in my childhood room. It felt as if I were stepping into a time capsule. Everything was tiny. My little twin bed still had the flowered sheets, the candy-striped wallpaper was a little faded, and the little desk was still by the window where I used to do my homework. I was glad that my parents didn't want to renovate anything; I was glad to find everything still the same.

Except when I closed the door. That was where a huge poster of Nick still hung. He was in his teens. His dirty blond hair was cut in a mushroom style that had been all the rage back then, and he was smiling and petting a golden retriever. This was the poster for that dog movie that I loved when I was young. So basically I'd had a crush on him since I was fourteen. How depressing.

This was going to be a hard breakup to get over, even harder than the first one, which I still didn't want to think about. One heartbreak at a time was plenty for me.

I took down the poster slowly, careful not to rip it. I couldn't bring myself to throw it away, and I ended up rolling the poster up and hiding it in the back of my dusty old closet.

Other than that small, painful reminder, I was happy to be back in my old room. I got under the covers of my bed and slept because I was so tired from the early flight.

After an hour, a bang on my door woke me up.

"Kiddo?" Dad called. "Lunch is ready. Wanna eat with us?"

"Yes," I replied. "I thought you'd never ask."

At the offer of food, I practically jumped out of my bed.

There was nothing like Dad's comfort food to get you out of a funk. Sure, I'd eaten in some of the finest restaurants around the world, but nothing compared to Dad's beef stew and crab cakes.

"You didn't mention on the phone whether Nick was coming for Christmas?" Mom inquired.

I tried not to cringe at the mention of his name.

For the past year, Mom had been waiting for Nick to propose. If I had to be honest, I was too.

So I had purposely forgotten to tell them. The plan for me to come home for Christmas was last minute, and of course they were thrilled, but I didn't exactly want them feeling sorry for me.

"His schedule is crazy," I said. "I'm not sure. He has this new movie coming out..."

"I can imagine," said Mom. "But I hope he can make it. He's never been to our town. It would be nice to show him around your old haunts, you know."

"Of course. It's too bad."

My family had met Nick on several occasions and they adored him. Dad was a big fan of Alive or Dead, the only action film Nick had ever been in. Mom was still bewildered that one of the biggest movie stars in the world was dating me.

I changed the subject.

"Is Mirabelle at work?"

"Should be," Dad said. "She always is this time of day."

"Great. I'll go and swing by the cafe after."

I couldn't wait to see my big sister. She lived only one block away and she owned the Chocoholic Cafe, the best cafe in town. They had the best coffee. I was the one who'd helped her pick all the beans before she opened the store after all — and yummy choco-late desserts to go with it. Their specialty was their organic hot chocolate. Of course, since I loved caffeine and chocolate equally, I made her invent a drink that combined the two, the hot chocolate latte.

On Samford Street, where all the best shops were, the Chocoholic Cafe was buzzing with locals. I couldn't wait to get my hands on all their fresh chocolate cakes, croissants and cupcakes during my stay.

When I arrived, Mirabelle wasn't behind the counter. There were two baristas making the drinks, Kate and Michelle. They looked busy, but I approached them to ask where my sister was over the sounds of coffee beans being ground to death and a latte machine making the sounds of a dying cat.

"She's out running a few errands," said Michelle.

"Great, I'll just wait for her then."

"Want me to make you something?"

"Thanks, but I'll wait in line so we don't get chewed out. You can't piss off people who are demanding caffeine or chocolate, or even worse—both."

Kate and Michelle laughed.

"Amen," said Kate.

While in line, I checked my phone to catch up on the news. Usually I avoided the entertainment section like the plague, but a fresh headline caught my eye.

Nick Doyle Dumps Emma Wild for New Victoria's Secret Angel.

Seriously?!

Nick was pictured smiling next to a laughing blonde. He was wearing a tux and the model was in a slinky red dress that showed off ample cleavage. I was used to wild rumors, but my jaw dropped at this one. Before me, Nick did date half of those angels. Now he was onto this child who looked barely twenty years old when I only moved out a week ago?

Nick Doyle stepped out in a dapper Armani tux yesterday night for the Sick Children's Charity Benefit. Sources say that his longtime girlfriend, singer Emma Wild, moved out from their Soho apartment recently and he is currently single and already mingling. Witnesses caught him in deep conversation with new Victoria's Secret Angel Tara Amberstone. They couldn't pull their gaze away from each other all evening. This isn't the first time Nick Doyle has been smitten with an Angel. In the past, he has dated...

I forced myself to stop there. I believed this article. Completely. Moving on this quickly was something that Nick would do. He'd done it in the past to ex-girlfriends. In fact, he'd only broken up with his supermodel ex-girlfriend a couple of weeks before he began flirting with me. Why did I think I would be any different?

Still, the article stung. I wanted to lock myself in a room somewhere and break down. This was so humiliating. Now everyone was going to know. My parents would find out eventually. Everyone would feel sorry for me.

Luckily, most of Hartfield's population were my parents' age. They were more into crossword puzzles than trashy celebrity gossip. I hoped.

Taking a deep breath, I closed my phone and put it back in my purse. I concentrated on the chocolate pound cake sitting above the counter next to a tray of gingerbread cookies.

Inhale. Exhale. Inhale. Exhale.

The guy in front of me turned around and gave me a weird look.

Yup, I was breathing too hard.

I looked at the colorful cupcakes, the muffins, the oversized cookies and breathed in the sweet aroma of the cafe. Chocolate would cure me. Caffeine would cure me.

I wasn't going to cry.

It was finally my turn to order. I could put on my pageant smile again.

The cashier was a lanky hipster type in his late teens or early twenties. With shaggy dyed black hair over his eyes, a ring dangling out of one nose, and heavy eyeliner, he looked out of place in this quaint cafe.

His name tag said "Cal."

"Hi, what can I get you—Emma Wild?"

His hazel eyes flashed with recognition when they met mine.

"That's me."

I was surprised that he knew who I was. He seemed the type to listen to heavy metal or punk.

"I...know you," he said somewhat awkwardly. "Mirabelle's sister."

"Oh, right."

That was why he knew who I was. Of course.

After placing my order, I stood with a bunch of people by the counter to wait. Since Cal had already given me my piece of chocolate pound cake, I started nibbling on it from the bag. I had also bought half a dozen chocolate chip cookies, two chocolate biscotti, a chocolate croissant, and three cupcakes. If they'd sold ice cream, I would've bought that too. I reminded myself to buy ice cream from the supermarket on the way home. There was none left in our freezer, if you could believe. And I wasn't going to share any of this stuff. It was breakup food.

I tried to remind myself that I didn't have it so bad. Nobody was immune to heartbreak in some form. Look at Kendra. I couldn't imagine losing a husband so young. This was nothing. After I had a good cry and stuffed myself full of sickeningly sweet desserts, I'd be fine.

I was sick of being heartbroken. And singing about it. My last two albums hammered this subject to death. The third one coming out was full of songs about love and loss too.

I'd been feeling this way since I was old enough to go out on a date. It was time to finally hang up this shtick and be in a relationship where I was treated like a queen. First, I'd make an effort to write some songs that didn't have to do with love and relationships.

Maybe for my next album, I would do something different. Maybe some brainless pop numbers, stuff that people would feel happy listening to. Or maybe I'll just stay single, put my career on hiatus and do some volunteer work halfway around the world for a while.

But who was I kidding? I loved music. I couldn't go a day without some new tune taking over my head. If this wasn't true love, I didn't know what was.

As I stood there thinking about all the career routes I could take with my musical direction, one of the baristas called out my name. My tall cup of hot chocolate latte was steaming and ready for me.

But before I could reach for it, a blood-curdling scream came from behind me.

CHAPTER 4

*T*he scream almost made me drop my box of desserts and my bagged piece of pound cake. I whipped around and faced a crazy Cheshire grin on a woman around my age. She had a blonde bob, wore a red tuque, and simply could not stop jumping and clapping her hands.

"Oh my God!" She stepped forward, invading my personal space by a nose hair. "Emma Wild! I heard that you're from here, but I can't believe that I'm actually looking at you in person! You're so thin! I mean, in a good way. And your skin. What's your secret?"

The other patrons looked in our direction and I blushed.

"Heeey." Now that I was in the presence of a fan,

I had to be on. "Um, I don't know. I try to sleep and eat well."

"I am such a big fan," she gushed. "Your last album is still on constant replay on my stereo. 'The Killer in Me' is just a phenomenal song. I was just singing that in the shower this morning! What a coincidence! Seriously though, you're really an incredible songwriter. Look at me, I'm totally blabbering, but I can't help it. You're, like, such an inspiration to me."

"Thank you so much." Pageant grin, check. Modesty, check. Incessant nodding, check.

As much as I appreciated meeting fans who enjoyed my work, I tried not to let their constant compliments inflate my head. I had to learn to be immune to what people said about me so that opinions, good and bad, didn't affect who I was.

"Soy latte?" Michelle, the barista, called out.

My fan signalled to Michelle that it was hers, but she was rooted in place before me.

"I can't believe you're here." She was still jumping. "I know I'm really not acting cool right now, but I love you so much. I can't believe you've been standing in line in front of me this whole time and I didn't know it. How long are you back?"

"Just for the holidays," I replied.

"Maybe we can hang out, you know? I always thought that we could be friends? I mean, I see you in magazines, and I think we have similar style."

"Oh?" I laughed awkwardly.

I really didn't know who this woman was, and I quickly tried to figure out a way to get out of this. If she lived in this town, she might want to hang out all the time.

"Well, I don't know," I joked. "You'll have to pass my test. What's your favorite TV show?"

"The Voice!" she said. "I think you should be a judge on that show. You're so much better than Shakira or Christina."

"Oh, that's not true. Those girls are super talented. I've met both of them and they're very nice. So you're from around here?"

"I live in Sanford actually, but I drive back home from work through this town and I absolutely love this cafe."

She didn't live in Hartfield. That was a relief to hear.

"What did you get?" I asked.

"The organic soy latte is seriously good. Have you tried it? What did you get?"

"I have. I love everything here, but my fave has got to be the chocolate latte. Have you tried it?

"No, but I will now that I know that Emma Wild likes it."

Even though I was waiting for Mirabelle, it was probably best to leave. I reached for my cup on the counter and moved to the area where all the lids were. She followed me with her drink and put a lid on her cup quickly. I hoped she didn't want to leave with me. Before I could give an excuse, she asked for an autograph.

"Sure." I prayed that she wouldn't ask for my number or to hang out again.

She began rummaging through her purse until she found a notepad and a pen. I put my cup on the counter to give her the autograph as she drank from her cup. When I gave the notepad back to her, I saw that her face had scrunched up.

"This drink tastes really weird. I think—"

She clutched her chest, yelping a little. Then she began to spasm. Her cup slipped from her fingers and her body fell after it.

"Oh my God!" I shrieked.

The crowd at the cafe circled around her.

"Call the ambulance," Michelle said to Cal.

"Is she having a stroke?" a customer asked.

"Is there a doctor here?" I shouted out to the sea of shocked faces.

A woman wearing blue scrubs under her winter coat stepped forward. "I'm not a doctor, but I am a nurse."

I moved out of the way as she crouched down beside the fallen fan.

"Everybody clear out," said Michelle. "Please give us some space."

The customers began to go reluctantly.

"Please!" Michelle urged again. "The ambulance is coming and we need to make room."

"I don't feel a pulse," the nurse said.

"The ambulance is on its way," Cal said. He stepped out from behind the counter, face beet red.

"What do you mean there's no pulse?" I exclaimed to the nurse.

I looked down in horror at the girl I'd just been chatting with. She'd looked so flushed and vibrant only moments earlier and now...

"She's...?"

"Dead," the nurse said. "I think she's dead."

A hush went through the crowd. Cal, Michelle and Kate all looked horrified.

I looked down again at the girl who had just claimed to be my biggest fan. She was now a corpse.

CHAPTER 5

I couldn't understand what had happened. One minute she was alive and full of energy and the next minute she fell to the ground. It didn't make any sense. I kneeled down and looked at her in that brown pool of hot liquid. Blonde hair covered her face and one of her arms was crossed over her stomach. She had mentioned something about the drink tasting strange before she fell...

"The ambulance is here."

I looked up and saw Cal. His nervous red face loomed over me.

"Please leave," he said.

I stood up and walked out the door, numbed by the whole incident. The chill of the winter cold numbed me further and I moved out of the way as the paramedics went in.

But what could they do if she was already dead?

The coffee shop crowd had more or less stayed put outside. I stood with them, watching and waiting.

"This is horrifying," an old woman beside me remarked to her friend.

"Poor thing," the other lady replied. "I hope she's all right. Maybe she just fainted."

All around me the townspeople talked amongst themselves. A couple of pedestrians stopped and asked what was going on. The two ladies tried to explain, but they ultimately said that they didn't know.

"Miss?" The first lady turned to me. "Do you know what happened? Did she have a stroke?"

I couldn't tell them that she was dead. "I don't know the details."

"I heard that you're famous or something?" The second woman asked. "I'm sorry, I don't recognize you, but the young lady did. Were you talking before she fell?"

"Well, yes, we were chatting when we were getting our drinks—"

Then it hit me. How could I miss this detail? She had ordered a soy latte. The cup that she drank from and then spilled was dark brown. She had taken the wrong drink. Maybe she'd been allergic to dairy and that was why she requested soy. What if she had been seriously allergic to dairy?

I walked back to the scene to tell the paramedics. The police were also inside, and as I went in, I noticed Cal was talking to one of the two policemen and all of them turned to me.

"Miss?" said the cop with a scruffy beard. "I heard you were talking to the victim before she fell."

"Yes," I said. "Is she really dead?"

The taller cop nodded grimly. "Unfortunately she is. We don't know why, but we'd like to know what took place between you two so we can find out more."

I repeated what we talked about, embarrassed to mention that I was a celebrity, and that I was giving her an autograph before she fell.

"Oh, I think I recognize you," said the tall cop. "You sang that song, 'Cornflower Blues.'"

He looked at me with more interest.

"That's me," I said, and then quickly changed the subject. I told them the victim had taken the wrong drink.

Her body had already been removed from the floor, but the cup was still lying there. A name was written on the cup: Emma.

I looked around for my cup, which was still on the counter where I left it. It also said Emma.

"That woman—her name was also Emma?" I asked the cops.

"Yes. Emma Chobsky."

I looked inside my drink and smelled it. Soy. It was the other Emma's soy latte.

"Our drinks got mixed up," I said. "She took my chocolate latte. Her drink was a soy latte. It could be that she had a severe allergy to dairy. I feel horrible."

"Nothing's confirmed yet," said the first cop. "Don't jump to any conclusions. It could've been a medical condition. These things happen. The coroner will do some tests and we'll certainly tell them what you've told us."

Mirabelle came in through the door, flushed from the cold.

"What is going on?" she exclaimed. "Emma? What's all this?"

Mirabelle sauntered over, clutching her pregnant belly. She was also a redhead and looked very much like me, except that she was a lot taller, with brown eyes instead of green.

I hugged her and explained everything.

"Wow," she said. "Are you okay?"

"Fine," I said. In truth, I was a little shaken up.

"No you're not," Mirabelle said, looking deep into my eyes.

Tears welled up and I nodded. Mirabelle always saw right through me.

"It might've been my fault," I blurted out. "It was my drink. There was something in that drink that made her ill, I'm sure of it. If it's not the dairy, then—"

"Then what?" asked Mirabelle.

"Poison," I said. "Somebody was trying to poison me."

CHAPTER 6

"Poison?" said Mirabelle. "No, Emma, come on."

"I know I sound paranoid, but crazier things have happened."

"Who would poison your drink in a busy cafe?"

"I don't know." I sighed.

Outside, the crowd was breaking apart as the ambulance drove away. The truck was in no hurry. She was dead, after all.

"A lot of people hate me," I said. "I've received more than a few death threats in the past."

"Oh, Emma, crazy people are always threatening celebrities. I'm surprised that you haven't had to file a restraining order on a stalker yet. But this is small town Ontario."

She was right. It was crazy for someone to do this

in a busy cafe. If someone wanted me dead, wouldn't there be a better way for them to do it? But I still couldn't shake the idea away.

The cafe door opened and in stepped the ghost of misery's past. A man in a black wool coat with the collars turned up walked my way. I hadn't seen him in nine years, but he looked the same. The same moody gray eyes, dark hair, and broad shoulders.

Sterling Matthews. My heart sped up and I turned red.

From age fourteen to seventeen, we were practically inseparable. We met each other in the first year of high school, since we shared many of the same classes. At first we were awkward toward each other, but once we started getting to know each other on various class assignments, we became fast friends. In groups, he never talked much, but when we were alone, that was when he shared the most.

I used to feel privileged that he would share everything with me. About his family, about how his father had left the family when he was five. How his mother was working her tail off as a single mother of five. Of how exhausted he was to be the man of the house, taking care of his two brothers and two sisters when he wasn't in school.

When he had the time to sneak away with me when we were older, I'd try to devour him with my eyes and with my passionate kisses. He was my life. My parents adored him and his mother adored me. We were so young, but if he had asked me to spend the rest of my life with him, I wouldn't have hesitated.

The only problem was that he didn't feel the same. A month before we were to graduate, he started acting more distant. When he saw me, gone were the excited smiles. I could read his body language, and it seemed as if he was always turning away from me.

At first I tried to ignore it, writing it off as the stress of final exams and graduation, but July came. He worked in a grocery store, and I was home most summer days, recording music on my computer. We were both waiting for fall to go to a university that was only half an hour's drive away.

I wasn't thrilled about going to university, but Sterling planned to study Criminal Justice and I took English because the school didn't have a music program. He'd tried to talk me out of going to his school before. I'd thought it was because he wanted me to study something I cared about, but it turned out that he just didn't want me hanging around altogether.

At the end of July, I couldn't take it anymore. I

asked him to meet me down by the lake. I'd shown up first and watched the ducks float along the waters. He came and hugged me from behind, yet I sensed that something was wrong. He had hugged me as if he was hugging me for the last time.

"Can I ask you something?" I asked

"Sure."

"Do you still want to be with me?"

I watched his face carefully. A dark cloud passed over his eyes and they were impenetrable. His silence told me everything.

It was then that I knew that we were over.

Then he tried to explain.

"I don't think you'd enjoy being at the same school," he said.

"Bullshit. You just want to date other girls."

Then he gulped. After a moment of silence, he took a deep breath and admitted it.

"You're right. We're too young to be tied down. It's better if we let ourselves experience different things."

"Or different girls, you mean," I said, standing up.

Sterling didn't come after me. He pulled out a fistful of grass and played with the blades in his palms, letting the grass and the soil stain his hands.

"I think you should do what you really want to do, not what I want to do."

He looked up at me and quickly turned away.

He had grown cold again, his shield against the world. I never thought he'd need it with me. I'd always been exposed to his soft side. But I'd been kicked out, and knowing Sterling, there was nothing I could do about it. He didn't want me and he wouldn't fight for me.

And I'd be damned if I stayed behind to waste my life in a small town and with a guy who didn't even care about me. Even though I was crushed, I did realize how stupid I had been. I was all set on throwing my dreams away so that I could be with this guy. I didn't want to study English. I didn't want to go to university. I had just wanted to stay by his side. As difficult as it was to lose him, I threw myself into my other passion: music. So I moved to New York and kept busy.

Friends kept telling me that I'd get over him as soon as I met someone else, but I always compared every guy I dated to Sterling. When he used to look at me, it was as if I was the only person who existed to him. When he hugged me, I felt completely warm, secure and cared for. It was hard being sent back out into the cold after that.

Then I met Nick. That was when I started forgetting Sterling more and more.

∿

Now Sterling stood in front of me. We stared at each other at a standstill, each waiting for the other to strike first. All those feelings of anguish and obsession came flooding back. The feelings had always been there, dormant; they'd never gone away. Last I heard, he had gotten married and had two kids. That was what stung most of all. He had long since moved on.

"Hi," he said.

"Hi," I said.

"Mirabelle." He nodded to her.

Mirabelle smiled, but stepped back. Even she could sense the heat in this room.

"What are you doing here?" I asked.

"I'm a detective now." He stepped in closer, under the light. Yes. He was as gorgeous as ever. A dark five o'clock shadow gave his face a more rugged look. When he grimaced, two dimples appeared at the sides of his mouth.

"Oh. You'd always wanted to be a detective. I guess you got what you wanted in the end."

My voice came out sharp, even though I hadn't intended it to be so. But I couldn't put my pageant act on for Sterling. He'd know that it was fake.

"So how are you doing?" he asked.

"Fine. Everything's great. Couldn't be happier."

"Having a good Christmas with your family then?"

"Yes. It's fun. Except for this grisly death."

Sterling looked at the spot where the body had been.

"Yes." He frowned. "Not a pleasant homecoming, is it?"

"I've had better."

"I'd like to ask you some questions."

I crossed my arms. "I've said everything I needed to say to your colleagues, but now that you are here, I have something new to share."

"What is it?"

I told him about my poison theory as Mirabelle sighed in exasperation beside me.

"How likely is it?" I asked.

"We'll just have to see," Sterling said. He didn't say anything else. He didn't say whether it made sense or if he thought I was crazy.

His vagueness made me angry all of a sudden.

"Then this conversation is over," I said. "Mirabelle, I'll see you at home."

Without giving Sterling another glance, I stormed out.

CHAPTER 7

After nine years, seeing Sterling still gave me anxiety. That guy still had a hold on me. The whole day had been one dramatic incident after another, and I was spent.

When I reached my street, I was crying again. How embarrassing to run into Kendra just as I was trying to wipe the tears away. She was walking her son home.

"Emma." Her eyes widened in surprise at the sight of me. "What are you—?"

"I'm sorry," I said.

Crying in front of other people was the worst. Not only was it incredibly humiliating, I hated to bring other people down.

"Is everything okay?"

I couldn't even look at her.

"It's nothing. I mean, it was just a crazy afternoon."

"Mommy, why is the lady crying?" her son asked.

"This is Blake Junior."

"Hi, Blake." I blew into a tissue.

"What happened?" asked Kendra.

I started sobbing again. My face was probably contorted into my ugly crying face.

"Maybe I shouldn't say this in front of your son."

"Say what?" she exclaimed.

When Blake Junior seemed distracted by a ladybug on the lawn, in a shaky whisper, I parlayed everything that had taken place earlier.

Kendra gasped. "Who died?"

"I don't know. This woman from another town. Her name was Emma too."

I heard Kendra inhale as I wiped my face with a new tissue from my purse.

"I think I need to leave," I said. "Coming back home was a bad idea. I've been here for less than twenty-four hours and somebody drops dead? It's not a good sign."

"Don't be silly," Kendra said. "I don't know what happened at the cafe, but you have your family here. And it's Christmas."

I looked up at her in gratitude for her kind words. It was unexpected of Kendra. Her face was still quite stony, but judging by the curves of her mouth, she looked like she was trying to cheer me up by forming what seemed like a smile.

"I read that your boyfriend broke up with you," she continued. "Is that why you're back?"

I nodded.

"That must be humiliating that he would dump you for some lingerie bimbo."

I cried even harder.

"You can't go back to that," Kendra said. "It's good to take a break from all that, don't you think? There are no tabloids here."

"Yeah, but there might be soon," I said. "As soon as word spreads that someone's been poisoned, it might be a media field day."

I didn't know why I was blabbering so much, but I couldn't help it. I was a wreck.

"Poison?" Kendra looked shocked.

"Mommy, what's poison?" asked little Blake.

"I'm sorry," I said. "There's no proof of that, so I didn't mean to say that in front of your son. It's just been a very crazy day."

Kendra nodded. "Right. It sounds stressful. Maybe you should go home and relax."

"Okay." I sniffed and wiped my last tear away. "Thanks Kendra."

With a heavy heart, I climbed up the porch stairs. My parents had probably gone back to work after welcoming me. Alone in the house, I decided to hole up in my room and try to take a nap.

With the horrible things that had been happening to me lately, I thought it would be best if I disappeared from everyone. No ex-boyfriends, no tabloids, no fans, no dead bodies. But where could I go? Did I even want to go? Christmas was a time for family, and I'd probably be more miserable stuck on a resort alone somewhere. I could call a few friends who were living in Toronto or New York, but I didn't want to spoil their holiday cheer in my emotional state. Then there were my industry friends. They partied like crazy, but I didn't feel up for the party scene either.

I let myself drift off.

I dreamt that I was standing in the field at my high school and Nick and Sterling were both facing me. Suddenly they started throwing snowballs right at me. They were trying to kill me, telling from the menacing looks on their faces. I didn't know who had thrown the last one, but it hit my throat, and I began to cough out blood. The red blood tainted the pure white snow.

I woke up coughing and grasping my throat.

Maybe that was how the other Emma felt before she dropped dead.

My cell phone rang. My head felt groggy, but I willed myself out of bed and reached into my bag. It was my manager, Rod.

"Hello?"

"Are you sick?" he asked. "I like that voice raspy. It sounds a lot sexier."

Rod was the kind of ostentatious New Yorker who wore fur coats and fedoras. He used to be a rock star, but retired to being a manager when the lifestyle got too fast for him.

"No, just been sleeping. What's up, Rod?"

"I'm hurt," he said. "I called Nick and he said you got out of New York and you didn't even tell me. I had to hear it from the tabloids that you guys had broken up."

"Yeah, well, it's not personal. It's not as if I went around telling everyone."

"How dare he cheat on you? I thought he was the good kind of bastard."

"I don't think he cheated," I said. "I broke up with him, but I really don't want to talk about that right now."

"Understood, honey. I just hope you're doing all right. Where are you now, anyway?"

I told him I was at my parents' house, but left out the part about the dead fan.

"Do I have a gig for you," he said. "A Middle Eastern prince wants to pay you half a million to sing at his birthday party next week."

"What? You're joking."

"No joke. Completely serious."

"Who is he?"

"He wants to remain unnamed right now, but I talked to a representative who says he's a spoiled party boy who just wants to have a good time. His birthday party is being held in this crazy lavish hotel in Dubai. Don't worry, all you have to do is sing. No putting out or anything. I made sure of that. It's a five-song set on the twenty-fourth. It's in and out. Just a very long flight, but you get to stay in this gorgeous hotel and everything."

"Next week? But it's Christmas."

"I know, but it's half a mil!"

This sounded perfect. I was thinking about leaving earlier, wasn't I? But now that the opportunity was presented to me, I wasn't so sure.

"It's just that it's...Christmas."

"This is really a no-brainer. That is, if you're Jewish, like me."

I laughed.

"I'll think about it. Can I call you back tomorrow?"

"Sure thing, doll. Sleep on it."

CHAPTER 8

*R*od was probably right. Who would turn down an offer for 500K to sing a few songs? I used to go around and beg for a chance to sing for people. But fortunately I was in a position now to make decisions where money wasn't a factor. And I also felt like I had a responsibility to stay.

The next morning I visited Mirabelle at her house. She was pregnant and she didn't need any more stress around this time of year. The cafe was closed until further notice and she was sitting in front of the TV, watching a cheesy soap opera and eating Cheetos.

"Want some?" She offered me the bowl.

"No, thanks."

I was apologetic about the cafe.

"Oh, what's to be sorry about?" she said. "I get a few days off. It's fine. These things happen."

"Do they?"

"Okay. It's not every day that someone dies in my cafe, but it's nobody's fault. I'm sure we'll find out soon that she just had some sort of medical condition. I think you worry way too much. You definitely got that from Mom."

"Why can't I be more cool and collected like you and Dad?" I sighed. "When do you think the cafe's going to be open again?"

She shrugged. "Maybe in the next few days. I should hear from the police soon. Once the coroner confirms that it was a health issue, we'll get the go-ahead to reopen."

I was still concerned that the cafe's reputation might be tainted by this, but I didn't say so. Mirabelle was so certain that there was no foul play, but I thought she was a little naive. She'd lived in this quaint town all of her life; she didn't realize that horrible things happened all the time. On my travels, I'd seen some crazy stuff.

"Ouch!" Mirabelle held her stomach. "The baby's kicking."

"Little Drew?" I called to her belly.

"Oh, the little rascal. Well anyway, just don't worry. Everything's going to be fine."

We watched the dramatic soap opera in silence. An evil twin was going to pull the plug on the good twin, who was in a coma, but she kept getting interrupted by visitors coming in and talking to the coma girl in the hospital room and the evil twin had to hide in the closet each time. The whole thing made me chuckle.

I didn't tell Mirabelle about singing at the prince's birthday thing. First of all, she would probably make fun of me. She might even encourage me to go, but I decided that I wanted to see her cafe reopened before I could say yes.

When I walked back to my family's house, a black Honda pulled up my driveway. Sterling got out. At the sight of him, I froze again.

"Hi," he said.

His two dimples made a brief appearance.

"Hello," I replied coldly.

"How you doing?"

"Fine."

He stood before me, looking as uncomfortable as I felt and trying to hide it.

"I'm sorry to intrude," he said. "I just thought it was best to tell you in person."

We were both hugging ourselves, freezing in the winter cold.

"Do you want to come in?" I asked.

"Sure, thanks."

My parents were both at work. Sterling looked around.

"Wow," he said softly. "It looks the same, like I'm traveling back in time."

"Wait till you see my bedroom," I said, but quickly regretted it. "I mean, do you want some coffee?"

"That would be nice."

I went into the kitchen to make a brew. It was really strange to have Sterling here. The bedroom comment had slipped out because we used to spend hours there, listening to music, hanging out and chatting. He'd been my best friend. I hoped he knew what I meant and didn't think I was insinuating hooking up. Which I didn't want. Certainly not.

I came out with two cups. One cream and two sugars. That was how we both liked our coffees.

He took a sip, then gulped the coffee down despite how hot it was. I stifled a grin, knowing that he liked it.

We sat on the couch next to each other, but I tried to stay as far as I could. Still, I could smell his cologne and I felt numbed by all the heat emanating from my nervous body. Whether he felt it too, I didn't know. He sat upright with his hands on his lap and looked everywhere but at me.

"I heard that you have kids now?" I asked.

"Yes, Maria is five and Sandy is two."

"Wow," I said. "I bet they're cute."

"They are." He nodded. "And I'm divorced."

"Oh...that's too bad."

Why he brought that up, I wasn't so sure. Mirabelle had already told me, so it wasn't a total shock. I wasn't sure how I felt about it. It certainly did hurt to hear that he had been married, that he was so in love with someone else that he took the plunge. But did I want him to be single? I wasn't so sure.

"So, did you find out anything new?" I asked.

"Well, yes," he said grimly. "I hate to tell you this, but the coroner came back with the results today and it's confirmed."

I held my breath. "What's confirmed?"

"She was poisoned. There was a lethal dose of cyanide in that hot chocolate. So you were right. Emma Chobsky was poisoned."

CHAPTER 9

I exhaled. "I knew it."

"My partner has been researching Emma Chobsky's background to see if she had any enemies, but she doesn't as far as we can tell. She was working as a personal trainer, she was single, had plenty of friends, and was generally well liked."

"That would explain the soy latte," I said.

"What do you mean?"

"She drank soy because it was the healthier option. As you know, we took each other's drinks by accident because we both shared the same name but didn't know it at the time. So really, I was the target."

"Yes, which is another reason why I'm here. You're right. You're a celebrity. You're much more of a target."

"I get people saying nasty things about me and to

me all the time, but I didn't think that anyone would actually try something like this. I just don't know why."

"That's what we're trying to find out, but your safety is a concern right now. We have two guards monitoring your home at all times. They're in unmarked cars, but they are there in case you need anything."

"What, you think the killer is actually going to break in one day?"

"Who knows? But I do know that this house doesn't have a security system. You need all the protection you can get."

I shook my head. "I just never thought that something like this would happen in Hartfield."

"Horrible things happen everywhere," said Sterling.

"I feel terrible for putting my family and everyone in town in danger. What's going to happen to my sister's cafe?"

"It needs to remain closed for now, but our main concern is to get this guy behind bars as soon as possible. Our main concern is your safety."

He looked into my eyes. The way he looked at me was so soft and full of concern that it pained me.

I nodded. "So what's on the agenda to catch this killer?"

"Well, we've questioned everyone who was at the

cafe. Unfortunately, there were so many people coming in and out that it was hard to keep track. The cafe has no security cameras, as you know, and there are none installed on the street."

"Any leads at all?" I asked.

"We have a list of the customers and we've questioned some of them and all the staff."

I could tell from the glint in his eyes that he had someone.

"Who do you suspect?" I asked.

"Well, what do you know about Cal?"

"The cashier?" I thought about it. "Nothing much."

"I questioned him earlier, and he set off some red flags."

"How so?"

"I asked him whether he saw anyone or anything suspicious. He must've thought I was insinuating that he did it."

I raised an eyebrow. "Did you?"

He shrugged coolly. "Whether I did or not, his reaction was suspect. He got defensive, saying that he would never poison you. But we're digging more into his life. He didn't grow up here. He didn't know anyone in Hartfield before he moved here a year ago. His family's from Toronto. Grew up there. Seems a bit odd that he'd pack up to move to a small town alone, don't you think?"

"It does, but what does he want with me? Kidnapping me for money or something, that makes sense, but trying to kill me?"

"Maybe he has some agenda with you. I want to look more into his background, see what I can dig up, but does he look familiar to you in any way?"

I thought about it. I met all kinds of people all the time.

"I don't know," I said. "All I know is that Mirabelle hired him a few months ago and she seemed to like him enough. I didn't meet him until the incident at the cafe. The line was so long that we didn't exactly have time to chat."

"Well, be careful. He's coming into the station and I'm going to grill him further. We'll get to the bottom of him. In the meantime, be on the lookout for anything suspicious."

"Okay."

"Here's my number." He slipped me his card with his phone number on it. "Can I take down your cell phone number in case I need to reach you?"

"Sure." I tried not to blush as I wrote down my number on a notepad from the side table.

Sterling stood up. I did, too.

"Thanks for your time, Emma. We'll be in touch."

"Yes. Good luck."

I could tell he wasn't sure whether to hug me and I just stood limp. He gave a small smile and left.

As long as we were just working together, I could stand it. Finding this crazy maniac who was trying to poison me took precedence over the awkwardness of reconnecting to an ex-boyfriend. Yet I felt woozy after Sterling's visit. This was the Sterling I knew and loved: strong, capable, caring. I tried not to let my body turn into jelly after I closed the front door.

I tried to concentrate on the case instead. Surely there was something that I could do.

I knew Sterling would do his best to get to the bottom of this because he always had a brilliant mind, but I had impatience on my side. If Cal wanted to kill me, there was surely proof of that, and I might as well go find it while the trail was hot.

CHAPTER 10

$\mathcal{I}$ could see why Sterling wanted to a be a detective. If I weren't a singer, it would be fun to be a spy. It would be such an adrenaline rush. When I was little I used to spy on neighbours and eavesdrop on conversations all the time. And I was never caught. I figured that since I wasn't doing much, I could speed up the investigative process by helping.

I called Mirabelle.

"Hey, where does your employee Cal live?"

"Why?" she asked.

"I'll tell you later. I just wanted to have a chat with him."

"Are you up to something?" Mirabelle asked.

"No, I just want to ask him a couple of questions about the whole cafe incident."

"Fine, I'll forward his phone and address to you on the phone."

"Thanks. Hey, does he live alone?"

"Yes, I think so. Why you need to know?"

"Just wondering. Gotta go." I hung up.

There was no need to sit and wait for answers when I could just go to the source. While Sterling had to play by the books, I could get down to business and do the real digging.

When Nick was training for his action film, I went to visit him in Queens for his training sessions. I even trained with his trainer for fun and now I was very adept at Krav Maga, this brutal form of combat and self-defense used by the Israeli army. So I wasn't afraid to be attacked; I could handle myself. If Cal was the killer, I could take him. I might look small, but I could pack a punch.

Cal lived only three blocks from the cafe, on the third floor of a little apartment building. I threw my clothes on—all black for the mission—tied my hair into a bun, and headed out.

I passed the Chocoholic Cafe on my way there, but the sight of the place closed down in the middle of the bustling street made me sad. I was going to get whoever did this. I had to. All the pink-faced and merry shoppers, the charming brick and mortar stores, the lovely residents—I loved this town. The locals didn't deserve to have their lives in jeopardy because of me. I had to help close this case as soon as possible.

I turned a corner and headed to the residential Swann Street, where Cal's place was.

A man was walking my way in the distance. As I got closer, I realized it was the man of the hour. Cal was walking towards me with his headphones on. He wore a grey ski jacket and had his hands in his pockets, looking melancholic. There was something tragic about him. His overgrown hair shaded one eye and he didn't seem to be aware of his surroundings.

My original plan was to break into his home, but now that he was before me, I could talk to him to suss him out.

"Cal!" I said loud enough for him to hear with his headphones on.

He blinked twice, and took off his earphones, stumbling to turn off his iPod.

"Hey, it's Emma," I said. "Mirabelle's sister?"

"I know who you are," he muttered.

"What are you listening to?" I asked with a smile.

"Oh, uh," he stuttered, "just music."

His eyes darted. He looked like he wanted to be anywhere but in front of me.

I chuckled. "Well, fancy meeting you here."

"I live here," he said, after a beat.

"I was just on my way to see a friend. Where are you off to?"

He buried his hands deep into the jacket pockets and looked down at his shoes.

"The police station," he said. "They have some questions about the, you know, problem at the cafe."

"Why would they ask you?"

He shrugged. "I guess they think I might know something, since I talk to everyone who comes in."

"They don't think you had anything to do with the death do they?" I asked casually, like a joke.

"I don't think so," he said seriously. "Because I had absolutely nothing to do with it."

Did I detect a note of defensiveness in his voice?

"Well," I said. "I'm sorry that the cafe's closed down. It's such a shame for everyone."

Cal nodded. "Yes, but I'm not worried about my job. You know, from what I gathered from the detective, someone might be out to get you. Are you afraid?"

He blinked twice and stared at me as he waited for my response. I felt uneasy, but I stared back, as if to answer a challenge.

"No," I said. "I have nothing to be afraid of. The only thing I'm wondering is why?"

He shrugged again. "I don't know, but there's a lot of psychos out there, you know?"

"Yes," I said.

His face was still blank and inscrutable. He turned to leave.

I could see why Sterling had his suspicions. Cal was a bit off. He was definitely secretive. I felt as if there was something he wasn't telling me, which was why I planned on breaking into his apartment.

I once read that you could tell more about someone by looking around his room than talking to the person. I really believed that. I mean, if you went through my room, you'd see how girly and romantic I was. If this guy was a killer, I'd know it by a glance around his living space.

Snowflakes slowly descended from the sky. The street was pretty calm except for an old man who went into Cal's building with a bag of groceries. I knew that Cal would be at the police station for a while, so I had plenty of time for a quick check-in.

I could've followed the man in, but there was a much easier way. This was Hartfield, a place ridiculously easy to break into. If Cal was like everyone else in town and lived in a house, he probably would've left the front door unlocked, as many of my neighbours and my parents did.

I quickly went around the side of the building to the back. The building had a fire escape, and I had to jump to pull the stairs down. I climbed as quietly as I could so that the neighbours on the other two floors wouldn't be disturbed, if they were there at all.

On the third floor, I peered into the window. The curtains were open, and nobody seemed to be inside.

Of course the window was unlocked. It was heavy, but I managed to lift it.

When the opening was big enough, I slipped in. I stood in Cal's living room.

It seemed like a place that a bachelor in his early twenties would live in. Mismatched furniture was carelessly arranged in the space, including a raggedy couch in an ugly shade of brown and a beat-up oak coffee table. A bong was on top. He owned a modest-sized TV and a collection of video games. There was an acoustic guitar by the corner. The fridge contained more condiments than real food.

I found a notebook on the kitchen counter. I was hoping it was his journal. I flipped through it and read a few pages. It was all poetry. Really cheesy poetry, the emo kind I used to write in high school. Many were about heartbreak and love. Poor kid.

Looking around, it didn't seem as if he could be the killer. Maybe we were wrong. Maybe he was just a sensitive kid who wanted to get away from the city for a while. Find himself and all that. I could relate to that. In fact, looking around the sorry excuse for a living room, I felt sorry for him.

Next I checked out his bedroom.

And that was when I freaked out.

My own face stared back at me from every angle of Cal's bedroom. Posters, magazine shoots, album covers, tabloid pictures, you name it. All my CDs were stacked on top of his stereo. He even owned all my singles and EPs. He was also the proud owner of most of the merchandise we sold from my last North American tour: T-shirts, buttons, tote bags. It was totally creepy. Flattering, but mostly creepy.

I had never seen anything like this. Sure I'd met many people who had claimed to be my biggest fan, but I doubted that they slept in a shrine devoted entirely to me.

What I didn't understand about obsessive fans was why they would turn on the very person they were obsessed with.

But what did I know? Sometimes the line between love and hate was a bit blurred.

I called Sterling.

"Emma?" he answered.

"Is Cal still at the police station?"

"Yes," he said. "I'm in the middle of questioning him, why?"

"Don't release him. I'm in his apartment."

"Why are you in his apartment?"

"I broke in," I said casually.

"Emma, are you out of your mind? You can't just break into people's houses!"

"Well, he wasn't here, was he? Do you want to know what I found or what?"

I told him about the Emma Wild shrine that I found. However there was nothing further to go on. I searched his drawers, bed, closet, everywhere. No poison, no weapons. The guy didn't even own a computer.

"Get out of there," said Sterling.

"Just keep him there a bit longer," I said. "I need to find something."

I hung up and kept searching. Maybe Cal had a secret hiding spot, like under a plank of wood on the floor or something.

After ten more minutes of searching, a voice piped up from the window. I jumped, startled by the deep voice.

"Emma." It was Sterling, looking a bit frazzled. "You nut. Do you have any idea how dangerous this is?"

"Oh, hi, Sterling." I smiled sweetly.

I was starting to get used to his presence. Sure, he had shattered my heart once, but maybe over the years I'd overblown that incident to monumental proportions. I'd always been a dramatic person. I was even comfortable enough to tease him a little.

"Are you my father? Relax, it's fine. I know self-defense."

He sighed and rubbed his face. "Let's see it then."

I showed him the room. He was impressed.

"A bit excessive, huh?"

"It's looking a lot clearer now," he said. "This might just be our creep."

"But the thing is, we don't have much proof. So far, he's just an obsessed fan."

Sterling crossed his arms. "There might be more to it. Apparently he used to have a drug problem when he was a teen. He even went to juvie for a few months after fighting with someone and almost pounding the other kid to death. He's obviously a troubled guy, possibly mentally disturbed."

"Why would he come after me?"

"For control. Maybe he's obsessed with you and knows that he can't have you. After all, you are with this hotshot movie star. Maybe he doesn't think he has a chance and would rather kill you than lose you to someone else."

He said it so matter-of-factly that I almost laughed.

"Seriously? That's what you can come up with for a motive?"

Sterling shrugged. "Just a guess."

This time, I really laughed.

"I just can't imagine it."

"Imagine what?" he asked.

"That someone would be so in love with me to want to kill me."

He pressed his lips together, staying silent for a couple of minutes, then he turned to me.

"Emma, maybe you don't know the effect that you have on people."

The humorous smile faded from my face. Sterling looked serious. And sad. Could he still have feelings for me?

"You're beautiful and talented. Your music is enormously popular. Certain guys will put you on a pedestal. It's not a good feeling when they're faced with something that they can't have. When they're so close."

I slowly nodded.

"You know," I said. "My life's not that perfect.

People think I have this lavish life, but I'm still the same person. There's just more people looking up to me. And I kind of resent that sometimes. I can't be this perfect role model all the time. Because frankly, they don't know how much of a mess I can be. How much of a mess I am. The media can adore me and easily turn on me, and that's the case with this case. Love can easily turn on itself, can't it?"

Sterling sighed.

He took me into his arms and hugged me.

He didn't need to say anything. These were the kind of moments when I really enjoyed his silences. Because I knew that he understood. And if he didn't, he was willing to try.

I pulled away.

"And my perfect relationship to the famous movie star? Well, that's over. Gone in a New York second, okay?"

"I'm sorry," he said softly. "What happened?"

"He wanted lingerie models."

The somber way I said it made him chuckle. "He's a shallow idiot."

"I agree."

"It's agreed then," Sterling teased. "Your life is terrible."

I scowled. "Yeah, yeah, I know. I hate it too when a celebrity complains. I know how good I have it."

"Someone's trying to kill you," Sterling said. "You

have the right to feel a bit apprehensive about your lifestyle."

"You're right. Thanks." I headed back out the window. "You coming? I really want to talk to this guy and get to the bottom of it already."

CHAPTER 12

"So I hear that you're a big fan of Emma Wild," said Sterling.

I watched Cal in the interrogation room from behind the one-way mirror as Sterling questioned him. Cal's eyes widened the way they did when he'd run into me earlier, as if he'd been caught doing something he shouldn't.

Cal didn't answer.

"Are you or are you not a fan of Emma Wild's music?"

He nodded. "Yes, I am."

"Do you have all her CDs?"

Cal paused. "Yes. I listen to quite a lot of her songs. That's not a crime, is it?"

"You just don't seem like the type."

"The type to what?"

"Listen to her music."

Cal looked offended. "And what's wrong with her music? It's well written, her voice is beautiful, and it's deep. She gets me."

Sterling crossed his arms and narrowed his eyes at him.

"Seems a bit suspicious that you'd come all the way to live in her hometown, where you know no one, and get a job at her sister's cafe. Is that what you came out here for? For a chance to meet Emma Wild?"

"No. I didn't think that would happen. I thought she lived in New York."

"But you knew that her family lived here, right?"

"Yes, but—"

"And what a coincidence that you got a job at Emma's sister's cafe. What a better chance to meet Emma than there, short of breaking into her home, right?"

"Really, I had no idea that Mirabelle was her sister until I got the job."

Cal's face turned red. Was he embarrassed or guilty?

"I want a lawyer," he said.

"You have plenty of experience with lawyers, don't you?" Sterling continued. "You had a slew of trouble when you were in your teens, and now you're on the straight and narrow?

"Yes," Cal said through clenched teeth.

"It just so happened that you abandoned the city where your friends and family live to move all the way to a small town where you know no one."

"Yes. If you really must know, the city was getting too crazy for me. And my family and I don't get along. It's true that I'm a big fan of Emma Wild. I knew she'd grown up here, and it sounded like a nice town, so I moved up here, to get away from everything. And it really was a coincidence that I got a job at her sister's cafe. Except that I wouldn't call it a coincidence."

Sterling leaned in on the table. "What would you call it then?"

A dreamy smile spread over Cal's face. "Fate."

Sterling raised an eyebrow.

"Fate wanted us to meet." Cal's face lit up the more he spoke. "And when we finally did, I was completely starstruck. I mean, I've been to so many of her concerts and I listen to her music all the time. In fact, I was listening to her last album when I ran into her on the street earlier. Imagine that! Emma Wild running into me and wanting to talk to me. I was so embarrassed that I didn't know what to say to her. I was afraid that whatever I said would make me sound like a blubbering fool so I said next to nothing."

"Why do you love Emma so much?" asked Sterling.

"My upbringing wasn't so good. It was true that I got into all sorts of trouble as a kid, that by the time I was twenty, I couldn't take it anymore. If I'd stayed in the city, I would've gone deeper with the wrong crowd. My drug addiction would've gotten worse. I needed to clear my head. The last straw was when my girlfriend broke my heart, man. I was in love with her for three years.

"We were finally together when I got my act together, but then she dumped me. Dumped me for some crappy asshole who works in I.T. Emma's music was what got me through it all. She saved my life. If I didn't have her music to get me through the horrible times I went through in the last few years of my life, I wouldn't be here right now. I travelled, worked on the road, went to her concerts, got my head straight. And now I'm here, in Hartfield. And I love it here. It's so peaceful. The people are so friendly."

Sterling seemed to be digesting his story.

"Look," said Cal. "I would never hurt Emma, I swear to you. I'm her biggest fan. Why would I hurt her?"

Sterling sighed. "Somebody I spoke to thought you were involved, or might know something."

"Who?" Cal frowned.

"I'm not at liberty to say, but you do come in

contact with everyone at the cafe. You do touch every cup when you write the customer's name on them."

"Yes," Cal said, exasperated. "I do write the names on the cups, but the baristas are the ones who make the drinks. They would know if the cups were filled. I don't leave the cash register once I give the cups to them. In fact the counter is quite far from the cash register."

"Do you think one of the other workers had something to do with it?"

"No, I don't think so." But something in Cal's expression told otherwise.

"Are you sure?" Sterling pressed.

"Except..."

"What?"

"Kate, one of the baristas. She hates Emma's music."

"Why does she hate Emma's music?" Sterling asked.

Cal thought about it. "I think she mentioned that she just didn't like her voice. That it gave her a headache. Oh, and she was the first one to leave after we were all questioned. She looked really ill and really shaken up. It could've been that she was shocked, but who knows? Maybe she was overdoing it as an act."

"Well, what do you think?" Sterling asked me.

"I believe Cal. He didn't do it," I said. "What do you think?"

"I don't think he did it either."

Cal was just a hardcore fan who was going through a difficult time. I was glad that my music was able to help him. Plenty of fans wrote to me to tell me about their breakup stories all the time. When you were hurt and vulnerable, you needed someone who understood, and I was the safe person who was close but far, who whispered sweet songs of comprehension in their ears and gave them reassurance that they weren't alone.

"I'll go visit Kate at her home," said Sterling.

"I want to come," I said.

"No. It's better if I do it. Don't want to put you in danger."

I sighed.

"Fine," I said. "I'll go home and ask Mirabelle what she knows about her."

I didn't know Kate well, but the few times that I'd talked to her, she seemed nice and friendly, but so were those journalists who used to interview me. To my face, they were adoring angels. Then later I'd find out that they'd written the most scathing review or the most damning interview. In all my years in the industry, I knew that people weren't to be trusted at face value. And I didn't trust Kate.

CHAPTER 13

Mirabelle was on the couch again, finishing the stale cakes from the shop ever since it closed down. Somebody had to finish the inventory. On TV the evil twin on the cheesy soap was caught in the act of trying to kill the good twin by her mother. The mother was in hysterics.

"So what's up with Kate?" I asked. "What's the scoop on her?"

"Why? Is she a suspect now?"

Mirabelle had already been informed by the police that the drink had been tempered with. I didn't try to rub in the fact that I was right, seeing what a terrible situation it was to gloat about.

"Well, maybe. I mean, she does hate my music."

Mirabelle's jaws dropped. "Really? Says who?"

"It doesn't matter."

"I hope that's not true. I play your music in my cafe all the time."

"Thanks, sis."

"I hope it's not Kate. It can't be. She's so nice."

"What do you know about her?"

"Well, she's two years younger than you."

"Did she grow up here?" I asked.

"Yes. But you've probably never seen her because she had twins at sixteen and had to drop out of school."

"Really?" I exclaimed. "Twins? Wow."

"No kidding. She'd been working odd jobs since then. Never graduated high school. Her boyfriend, the father of the kid, skipped town five years ago. Terrible. So I was happy to give her a job at the cafe just when she was broke and getting kicked out of her apartment."

"Are you close at all?" I asked. "Does she talk a lot about her personal life?"

"Well, she talks about the kids, and sometimes who she's dating. So yes, I guess you could say that we're friends. She's closer to Kendra. She's her cousin, you know."

"Kendra? I didn't know they were related."

"I don't think they were close growing up. Kendra used to distance herself from Kate because she got pregnant so young and Kendra didn't want to be associated with all of that. But now, as far as I can tell, they're pretty close. Kendra comes in to chat all the time."

"I need to go talk to Kendra then."

Mirabelle put down the piece of cake and gave me a look.

"You're not going to tell her that Kate's a suspect are you? I mean, you can't just accuse her cousin of trying to poison you."

When I knocked on Kendra's door, I heard Blake Junior screaming in the house.

Kendra was shouting at him to pipe down when she opened the door.

"Hi," I said. "I hope it's not a bad time."

The kid was banging on a pot and singing at the top of his lungs in the kitchen.

Kendra was surprised to see me. She hesitated at the door.

"No," she said. "Come on in."

She cringed when her son sang a high note.

"Blake! I'll give you a dollar if you go upstairs and keep quiet."

"A dollar? Yay! I can buy ice cream!"

The kid with chocolate on his face happily went up the stairs.

Kendra rubbed her temples. "Ugh. I have a headache."

"How old is Blake?"

"Four. It's hard to keep up with him, and he still has all this energy even after running around in daycare all day."

"I didn't mean to intrude," I said.

She narrowed her eyes at me. "Why are you here?"

"We've been trying to get to the bottom of this whole case at the cafe, as you know. And it has been confirmed. Someone did poison the drink."

Kendra looked shocked.

"Oh my God."

"Yes. Cal mentioned that Kate might know something and I was wondering if she told you something?"

"Kate? No. What would she know?"

"We just don't want to leave any stones unturned, that's all. Kate's at the police station, being questioned right now. I just wanted to know if she'd mentioned something strange. She's closest to all the action, and maybe she mentioned whether she suspected someone, or knew something that she wasn't telling us?"

"Or if she did it herself you mean?" Kendra asked. "Is that what you're trying to say?"

"No. Of course not." I chuckled.

"Why would she want to kill you?" Kendra had her hands on her hips. Oh lord.

"I'm not accusing her."

"Sure, she has a temper sometimes. Sure, Kate hates your music and your looks and the fact that you stole her man, Nick Doyle."

I gasped. "What?"

"She's obsessed with Nick Doyle. She loves all his movies."

"Oh."

"And she's jealous that you're with him. Plus, sometimes Kate can get a bit stressed out. Her life is in shambles, has been ever since she had those twins young. Losing the best years of her life to raise kids? Brutal. She's had more than a few nervous breakdowns. Boyfriends just come and go. The baby daddy's long gone. And she sees you and your perfect life, and well..."

"What, so she does hate me?"

Kendra paused. "Hate is a strong word."

I was expecting Kendra to defend her cousin, to say that she was sweet and caring, and that she would never hurt a fly. But this just got interesting.

CHAPTER 14

$\mathcal{I}$ called Sterling, but he was probably still questioning Kate. After getting her address from Mirabelle, I set off for her house.

I had to pass through Samford Street because she lived on the other side of town, but a crowd of paparazzi had shown up. They were at the cafe, taking pictures.

My instinct was to run away, but I was so surprised that I froze and watched them.

Until it was too late. One of them saw me and began running towards me.

"Hey! Emma!"

"Is it true that someone was trying to poison you?"

"Who do you think is the killer?"

"Is it true that Nick dumped you for that hot model?"

They had cameras, and one of them even had a video camera. I began to run. For a small woman with short legs, I could run really fast. As I did, my phone rang.

"Emma," Sterling said. "What's going on? What's all that noise?"

He was referring to all the commotion behind me. The townspeople were looking at me, while the hound dogs were hot on my trail.

"Paparazzi scum," I said. "They're here."

I explained that I was literally on the run as I spoke.

"Where are you?" he asked.

We made plans to meet two blocks away, so I ran even faster. All the time at the gym working out paid off. I silently thanked my trainer. By the time I reached my destination, those scum were eating my dust.

Sterling pulled up in his black Honda. My getaway ride.

"Thanks." I jumped in and he sped away.

"How did they get here?" he asked.

"I should ask you. You're the detective."

"It could be anyone," he said.

"That's how it always happens. Where should we go?"

"Well..." Sterling raised an eyebrow. "Are you hungry?"

He drove outside of town until we were surrounded by farm land covered with snow.

"I know this great diner that just opened up," he said. "I bet you've never been."

After a few more minutes, he pulled into The Burger Shack.

"This is nice," I said. "Away from all the commotion."

We slid into a booth. When the waitress came, I ordered a cheeseburger and a chocolate milkshake, and Sterling ordered the same.

"I see your taste buds haven't changed," he said.

I made a face. "What, you think I would live off salads with low-fat dressing now?"

"Isn't that the celebrity diet?"

"Yeah, well, I do admit to that, although I reserve my weekends for junk food. I also have a dozen people working on me at all times. It's all part of the job unfortunately."

"You look great either way," he said. "But I always liked you better with no makeup."

"Thanks. I do too."

We shared a moment of looking into each other's eyes.

"So this is your life, huh? Is it always that chaotic?" he asked.

"Worse," I said. "There's usually one or more of these paparazzi bastards trailing me whenever I go outside. Which is why I stay in a lot of the times. I thought I'd get some peace in Hartfield, but they found me."

"Don't worry." He grinned. "I'll protect you."

I grinned back.

"Did you talk with Kate?" I asked.

"Yes. But I didn't get much out of her. She said the reason she left so abruptly that day was because she was sickened by the whole thing and went home because she was nauseous."

I told him what Kate's cousin told me.

"Unstable, huh?" he said.

"Yes. Do you think that she has access to cyanide?"

Sterling thought about it. "I thought I saw her some time ago with this guy who worked at the pharmacy. But they broke up a year ago."

"But she might still have access to it?"

"Maybe. Sure."

"But I still don't understand her motive. Does she hate my music so much?"

"Maybe it is jealousy," Sterling said. "She's a single mom of two kids with no education and tons of debt.

She has to work two jobs. And here you are, wealthy, loved, dating rich movie stars."

His eyes clouded over. Maybe Sterling was the one who was jealous. If only he knew how much I was in love with him, how hurt I was when he dumped me...

"That's what Kendra said," I said.

The waitress brought our food and we dug into our burgers. We were both famished.

"I want to search Kate's house as well," I said.

"Let's not have another B&E," he said. "I'll get a warrant this time."

CHAPTER 15

The next morning, Sterling and his team went over to Kate's house. I wanted to be there, but he wouldn't let me come.

It was a Saturday morning, and I stayed in baking gingerbread cookies with my parents instead.

By the time the cookies were in the oven, Sterling called me, excited.

"It's her," he said. "We just found the bottle of cyanide hidden inside her toilet."

"No way!"

"She's been arrested by the police."

"So you'll be at the station soon?" I asked.

"Yes, but—"

"I'm coming."

Sterling sighed. "I guess I can't stop you, can I?"

"Don't you know? I'm a celebrity. I can get in anywhere."

"I bet you can."

"Come on, please?"

"Fine. Come on over. Maybe you'll be an asset."

"It's not me! I swear," Kate shrieked as they brought her up the steps and through the front door of the police station.

Her brown hair was a mess over her face and her hands were handcuffed behind her back. She sobbed and snot dripped down her nose. Once she was inside, the police uncuffed her and Sterling gave her a tissue.

"Emma!" she said when she saw me coming in the front door. "I didn't do it. You have to believe me."

I signalled to Sterling to bring her into the interrogation room. I wanted to talk to her, too.

"If you didn't do it, why is there a bottle of cyanide in your house?" I asked.

"I was framed."

"By whom?"

Kate cried louder.

"Who, Kate?" My voice rose.

"Kendra."

"Kendra?" I gasped. "Why?"

"I wasn't sure if it was her at first, but nothing else explains it."

"Start at the beginning," Sterling demanded.

"I remember seeing Kendra that day at the cafe. She was just leaning in to chat, said something about cooking dinner the next day. It happened so fast that I didn't think of it."

Kate blew her nose.

"So you didn't see her poison the drink," I said.

"No, but when the woman died, I got suspicious. I went to Kendra's house immediately after to ask her about it."

"Why did you immediately jump to the conclusion that your own cousin did it?" Sterling asked.

"Yeah," I added. "I thought you were close."

"We are," said Kate. "Which was why I suspected her. You see, I know how much Kendra hates you, Emma."

That stung. "Why does she hate me so much?"

"She blames you for her husband's death."

"*What?*"

"She has to blame someone and you were easy. The thing is, her husband killed himself. He was depressed for a long time and he used to listen to your music all the time. He said you had a voice like velvet. Kendra hated that even when he was alive. They used to get into fights when he listened to your music in front of her. She was so jealous. He said that you were the only one who understood him. Then finally, he poisoned himself and left a note, which Kendra destroyed."

"Wow." I leaned back in my chair. "What did the note say?"

"I don't know," Kate continued. "She only told me about it, but not what it said. She didn't want anyone to know that he had committed suicide, which was why she didn't even hold a funeral. Since that day, a bitter seed was planted in her heart and it grew bigger and more powerful every day. Every time I saw her she mentioned how much she hated you and wanted to kill you. I thought she was just venting. I really didn't think she was serious. I know that deep down she blamed herself, but it felt good for her to blame you."

"So when you talked to her, what did she say about it?" asked Sterling. "Did she admit to it at all?"

"Kendra was totally defensive about it. She played dumb and said she didn't know what I was talking about. But I knew her husband had poisoned himself with cyanide and she still had the bottle. I just didn't know that she would turn around and frame me. All I'd ever done was try to protect her."

Sterling shook his head.

"You wanted to protect her so much that you were willing to put Emma's life and the lives of other people in town in danger? You should've come forward with this information sooner."

Kate sobbed.

"I knew how much she'd been through. I was her maid of honor. I thought we were close. I can't believe she'd frame me like this. Why?"

Sterling and I looked at each other.

"We'll have to ask her, won't we?" I said.

CHAPTER 16

When they brought Kendra in, I decided to bring her a cup of hot chocolate from the station's lunchroom.

She looked up, surprised to see me. I gave her a smile that she didn't return.

"What's the matter?" I said. "You don't like hot chocolate?"

Kendra stared at me with that chilling dead look of hers.

"Not your drink then." I took a sip of it. "But you know it's mine."

This was the first time I drank hot chocolate since Emma Chobsky was poisoned. I had to say, it was delicious, but of course it wasn't nearly as good as Mirabelle's.

"How long have we known each other?" I asked.

Kendra shrugged. She looked lifeless sitting in that chair. She acted as cool as a cucumber, but I knew she was scared.

"Since we were eight," I answered for her. "I remember the first time I met you. You had your own little clique, your band of followers even then. You almost tore my hair out for sitting at your lunch table."

"It was an exclusive table," she replied. "And I never gave you permission to sit there."

"Little Kendra. Always a control freak. When did Blake die?"

"It will be seven months this Saturday," she said. "Can I go home? I'm getting tired."

"Tired from what? You don't do anything all day. Blake's insurance gave you a good chunk of money."

"Well money doesn't buy happiness," she snarled.

"Why did he die?" I asked.

I could see the steam rising to her face. She turned red, seething.

"He was sick," she finally said.

"What was he so sick from?"

She composed herself. "I'm not going to talk about this."

"It was poison, wasn't it? Cyanide?"

Her face was beet red, but she still wasn't talking.

"You came home one day and your husband was found dead by his own hand in the bedroom. My first album was playing when you got there. How did that make you feel?"

Kendra shot me a hateful look. "How would you feel if the love of your life died?"

"It would be excruciating. Is that why you tried to kill me? Did you hate me that much?"

"No. I didn't try to kill you."

I locked eyes with her.

"Eyes don't lie, Kendra. There's hate in your eyes and it's directed at me. Now isn't it funny how someone tried to poison my drink with cyanide? The cyanide that remained from your husband's suicide?"

"It wasn't. You already got your perp. Kate."

"Your own cousin? Really, Kendra?"

"Kate's a liar! She belongs in a psychiatric ward!"

"For what?" I spat out. "For trying to protect you? I agree. She is crazy for trying to cover up a murder in your family. Can you imagine how Emma Chobsky's family feels?"

"That was an accident!" she blurted it out.

It was too late for her to take that back. The jig was up.

"Come on, Kendra. You framed your own cousin. You tried to poison and kill me in public — how did you ever think you were going to get away with that?"

Kendra stood up. I was wearing my flats and she loomed over me.

"It was all your fault," she spewed out. "The

moment you stepped into town I wanted to rip you apart. It wasn't planned. In fact, I would've tried to kill myself if I didn't have Blake Junior to take care of. I hated you so much for what you've done to my family. So I followed you. The cafe was so crowded that nobody saw a thing when I poured the poison, especially when people were distracted by your screaming admirer."

"Whom you killed," I retorted. "You killed an innocent young woman."

"Like I said, it was an accident!"

Kendra lunged toward me and Sterling burst in and stood between us.

"Sit down, Kendra," he said.

"My husband is going to hell because of you," Kendra continued. "Suicide! Nobody gets into heaven with suicide. And you did it. You made him do it with your depressing songs. He kept replaying that one song, 'Die For You,' over and over. And the other one, 'The Killer in Me.' I thought I was going to go mad, too. Are you proud of that? Are you proud of what you've done?"

The blood drained from my face. To be accused of being responsible for someone's death was so vicious. Kendra could see that it affected me, and that encouraged her.

"I was doing the world a favor. How many more

people are going to kill themselves because of you? Shame. Shame!"

Sterling pushed her to the wall. Two policemen came in and cuffed her again.

Sterling saw how shaken up I was and he embraced me.

"I was doing God's work!" Kendra railed. "Blake and I loved each other. We were supposed to grow old together. My son is fatherless because of you. All thanks to you and your devil's music. Go to hell, you murderous bitch!.I still have another plan to kill you. To bury you. Go to hell!"

Sterling took me outside, but I could still hear her screaming in that room.

I sobbed in his arms.

"Don't listen to her," he said. "It's not your fault."

"It is partly my fault. My music triggered something in him that—"

"Shhh, Emma. Your music brings joy to so many people. Blake was mentally ill. I'm sure Kendra blames herself more. She's just taking it out on you. I'm sure she felt as if she failed as a wife. If they were so in love, why would he kill himself? There was nothing she could do. She was helpless. She just needed someone to blame."

I nodded. It knew that he was right, but I still couldn't shake off the guilt.

"What you have to offer the world is amazing," Sterling said. "You're amazing."

It did feel better to be in his arms. I felt protected. I'd always felt warm and safe in Sterling's arms. God, how I'd missed him.

CHAPTER 17

Kendra was locked up and awaiting trial. The paparazzi stuck around and were all over the scoop while I holed up at home and ordered Christmas presents online. It had been a crazy December. Emma Chobsky's funeral took place last weekend. I was invited and I decided to go out of respect to pay tribute. I even sang a song. The family wept. So did I. I was pretty glum for a few days, but things cheered up when we got closer to Christmas.

I tried to focus on the positive. I had a lot to be grateful for. The killer was behind bars, I was safe, and I had my lovely family to celebrate with.

On Christmas Eve, most of the paparazzi had left. Hopefully they had family of their own to spend time with.

Mirabelle and her husband Sam were over at my

parents' house. After our traditional Christmas meal where we stuffed our faces with all sorts of comfort food and desserts, we carried the party into the living room to drink eggnog and open presents.

"This one's for you, Mom." I passed my present to my mother and watched her open the pink box.

"A new knitting set! Is this real silver?"

"Yes."

My mom was in a knitting circle, and I figured this would score points with her ladies. Who didn't envy someone with the hottest knitting needles?

"You're next." Mirabelle gave me a red box.

I shook it first, then sniffed it.

"It doesn't smell like chocolate," I said with disappointment.

"It's better," she said.

I opened it. "The Super Kid's Detective Kit!"

It was a set for young sleuths in the making. It came with a spyglass, a notebook, finger print powder, and a book of codes.

"Thanks! I love it. I'll put it to good use. Didn't I have one of these as a child?"

"You did," said Mirabelle. "That's why I got you an updated version. You used to drive everyone crazy trying to dust fingerprints all over the furniture with all that white powder."

I laughed at the memory.

"I always wanted one of those Sherlock Holmes hats," I said. "And the cape to match."

"Well, that's a present for next year," said Dad. "Come on, let's sing some songs."

He began to play the piano rendition of Wham!'s "Last Christmas." It made us all cringe at first, but we sang along anyway. When Dad transitioned into Mariah Carey's "All I Want for Christmas is You," the doorbell rang.

I stood up to get it. When I opened the door, boy did I get a nice surprise.

Sterling.

"Hi," I said.

Those old butterflies came fluttering back into my belly.

"Hi." He grinned.

"I hope you're here to give me my present."

"I am."

"Come on in."

He pulled at my arms. "I can't stay long. I just came to see you."

"Oh?"

I stepped out and closed the door behind me.

It was snowing lightly and the street looked so peaceful and gorgeous.

Sterling looked very handsome in his dark coat. His bright grey eyes shone under the lights.

"So where is it?" I asked. "Where's my present?"

"It's here."

He pulled me in. His lips softly touched mine. One hand lightly touched the small of my back as the other rubbed below my neck. It was the kiss that used to make my head spin as a teenaged girl.

When he pulled away, my legs felt like jelly.

"Emma, I know that after Christmas you might be going back to New York, so I have to tell you."

I looked at him expectantly. "Tell me what?"

"I know that I've been an idiot. It's hard for me to express myself. I know that. It's the reason that I got divorced, well one of them anyway. It's also one of the reasons I lost you to begin with. I know I need to learn how to tell people how I feel, and now I'm telling you."

I gulped and waited. The smell of him was intoxicating. My heart pounded like crazy.

"You know why I broke up with you?" he asked.

I frowned, not wanting to think about it. "Because you didn't love me and wanted to date other girls."

"No. That wasn't the reason."

"So what was it?"

"I did love you," he said softly. "I was crazy about you. I knew that you could do whatever you set your mind to, and I knew that you'd stay in this town for me. Except that I also knew that you had more to offer the world. So I had to let you go."

"That's ridiculous. So that was why you were so cold? So I would think that you didn't love me?"

Sterling nodded. "And I was right to. You know? You had all that success—success that I knew was in you. You'd always been so passionate about music and you couldn't sing at birthday parties for the rest of your life. I'm glad I don't have that on my conscience —the guilt that I had held you back."

I took a breath. "Sterling, that is just so cruel. How could you? You broke my heart. All these years I thought you didn't love me. And I wrote all those songs about it."

"I'm sorry. I wanted the best for you and I just thought this town was too small for you. I wasn't enough for you."

"How could you say that?" I exclaimed.

"I thought that you would get over me and be with someone else, someone on your level. And you did."

"But I spent years trying to get over you. You don't know how much I cried and suffered over you!"

Now it was his turn to look surprised. "Really?"

"Yes. I wrote so many songs about our breakup."

"I didn't know that you felt so strongly. When you came back, I was unsure at first, but being around you again...I knew that I didn't want to let you go again.

I laughed. "I can't believe it. I mean, I really

thought that you didn't care. I avoided this town because of you! You really are cruel. All those years of torture. You know that you're going to make up for all the heartache you've caused me, right?"

"I'll be glad to," he said.

Then he kissed me again. Hard. In his arms, I simply disappeared. Gone was the street. The houses. The earth. It was just me and Sterling. This could possibly be the best Christmas ever, despite all that had happened.

When we broke apart, I saw a man down the street out of the corner of my eye. Sterling and I both turned to him.

"Emma?" The voice sounded awfully familiar.

He came closer and a face emerged.

It was Nick Doyle. My ex.

CHAPTER 18

"*N*ick? What are you doing here?"

Nick's face was contorted in shock. And hurt. His dirty blond hair was combed neatly to one side. He wore a black designer winter coat, and he looked like he had just stepped out of a magazine spread.

"I came to see you," he said. "Aren't you going to introduce me?"

I noticed Sterling's jaw tense.

"This is Sterling," I said slowly. "Sterling, this is Nick."

Sterling put out a hand, but Nick didn't take it.

"You've moved on already? With him?"

I crossed my arms. "What's it to you?"

"I'm here because I wanted to see you and talk to you."

"About what? A simple phone call couldn't suffice?"

"I tried your cell phone, but you didn't pick up. Your manager told me where you were. Then I saw some tabloid pictures in the papers and got worried. Someone was trying to murder you?"

"The killer's been caught," I said. "I'm fine now."

He gave Sterling another steely once-over. "I can see that."

"We're over," I told him. "Yes, I am with Sterling. I have the right to move on. Just like you moved on with that Tara, right?"

Nick groaned. "You should know as well as anybody that tabloid stories are false. I went to Tom's birthday party, and some models were there. They're usually everywhere. We just took a picture together."

"It doesn't matter," I said. "I'm not going to interrogate you about what you did or didn't do. That wasn't the reason we broke up."

Nick sighed.

"I know," he said softly. "I messed up. I wasn't willing to fight for you. I took you for granted. Which was why I came here."

He reached into his pocket and took out a small box. He opened it. The most dazzling diamond ring shone back at me.

"I planned to propose."

My jaw dropped.

"But I see that you're busy with loverboy here."

With that, Nick turned away. I only stood there, aware that Sterling was watching me watch him.

RECIPE 1: HOT CHOCOLATE LATTE

Ingredients:
- 4 cups brewed hot coffee
- 1 cup half-and-half
- 1/4 cup chocolate syrup
- 1/2 teaspoon vanilla extract
- 2 tablespoons sugar

Stir everything in a pan over low-medium heat for five minutes or thoroughly heated. Serve with whipped cream!

RECIPE 2: ORGANIC HOT CHOCOLATE

Ingredients:
- Organic milk or unsweetened nut milk
- 4 to 8 pieces of high quality chocolate (preferably organic)
- Cream (optional)

Pour milk in a mug, leaving two inches for the chocolate. Heat this the milk on a stove. Meanwhile, chop up the chocolate. When the milk is warm (not boiling), throw the chocolate in. Pour back into the mug and enjoy! You can try this recipe with different flavors of chocolate, such as mint or orange, if you are feeling more adventurous.

RECIPE 3: HOT CIDER NOG

Ingredients:
- 1 cup apple cider
- 1 cup milk
- 2 cups half-and-half
- 2 large eggs
- 1/2 cup sugar
- 1/4 tsp ground cinnamon
- 1/8 tsp ground nutmeg
- 1/8 tsp salt
- 1/2 cup whipping cream, whipped

Whisk all ingredients except whipping cream in a saucepan over medium-low heat. Whisk occasionally until mixture thickens and coats a spoon (around 15 minutes). Top with whipping cream. Garnish with a cinnamon stick if you'd like.

BOOK 2: NEW YEAR'S SLAY

CHAPTER 1

*I*f I hadn't known any better, I would've thought that Martha Owens got staked through the heart by a vampire slayer. That was the first thought that came into my mind when I saw her limp body on the ground in the Sweet Dreams Inn. But it wasn't a wooden stake through her heart; it was simply the largest knitting needle I had ever seen. It stuck right out from her chest while blood stained the lower part of the needle, along with a good portion of her lavender cardigan set.

"Oh my god," I gasped.

A police officer stepped in front of me before I could get any closer to the body.

"Ma'am, you're not allowed to be here."

Before I could protest, Detective Sterling Matthews stepped forward and waved him away.

"It's okay, Peter, she's with me."

Sterling smiled and winked at me. He raised his arms for a hug, but his arms went right back to his sides when he saw that I wasn't making my move to greet him the usual way—with a big hug and a kiss on the lips.

"What a way to ring in the new year, huh?" Sterling said.

"Who would do this?" I asked.

"I was just asking your friend the same thing."

I looked up at Nick Doyle—the movie star and my ex—standing in a corner of the living room. Eyes wide and hugging himself, he was clearly shaken.

Sterling had been questioning Nick before I showed up, which was why Nick called me right after he called his lawyer. Nick was the only guest at the inn, and the only person who saw Martha last before her death. And he was the prime suspect.

I didn't know Martha Owens too well, but I knew of her because she owned the only inn in Hartfield. The only other lodging for visitors was a seedy motel a half hour's drive away. Martha was also in my mom's knitting group, but from the way my mom talked about the dynamics of the group, it didn't sound like she was very well liked. Even Mom, who generally got along with everybody, hardly ever invited Martha over.

Funny enough, I did speak to Martha three days before she was murdered when I went to the inn to talk to Nick.

When he showed up in Hartfield on Christmas Eve, he caught me kissing Detective Sterling Matthews in front of my house. Nick and I had broken up a few weeks before and I had moved out of the New York penthouse apartment that we shared. After holing up in a hotel for a week, I decided to come home to Hartfield to spend time with my family for the holidays.

I didn't expect to reconnect with Sterling, who was my high school sweetheart and my first love that I never completely got over, but I did and I was happy, until Nick arrived with the most beautiful diamond engagement ring I had ever seen.

I thought that Nick would go back to New York and never speak to me again after finding out that I had moved on with Sterling, but he surprised me by staying. Nick was angry at first, but he took a couple of days to cool off. He wasn't the type to stay angry for long, and he knew that I wasn't to blame because we had already broken up and I was under the assumption that he had already moved on with a Victoria's Secret model thanks to the tabloids. However, it turned out that the rumors weren't true.

I never expected Nick to come here and propose. For a while, I believed what the press said about him —that he was heading to a lifetime of bachelorhood à la Leonardo Dicaprio. I was pushing thirty and Nick hadn't proposed after four years of living together, so I gathered my pride and my designer clothes in a suitcase and left him. But now it turned out that he did want to marry me. Practically every girl wanted to marry Nick Doyle. But I couldn't just drop Sterling; I had feelings for him too.

As one of the biggest movie stars in the world, Nick was used to getting what he wanted. I guess when I left he realized what he had taken for granted. I had to be careful with him. Who knew if Nick really meant it? Sterling and I were starting to have a good thing going. I'd never stopped loving him. But I never stopped loving Nick either. The decision to be with Sterling had been easy when I believed that Nick didn't love me enough. Now, I was beyond confused.

Nick called me a few days after Christmas and told me that he was still in town.

"I thought you'd be back in New York by now," I said.

"You can't get rid of me that easily. I waited a while to call you to get my head straight."

"Are you mad?" I asked.

"I was, but I want to talk to you in person. Can we meet?"

I was hesitant. While we weren't official, I was back with Sterling, but I knew that I owed Nick a face-to-face chat if he had come all the way to Hartfield with an engagement ring.

"Sure. Where are you staying?"

"The Sweet Dreams Inn."

I stifled a laugh. Somehow I couldn't quite picture Nick staying in Martha's quaint little B&B when he was used to five-star accommodations. With her floral wallpaper, ornamental plates on walls, pink bed sheets and an excess of pillows and cushions, Sweat Dreams was a grandmother's dream.

"There are no other hotels in sight," he explained. "Where else could I stay?"

"True," I said. "Should we meet there then?"

"Yes. There's no one else staying here at the moment."

"Did anyone recognize you?" I asked.

"Martha has no clue. I only told her that I was in town alone nursing a broken heart so that she'd feel sorry for me."

"You didn't." I laughed.

"Now she wants to set me up with the daughters of a few of her friends."

"Hmmm."

"Since you're taken, I might take her up on that offer."

"If that's what makes you happy," I said.

"Glad to have your blessing," Nick joked.

At least Nick was back to his jovial self. He was like a cat, always landing on all fours whenever he was thrown. If I stayed with Sterling, Nick would be all right. The question was, would I?

We made plans to meet at the inn for afternoon tea.

Sweet Dreams was on the outskirts of town, near the lake. It was run by Martha Owens. Ever since Martha's divorce ten years ago, she'd been running the inn alone. Her husband had moved to Vancouver and got remarried.

Tourism had dwindled in recent years. But Martha had too much of a sentimental attachment to the inn to ever sell it. She had grown up there, and her son had grown up there as well. Maybe Martha was fine living in what was really an empty Victorian mansion.

The upside to the lack of business was that Mom's knitting circle was welcome two times a week in the inn's lounge, a.k.a. the living room. The group had nineteen members and the inn was one of the few places in town that could host such a large group of chatty senior ladies armed with sharp needles.

I passed by Samford Street, where the massive Christmas tree and all the decor and lights on the lampposts and shops were still up. Boxing Week was still going strong. The locals went into stores in droves and came out with more shopping bags than they had before Christmas. My sister's cafe was as busy as ever, and I waved to her outside the window when I passed by, but she didn't see me. I was relieved that the murder last month in her cafe hadn't affected sales, but the whole incident was another story—something I was trying to push from memory going into the new year.

When I reached Sweet Dreams, Nick was standing on the porch waiting for me.

His dirty blond hair was neatly parted and combed, reminding me of that rockabilly character he played in one of his movies. He was tall and fit, especially coming off filming the sequel to his action film Alive or Dead. His hands were shoved deep into the pockets of his black wool jacket and he was shivering.

Even though he was thirty-three, he reminded me of a boy who needed to be taken care of, and I supposed he brought the maternal instinct out in most women, which was part of the reason why he was such a hit with them. I wanted to scold him for not wearing a scarf in December weather, yet wrap my arms around him to warm him up.

When he saw me, his blue eyes lit up and he cracked his dimpled smile that made me—and every other girl in the world—melt. I smiled back, but I really wanted to sigh in frustration. Why did he have to be so good looking?

He came down and hugged me. "I missed you."

"Let's go inside," I said. "You look like you're freezing."

"Is it always this cold in Canada?"

"You have to ask? Winter barely just started here."

The inn was beautiful, but in that creepy Victorian way. As a child, I used to be afraid of it because rumor had it that it was haunted. The outside was painted a dark teal with even darker window shutters. The interior was like the inside of a dollhouse. Everything was perfect and antique. Martha was in her rocking chair, knitting away. Time stopped inside that place.

When Martha saw me, she got up and greeted me.

"Beth's daughter," she said. "I haven't seen you for a while. Heard you ran off to the city and became a singer."

Martha was nearly sixty. Her curly short hair was dyed an orangey blond color and she wore bifocals that enlarged her brown eyes. I didn't know what to make of her. She'd scared me as a child because she always seemed cranky and I was told not to get on her bad side because she had a temper. Kids always knew to stay away from her place on Halloween if they didn't want day-old fruit and a lecture about candy causing cavities.

"I did," I replied.

"I always saw you singing around town and now I hear you're singing in New York?"

"That's right."

"I hope that you're making a living. Are they paying you well?"

Nick and I both tried not to laugh. Martha didn't seem to have a clue that I had two best-selling albums and a Grammy award for best album of the year.

"Yes," I said. "They are."

"Good." She smiled. "Your mom said you were doing well." Martha turned to Nick. "See, young man? I told you that there are plenty of pretty young women for you in this town. You'll get over that nasty ex-girlfriend in no time."

I raised an eyebrow. "Oh?"

Nick chuckled nervously. "She wasn't all that bad, Martha..."

"She sounds awful," Martha said vehemently. "Who could break this handsome young man's heart and jump into the arms of another young man? A floozy, that's who."

"She sounds horrible," I said, not sure whether to laugh or get mad.

"You deserve better," Martha said to Nick.

"Er, thanks." Nick rubbed the back of his neck. "We'd like to have some tea, please."

"Oh, sure," said Martha. "I didn't mean to intrude on your date. Of course. Sit yourself in the library and I'll bring you some tea and desserts. I just made fresh blueberry scones this morning. Do you like those?"

"Yes," we said in unison.

"Then I'll put on the kettle and bring you everything when it's ready."

The library was a nook around the corner from the living room. Two walls were lined with books, mainly mystery novels and a very heavy encyclopedia set. There were three sets of tables and chairs, all empty, and we sat at one table.

"I'm sorry about that," Nick apologized.

"So you've been talking about how awful I am, huh?"

"I was mad when I first saw you and that guy kissing, so I vented a bit, but—"

"It's fine," I said quickly. "I get it. It's a complicated situation and I didn't mean to hurt you."

"You know why I'm back," Nick began. "I didn't know that you would move out so suddenly. I mean, I really didn't see it coming."

"That was one of the problems," I said slowly.

"I know, I know." He sighed. "It's difficult for me to have a relationship, with all the traveling that I do. I always have a million things going on."

"Yes, well, I didn't want to get in the way."

Nick leaned forward on the table and took my hands. "You weren't. I was the idiot. I realize that I took you for granted."

His hands felt warm over my cold hands. How did he manage to warm them up so fast when he'd been freezing outside only moments earlier? I didn't move my hands away, but I didn't say anything either.

"I realize now that when you were talking about marriage and everything, you meant it. I was so stupid. I didn't think you were serious because we were living together and we were happy. Or I thought we were happy. Heck, I thought I was committed because you were the first girl and only girl I'd ever lived with. Aside from my mom."

I laughed. Nick never failed to make me smile even in serious situations.

"You have to admit that all things considered, living together was rather a big step for me."

"But we'd been living together for four years," I said. "For some girls, that may be enough, but I'm a traditional, small town girl. I want to get married and have kids. But aside from that, it just didn't seem as if I was a priority in your life. All the filming, the promotional tours, the charity events—I understand that they're all important to you, but for a while, we were roommates who hardly saw each other. I was the one flying out to you most of the time."

"Which is why I'm here," he said. "I'm ready to make a commitment. Come on, Emma. Please give me another chance. I love you."

His last words seemed to echo in the little library. I had to take into consideration that he was an actor, and that he could say a line pretty well. But I also knew him well: Nick wasn't the type to lie.

"What about those lingerie models?" I asked.

"The thing with models is that they are, well, for a lack of a better word, easy. They're pretty and they're fun, and I dated them when I was younger when I wasn't looking for something complicated. But now I'm ready. I want to be in a meaningful relationship with a complicated girl. The ring is still for you. What do you say?"

If Sterling weren't in the picture, I would've said yes. But I was hung up on Sterling. Most of my songs on my first album were about him. You never forgot your first love.

When it rained, it poured. Just weeks ago, I thought I was better off single because I couldn't find a guy to commit, but now Sterling also wanted to be in a serious relationship with me. He said so on our last date.

"You know that I'm dating someone else," I said finally.

Nick sighed. "But whoever that guy is, he's a rebound and you know it."

I shook my head. "He's actually an ex-boyfriend. We've known each other since high school."

"High school sweethearts, huh?" Nick's smile fell and there was a harsher note in his voice. "Are you spending New Year's Eve together?"

I nodded. "I'm sorry, Nick."

On New Year's Eve, my family was throwing a party with close friends, and Sterling was coming over. I couldn't invite Nick too.

He looked crestfallen, but he kept his hands over mine.

"Then I'll be here," he said. "I'll wait right here at this inn until you're ready."

"Why would you assume I'll be ready?"

"Because you haven't said no."

He was right. I hadn't said no. He still had a chance, and he knew it.

"Like I said, Emma. I'm going to fight for you this time. I don't care who this guy is, and how long you've known each other. You love me and I love you. It's as simple as that."

I wasn't so sure about that. I never knew love to be so simple, and that belief was evident in my songs.

CHAPTER 2

The Wild house was pumping with cheesy eighties music. Dad was dancing to Cyndi Lauper's "Girls Just Wanna Have Fun" and trying to get Mom to join in. We'd invited fifteen guests comprised of close friends and family. My very pregnant sister, Mirabelle, was here with her husband, and our childhood friends Suzy and Leslie and their boyfriends. Most of the other guests were invited by my parents. Sylvia and Rhonda, Mom's closest friends from her knitting group were over as well.

I was relieved that Martha wasn't here. Because Sterling was invited, I didn't want her slipping in the fact that I had been on a "date" with Nick at her inn. Things with Sterling were still new and I wasn't exactly sure what to do. For now, I did want to give

Sterling another chance. There was a lot of catching up we needed to do.

He showed up clean-shaven and smelling like the ocean. He offered me a bowl of mashed potatoes, sheepishly admitting that he'd made it with his daughters earlier that afternoon.

"This looks great," I said.

He beamed and quickly kissed me before anybody behind me noticed he was here.

"Sterling," my mom said. "Glad you could make it."

My parents knew by now that I had broken up with Nick. I didn't tell them—Dad had stumbled onto an article about our breakup when he was on the Huffington Post website—and they had a good idea that I was still sweet on Sterling.

Mom took his coat and winked at me when she thought Sterling wasn't looking. I stifled a groan.

While there was more than enough food and drink for our guests, everybody brought a dish of their own and the party turned into a potluck. After I introduced Sterling to the other guests, I put his mashed potatoes on the kitchen counter already crammed with other bowls and plates of an assortment of dishes, appetizers and desserts.

"Help yourself if you're hungry." I pointed to the self-serve plates and utensils.

"Don't mind if I do." Sterling grinned at the selection and began loading up his plate.

"That's too bad your girls couldn't come," I said.

"They're with their mom," he said, "at their grandparents' house. But they're with me next weekend. Would you like to come over and meet them on Saturday?"

"Sure!" I said. "I'd love to."

I thought it was sweet that Sterling was so close with his daughters and I did want to meet them. He had divorced a couple of years ago, but seemed to have a civil and practical relationship with his ex-wife. I never knew his wife because he'd met her in college, and in a way I was curious about her.

I didn't mind that Sterling was divorced. It was so commonplace to have starter marriages now, especially when people married young. I thought it was great that Sterling became a dad. I'd always thought that he would make a great dad.

Maybe I was getting too ahead of myself, but I considered the possibility of becoming a stepmom. Would his daughters like me? Or would they resent me? What if I wasn't good with kids?

I told myself to relax. So far I'd only been on two official dates with Sterling.

Suzy and Leslie's boyfriends came by the table and began to chat Sterling up. There was a shortage of men at the party, so they stuck together. They talked about hockey, beer and whatever else it was that men bonded over.

I quit listening to the boys and wandered over to Mom and her knitting friends. When Mom got pulled into another conversation by one of Dad's golf friends, Sylvia and Rhonda teased me about my date.

"He's certainly a handsome fellow," said Sylvia.

At seventy, she was the oldest member of mom's knitting group. With her white hair, friendly face and cheerful demeanor, she reminded me of Betty White.

"If only I were forty years younger," Rhonda said. She was tall, big-boned and had shoulder-length gray hair.

Sterling was certainly handsome of the tall, dark variety. He had stormy gray eyes that made him look like he was constantly brooding. How different he was from Nick, Hollywood's golden boy. While Nick was outgoing and charming, Sterling was quiet and thoughtful. Nick was a popular celebrity, while Sterling stayed in the shadows to dig up the cold hard truth for his line of work.

Trying to choose between them was like picking between apples and oranges, but both had enough hold on me to break my heart. What they had in common was that they both did at one point. I'd written enough songs about those heartbreaks. But it was almost the new year. I would start fresh and leave the past pain behind. The question was—who would I choose to spend my future with?

Sylvia giggled. "He looks just like this boyfriend I

had when I was in my twenties and living in Rome for the summer. Is he Italian?"

"I don't think so," I said.

I was so amused that they were giggling over Sterling like schoolgirls that I got pulled into it too. For a while, I gushed about what Sterling did and how great he was. Then I asked them about how their knitting group was going.

The knitting gang met every Tuesday and Thursday at Martha's inn and Sylvia wasn't happy about the location.

"I keep telling the group that we should change venues," she said. "I don't like that inn of hers."

"Why not?" I asked.

"It's haunted," she said matter-of-factly.

"Oh, don't mind her," Rhonda said. "Sylvia thinks a lot of places are haunted."

"It's true," Sylvia protested. "This town was built on an Indian burial ground."

"Have you seen a ghost?" I asked. While I didn't know if I believed in ghosts, I was intrigued by the whole thing.

Sylvia nodded. "When I went in to the bathroom once at Martha's, I was washing my hands and saw a white figure reflected in the medicine cabinet mirror, but when I turned around, there was no one there."

"Maybe because there was no one," Rhonda said. "It could've been your overly active imagination."

"I saw it," Sylvia insisted. "You couldn't pay me to sleep in that house. No wonder the place hardly ever has guests. I would rather stay on someone's couch than that creepy place. I just get a really bad feeling every time I go there."

"Who do you think is haunting the place?" I asked.

"I don't know," said Sylvia. "But whoever is there is bringing a very heavy energy."

"We began holding meetings there when I couldn't host at my daughter's house anymore," said Rhonda. "My daughter had kids and the house became too chaotic for so many old ladies. Plus, I thought that since Martha had so much space, we would open the group up to new members, but it didn't turn out that way."

"I voted to let in new members too," Sylvia exclaimed. "Knitting has become popular with the younger women in town and some of them had expressed interest in joining. I thought it would be nice to have some young blood in the group, but Martha simply refuses."

"It's like she's in charge now!" Rhonda huffed. "Just because she's hosting doesn't mean she calls the shots. Sylvia and I are the founding members. It's completely unfair, so at the next meeting, we're going to insist on having a vote about this matter. And if Martha doesn't like it, well, we'll just have to find a new venue."

I nodded sympathetically. "I wonder if Mirabelle's cafe can be a potential venue. It's just so busy most of the time, but otherwise, I'm sure she would love to host you."

"We'll see, dear," Sylvia said, smiling. "It's just that there are so many of us that most establishments don't allow it. Your mom offered your home, which is very nice of her. We might take her up on it. We would fill the whole living room, but if worse comes to worse, at least we have a backup plan."

"I hope our house is not haunted," I joked.

"It's not," Sylvia said with a serious expression. "If it was, I would tell you."

"We used to meet in the town library," Rhonda said. "But that place is too quiet for a bunch of noisy old ladies like us. Plus the librarians disapprove of us because of our knitting needles. They say it's dangerous around the kids."

"Imagine calling us dangerous," Sylvia said, chuckling. "But I guess they have a point. It could be dangerous if a child took one of our needles from our bags without any of us noticing and ran around with it."

"Well, I hope things work out," I said.

"It would be great to include new members and pass down our techniques," Sylvia said.

"Knitting secrets." Rhonda winked. I laughed.

"It's just a matter of the members voting and agreeing on some things," Sylvia. "It's so silly. All the knitting politics."

Rhonda looked at her wristwatch. "My, it's getting late."

"But it's only ten forty-five," Sylvia said.

"I'm sorry, ladies. I promised my daughter I'd go home to count down to the new year with the family."

Rhonda said farewell to us and the rest of the guests while Sylvia and I continued to chat.

"I sure hope to get out of that inn." Sylvia shuddered. "It gives me the creeps. Have you noticed that crows always like to stand on the roof over there? That's never a good sign."

Aside from her ability to see ghosts, Sylvia surprised me by announcing that she could also read palms. She told me that I would have a long full life. I'd marry and have up to four children if I wanted to.

"Would it be soon?" I asked.

"It's up to you," said Sylvia. "You still have free will of course. This is just a guideline of what's in store for you. Lines do change however."

"Really? Lines can change on a palm?"

"Why, certainly."

I looked over at Sterling, wondering if he was the guy I'd end up with. He already had two children. If we married, I'd only have to give birth twice to have the big family that I wanted. That was, if his first wife didn't mind me spoiling her daughters.

But I also wondered how Nick was getting on. Was he still in Hartfield? If he was, he would be spending New Year's Eve alone. I knew it was silly, but I also worried about whether the inn really was haunted. When I was there last, I did sense a certain Victorian creepiness about the place, but I was there in the daytime. I was sure that it was much spookier at night.

I checked my phone. Nick did call. I listened to my voicemail. Nick left a message, wishing me a happy new year. He didn't say where he was. Wherever he was, he sounded lonely.

When the countdown began, everyone was so drunk and happy. Sterling pulled me in close and gave me a slow, sensual kiss when we reached midnight. I would've been lost in that kiss if I wasn't aware that my parents were hovering around us somewhere in the living room.

Was he a better kisser than Nick? I didn't know. They were just...different.

But I couldn't help but think about Nick and what a great time we had last New Year's Eve in Aruba, partying it up at a hotel party with a group of our friends. Nick was fun, which wasn't to say that Sterling wasn't, but I wondered about our lifestyle compatibility. Sterling was rooted in Hartfield, while

I needed to travel and tour the world for weeks or months at a time. Either way, I had a busy lifestyle to work around.

I decided that my New Year's resolution would be to not worry so much. For now, I tried to enjoy the moment.

But I kept itching to call Nick back because of how sad he sounded. I restrained myself.

On New Year's Day however, Nick called me, but his news was more bizarre than anything I expected to hear.

CHAPTER 3

"I didn't kill her," Nick said.

It was ten o'clock in the morning on New Year's Day. There was panic in Nick's voice. I didn't blame him when I heard what had happened.

When he went downstairs for breakfast in the morning, he stumbled onto Martha's dead body and stepped into her pool of blood.

"Of course you didn't kill her," I exclaimed. "I totally believe you."

"Can you please come down and tell that to your boyfriend?"

Oh no. Sterling was there already. I jumped out of bed and pulled out some clothes from my closet.

"I'll be there as fast as I can," I said.

After gargling down some mouthwash, dressing and twisting my red hair into a messy bun, I ran down the stairs, grabbed my coat and started running to the inn.

I saw Martha's body with that big knitting needle still stuck in her chest as soon as I ran through the door. A photographer was snapping away at the body as if this were one of my magazine cover shoots. Sterling stepped away from interrogating Nick to tell the policemen blocking my path that it was okay that I was there.

"This is unbelievable," I said.

Nick looked pale. He had dark circles under his eyes and his hair wasn't neatly combed and gelled as it usually was. He came over and hugged me.

"Are you okay?" I asked Nick.

"Fine." He tried to look brave, but it was obvious that the scene made him queasy. I took him into the library, while Sterling hovered nearby.

"What happened?" I asked Nick. "Start from the beginning."

He sighed. "Yesterday night, I ate dinner with Martha. I didn't really feel like celebrating the new year. Martha was kind of glum too because her son had plans and hadn't spent New Year's Eve with her. So we both decided just to retire early. I went up to my room and dozed off. Never heard a thing. Then I found her like this in the morning..."

I nodded, knowing that when Nick was asleep, it took a lot to wake him. It was why he usually set three alarm clocks when he needed to wake up for early shoots or important events.

"Poor thing," I said. Nick's eyes were rimmed with red and he was rocking from heel to toe as he spoke as a way of soothing himself.

"Your boyfriend seems to think I had something to do with it," he continued.

"I just want to get all the facts," Sterling said. "You were the last person to see Martha and the first person to find her dead. It seems a bit odd that you didn't hear anything. There was a sign of struggle. Martha could've been screaming for help. You're telling me that you didn't hear her scream or hear any voices at all?"

"Like I told you," Nick said through gritted teeth, "I'm a deep sleeper. Plus my room is at the end of the hall. It wouldn't have been loud enough to wake me."

"It's true," I told Sterling. "Nick doesn't wake up very easily. I can attest to that."

"There's no sign of a break-in," Sterling said. "Nick's fingerprints are everywhere and I wouldn't be surprised if they were on those needles as well."

"I'm a guest here!" Nick exclaimed. "Of course my fingerprints are going to be everywhere. If they weren't, I'd be a ghost. But I can assure you that they are not on those needles. I've never even seen those needles before. She usually knits with normal needles."

"We'll see about that," Sterling said. "Didn't you have some anger issues on the set of a film a few years ago? Where you reprimanded a crew worker and there was a recording of you swearing and having some sort of nervous breakdown? Maybe that temper of yours got the best of you. Maybe Martha didn't make your chicken dinner the way you liked it and you got peeved."

Nick's face grew red. "Not that this is any business of yours, but there was a reason I was angry at that crew member."

I knew the story. The crew member in question had been secretly filming Nick on set and selling gossip about him to the tabloids. The guy ultimately got fired, but unfortunately, his video of Nick freaking out over his invasion of privacy still leaked and went viral.

"I'm not some spoiled actor. Martha and I got along great. Emma can attest to that. She was here a few days ago."

Sterling looked at me in surprise.

"I was here," I admitted. "Nick wanted to talk so I came over for tea. He was indeed very friendly with Martha and she seemed to like him. There's no reason why Nick would want to hurt her."

Sterling grew silent, his gray eyes brewing a storm. I could feel him tensing up.

"Even so, the circumstances surrounding Nick are

questionable." Sterling turned to Nick. "As much as I hate to say this, you have to stay in town until we find out more."

With that, Sterling turned back to the scene of the crime to rejoin his team. Nick rubbed his face with his hands.

"It's okay, Nick," I said. "We both know you're not guilty."

"This is a disaster," he said. "How can she be murdered?"

"Is the door locked at night?" I asked. "Or did Martha keep the door open for any last minute guests?"

"She locked it," he said. "At least she usually did. She had a curfew. At ten o'clock she would lock the doors, so if I ever needed to go out, I had to tell her so she could give me a key to let myself in late at night. I remember her giving me a lecture about not staying up late or doing anything 'sinful.'"

"And what time did you go to bed?"

"Around nine thirty."

"Did you sleep right away?"

"No. I was probably up until 10:30 p.m. watching TV before I dozed off."

I smiled, imagining Nick falling asleep in front of the TV. It was a common habit of his and I usually had to turn the TV off and put a blanket over him.

"This means that she must've let the killer in," I said. "It was probably someone she knew."

"She didn't seem to be too well liked," he said. "She constantly complained that she wasn't invited to any New Year's Eve parties."

I recalled what Sylvia and Rhonda had said about her and how my mom hadn't invited her to the party because she was too much of a downer.

"It does sound like she butt heads with others a lot," I said.

"She could be very judgmental," Nick said. "And I think she had a lot of bitterness built up, but ultimately I think that she was a vulnerable person. As far as I was concerned, she was nice to me."

"And to me too," I said, recalling how attentive Martha was when I was over for tea.

"She's just someone who's used to getting her way and hates it when others ignore her."

I was touched by how much sympathy Nick had for Martha. He always treated older women well. He was very close to his mother.

"Well, it looks like you don't have a place to stay now," I said.

"That's right."

"You're welcome to stay with me," I offered.

"Sure," he said softly. "That would be great."

Nick smiled at me in gratitude. I smiled back. He was close enough to kiss me, but I stood up from the table. I took a peek out at the crime scene. The photographer had left, but a new man had entered the house.

He wore chunky black-rimmed glasses and, when his back was turned to me, I noticed that he was starting to go bald. His face twisted into an expression of pain as he looked down at Martha's body. Sterling reassured him and took him aside.

"Who would do this?" he cried. "Who would ever want to kill my mom?"

The man began to sob into his hands.

"I can't be here," he said. "I can't look at her."

Nick came up beside me.

"Shoot," Nick said. "It's Cal, Martha's son. Poor guy."

Sterling took Cal outside.

I turned back to Nick.

"Get your stuff so we can go to my house."

While Nick went upstairs to pack, I looked around the place. The forensic team was all over the living room, so I sneaked into the kitchen and looked around. All the dishes had been done. The glasses on the drying rack were all spotless. Martha must've been a clean freak. I checked the garbage can. It was empty except for a white knitted scarf. I could tell it was homemade and it had cable stitching. Maybe Martha threw it out because she was dissatisfied with the results, although I saw nothing wrong with the scarf.

Nothing else seemed to be out of place and I was disappointed that I had nothing more to go on.

Nick came downstairs with his leather duffel bag, ready to go. There was little else to do except to find out more about Martha Owens.

CHAPTER 4

We passed Sterling and Cal in deep conversation on the porch on our way out. They didn't notice us so I didn't say good-bye. I felt sorry for the guy. Imagine seeing your own mother's murdered body.

"They shouldn't have let him see her body like that," Nick said. "That's not right. It's traumatizing."

"I can imagine." I had also seen another dead body recently and it wasn't exactly pleasant.

We walked for a good ten minutes back to my house, passing the charming, snow-blanketed town. It was bittersweet walking with Nick through Hartfield. I'd often pictured us doing this but didn't think we'd do so broken up and leaving a murder scene.

"I heard that the inn is haunted," I said as we walked past the shopping area.

"Haunted?" Nick raised an eyebrow. "Really?"

"So you didn't notice anything weird? No strange noises, shadows, or anybody pulling off your bed sheets in the middle of the night?"

"No. Do you believe in that?"

I shrugged. "Not really, but it's fun to think about."

"I guess being in that big house knowing that the other rooms are empty can be kind of creepy. I didn't exactly want to hang out in the hallway alone in the middle of the night. Why? Have there been ghost sightings?"

"This lady from my mom's knitting group claims to be sensitive to spirits and that she saw something once in the bathroom."

"Ohh, a toilet phantom."

I cracked a smile. "Don't worry. There are no ghosts at my place. Just a couple of elves living in the attic."

Both of my parents had met Nick on many occasions and seemed to like him, but this was the first time that Nick ever visited me in Hartfield.

When Mom answered the door, she was shocked to see him. She knew that we had broken up and she wasn't aware that he'd been in town all this time.

She quickly covered her surprise with a warm smile.

"It's a lovely home you have, Mrs. Wild."

My dad came in from the kitchen. "Nick?"

He looked confused as well. They both knew that I was dating Sterling now.

I explained that Nick was here to visit—although I didn't say that he'd brought a diamond ring along— and told them what had happened to Martha the night before.

"Oh dear," Mom exclaimed. "Poor Martha."

She sat down and looked pale. Dad went to get her a glass of water.

"Nick has to stay here for a while," I said. "He's a witness. I hope that's okay."

"Of course it is," Mom said. "Who would do this to Martha?"

"We don't know yet," I said.

Mom stared into space and looked to be in deep thought about who Martha's killer could be. I wanted to grill her about what she knew, but thought it was best to let her think for a bit.

I led Nick up to the second floor and showed him the guest bedroom, the one next to mine. The room used to be Mirabelle's, who now lived with her husband in a house in the same neighbourhood. Even though Nick and I had lived together for years, having him in such close proximity made me nervous. What if the temptation to be together was still there?

"I'm sorry you had to get mixed up in all of this," I said.

"Who knew small towns could be so dangerous? In all my years of living in New York, I had never seen a dead body or knew of anyone who was murdered. The irony."

"Why don't you lie down and have a rest for a bit? I'll go down and see about lunch. I'll come and get you when it's ready."

"Thanks, Emma." Nick smiled.

I couldn't help but feel responsible. If it weren't for me, Nick wouldn't have had to stay in that inn. Taking care of him was the least I could do.

Downstairs, Dad made his famous chili, while Mom was still on the couch, digesting the news.

"This is horrifying," she said to me. "To think that this could happen in Hartfield. I wish there was something that I could do."

"I'm sorry, Mom." I hugged her. "Maybe we can do something, by figuring out who would hurt her."

"That would be difficult because Martha didn't get along with a lot of people. Even I didn't particularly see eye to eye with Martha most of the time. She could just be so negative and overbearing that it drove you nuts. But even so, she meant well, and she could be generous under that rough exterior. She didn't deserve this."

"Of course not, Mom. I'm sure we'll catch the killer. Sterling's investigating right now."

She looked up at me. "What is Nick doing here? I thought you two had broken up."

I slowly explained that Nick had been here since Christmas, and that he wanted to get back together.

"Why, that's wonderful. Although, Sterling..."

"I know, I know. I'm trying not to think about it right now."

She patted me on the knee. "Don't worry, honey. You'll know who the right one is when it's time."

"Thanks. Right now I just want to help catch this guy."

"If I tried counting all of Martha's enemies on my fingers, I wouldn't have enough hands."

"Was there anyone that Martha particularly hated?"

"Well, I only know Martha through the knitting group. Otherwise, we're not close enough to spend quality time together."

"Did she butt heads with a lot of the women in the group?"

Mom thought about it. "Yes. She had plenty of disagreements with Rhonda and Sylvia, because they are the founding members of the group, and Martha was starting to boss the group around more and more, but I've known Rhonda and Sylvia for years. They wouldn't kill her."

I didn't comment on that. Sometimes the person you least suspected could surprise you the most.

Instead, I told Mom that Martha was stabbed with a gigantic knitting needle.

"Just how big was the needle?" Mom asked.

"They were the thickest I'd ever seen. As thick as my wrist."

Mom's eyes grew wide. "Martha didn't own those needles. They're Rhonda's."

"What? Really?"

"Yes. You can't find those needles in Hartfield. Rhonda had to order them from an online knitting store and it took quite a while for them to be shipped here."

"Maybe Martha ordered them too."

Mom shook her head. "I don't think so. Rhonda had them during the last meeting, and she was showing them off quite a bit. Martha really wanted them. If Martha ordered them that day, the needles wouldn't have gotten here so fast, especially with delivery being so slow around the holidays."

"What about express shipping?"

"She would never pay for express shipping. Martha was, well, cheap about those kinds of things."

I stood up and paced. "Do you think that Rhonda could hate her enough to kill her?

"Rhonda's one of my closest friends!" Mom exclaimed.

"I know, Mom, but sometimes people do regrettable things when they're angry. I'm not saying

Rhonda did it; I just want all the facts to piece this together. Can you tell me more about what they argued about?"

Mom slowly nodded and considered her words carefully. "Rhonda and Martha have had their disagreements, but they usually tried to be civil about it. Sylvia and Martha butt heads a lot, and Rhonda usually comes to Sylvia's defense, so Martha tends to feel a bit outnumbered sometimes. But Martha can be bullheaded and downright aggressive when she argues. She can be a bully to many members of the group."

"Sylvia was at our party on New Year's Eve," I said.

Mom nodded. "And your father drove her home."

"Rhonda left early. She said she was going home, but she could've stopped by Martha's easily."

"To think that Rhonda could murder someone..."

Mom still couldn't wrap her head around this possibility, but the evidence was starting to point Rhonda's way. I recalled the scene this morning at the inn. A new ball of lavender yarn had rolled loose on the floor, and a bunch of regular needles poked out from a bag. A yellow scarf was in the process of being completed with a pair of these normal-sized needles and it rested on top of the bag. It meant that Martha was already working on something. Maybe Rhonda came in, there was a scuffle and she stabbed Martha at the height of her anger.

Dad poked his head in from the kitchen door. "Lunch is ready. Emma, do you want to call Nick down?"

"Sure, Dad."

I ran back up and knocked on Nick's door. He had fallen asleep and groggily sat up when I came in.

"Nick, did you ever see Martha knit?"

"Yes, all the time."

"Did you ever see her knit with those big needles?"

He thought about it. "I recall Martha talking about knitting. She said she was finishing a scarf to donate to sick children at the hospital. Those were with regular needles, I think. That was yesterday. I don't know if she was knitting with those big needles or not."

"But you would notice if she were knitting with big needles, right?"

"Maybe," said Nick.

He wasn't the most reliable guy when it came to details. Sometimes he'd go days without noticing that I had gotten my hair cut.

The only way to find out whether those needles were Rhonda's was to go to the source.

CHAPTER 5

I knew that Rhonda was in her late fifties. She lived with her daughter's family and owned a cheese shop on the corner of Samford Street and Marble Avenue.

I didn't want to tell Sterling about the needles belonging to Rhonda just yet. I was afraid that he'd be too tough on her and frighten her with his questions when all I wanted for now were some simple answers. If Rhonda was the killer and she was comfortable speaking to me, she might let something slip.

Another reason I didn't want to talk to Sterling was that I wasn't ready to talk to him yet. I was sure he was mad at me for seeing Nick, and he would be more upset to know that Nick was staying with me now too. I knew I had to talk to him sometime, but not before I gathered the info that I wanted to support my case.

Many of the shops on the main shopping streets were open on New Year's Day, including Mirabelle's Chocoholic Cafe. Rhonda's cheese shop, Cheese, Please, was also open. I was glad because I had an excuse to see Rhonda.

I picked up a few things from the supermarket to make it seem as if I was just shopping before I entered *Cheese, Please*.

"Hi, girls," I said brightly.

Sylvia and Rhonda were both behind the counter wearing red gingham aprons. They were all smiles at the sight of me.

"Hello, dear! Have you tried our cheese of the week?" Sylvia pointed to the cheese samples on the counter.

"Mmm, Gouda." I didn't even like cheese that much but tried one anyway.

"Food shopping, already?" asked Rhonda. "Thought you had plenty after last night's bash."

"Actually, most of the food is gone," I said. "Everyone kept eating well into the morning."

"Sounds like some party," said Rhonda. "I guess things really began to heat up after I left."

"Are you looking for anything in particular?" Sylvia asked.

"I'll take this," I said about the Gouda. "Dad loves cheese. I'm sure he'll like this one."

"It's from The Netherlands," said Sylvia.

"Do you know that they have a little cheese museum in Amsterdam?" said Rhonda. "I would love to visit sometime."

Guessing by their cheerful demeanors, they hadn't heard about Martha's death. Or perhaps Rhonda was simply feigning ignorance.

"Have you heard about Martha?" I said.

"What about Martha?" Sylvia asked.

I told them that a guest at her inn found her murdered this morning.

Shock splashed across both of their faces. Sylvia gasped.

"Oh my God," said Rhonda. "How?"

"She was stabbed with a knitting needle. A very chunky needle the size of my wrist."

Rhonda turned white. "Oh, Jesus."

Sylvia turned to Rhonda with her mouth open and I held my breath, anticipating Rhonda's admission. How would she get out of this?

"Those are my needles," Rhonda admitted.

"Your needles?" Sylvia said. "How can you be sure?"

"Because I let Martha borrow them."

"When?" I asked.

"Last night," Rhonda said, her voice shaking. "I

had agreed to let her borrow them, but I'd forgotten to give them to her yesterday. When I opened my trunk to store my empty Tupperware from your party, I saw the needles there, and I decided I'd just go and give them to Martha, since her inn was on the way home."

Sylvia frowned. "But you just got those needles. Why would you let her borrow them?"

Rhonda hung her head a bit. "Well, I didn't want to tell you, but Martha wanted to kick you out of the knitting group."

"What?" Sylvia exclaimed.

"She was trying to convince the other members that you were...crazy. Martha was very offended that you kept calling her house haunted and creepy, and wanted to vote you out of the group."

"But..." Sylvia looked hurt. "How could she?"

"You know how vindictive she can get when she feels wronged. I was trying to talk her out of it, to not start any drama that would cause more arguments in the group. That was the only way the group could survive. As a peace offering, I lent her the needles, knowing how much she liked them. She planned on making a shawl with them. That was the deal. She got the needles until hers came in the mail, and she'd drop this little war on Sylvia. I think what she really wanted was control, because she was so lonely. Her son moved out and she had nobody to listen to her anymore, except us. I knew she didn't have anywhere to go on New Year's Eve. She wasn't invited anywhere. It was late, but her light was on, so I went to see her. I thought she would welcome the company, so I chatted with her a bit about her knitting project. She was cranky when she answered the door, but she was in a better mood when I left, probably because someone actually came to visit her. Although she'd be too proud to admit any of this."

"Was anyone else in the inn?" I asked.

"Not that I was aware of. I heard no voices. Although..." Rhonda paused, something obviously striking her. "When I was driving away, I did see a pickup truck pull up in front of the inn."

"Did you see who it was?" I asked.

"No. It was too dark, and I didn't think much of it."

"What color was it?"

"I don't know exactly, but it was a dark color."

"You know who it could be?" Sylvia said.

"Martha's ex-boyfriend!" Rhonda exclaimed.

"Right. What was his name?"

"Edward...Edward Herman. He's a dairy farmer."

"When did they break up?" I asked.

"About six months ago," Rhonda said. "We saw him only once the entire time we started holding knitting group meetings at the inn. After their breakup, Martha became more and more bitter."

"I don't think their breakup was very civil," Sylvia. "But with Martha, she made a big drama about everything. She was angry a lot."

"Did she ever mention why they broke up?" I asked.

"No," said Rhonda. "Martha never spoke about her personal life. She was hoping to get remarried, and she would rant about how all men were scum anytime one of the knitting group members would start talking about their husbands or boyfriends."

"So you don't know much else about him?" I asked.

Rhonda shook her head. "No. He doesn't live in Hartfield. At least I'd never seen him in town."

"So he lives on a farm, huh?" I said.

"He's a dairy farmer. Not sure where he lives."

Sylvia's eyes were as big as saucers. "Do you think he's the killer?"

Rhonda went pale. "To think that we met a killer!"

"Is Sterling on the case?" Sylvia asked me.

"Yes," I said. "I'll be sure to tell him to look more into Edward Herman."

I paid for the Gouda and thanked the ladies. I was relieved that Rhonda didn't have anything to do with it. Unless of course she was a very good actress sending me on a wild goose chase.

After I left, I immediately called Sterling.

CHAPTER 6

"We need to talk," I said when Sterling answered his phone.

"About?" He sounded nonchalant, but I knew it was only because he was still hurt.

"I have news about the case. A new lead."

"Okay." He sounded surprised, but he shouldn't have been. He knew how much passion I had for solving mysteries. "Shoot."

"Can I meet you?"

"Well, I'm finishing up my lunch at the office."

"Can I come by?" I asked.

"Does it even matter what I say?" Sterling sighed. "I know you're going to come whether I say yes or not."

I grinned and started heading over to the police station. One of the reasons why I loved Sterling was that he got me, completely. And I got him. Beneath that hard shell, he was a sensitive and intuitive guy who could empathize with people. Which was why I felt guilty for hurting him. But romance wasn't on my mind right now.

Sterling had his arms crossed when I entered the office. A frosty reception, but I tried to focus on the matter at hand.

"What did you find out?" he asked.

I told him that I had just spoken to Rhonda and Sylvia, and about Edward Herman.

"He's on top of my suspect list too," Sterling said. "Martha's son mentioned that this Edward Herman got into many arguments with Martha when they were together. Once he even laid his hands on her."

"Oh, really?"

"Slapped her right across the face."

"What else did her son say about this guy? Does he know much else about him?"

"Edward wasn't very personable. He doesn't have children of his own, and didn't make much of an effort in getting to know her son. Cal, Martha's son, said they were together for about six months, but they had frequent screaming matches."

I pulled up a chair and sat across from his desk. "What did they argue about?"

"Martha used to get jealous a lot and often accused Edward of cheating on her."

"Was he?" I asked.

Sterling shrugged. "Cal seems to think so, but he didn't have proof. He didn't stick around to hear them fight."

"Doesn't sound like this Edward stuck around long for the fights either," I said.

"Funny enough, before you came in, I was doing a background check on this guy. He lives alone on his dairy farm thirty minutes from here. He does have a few employees, but they don't live on site. I was just going to go visit him."

"And you're taking me with you, right?"

He shook his head. "I don't think so, Emma."

"Please," I said. "If he's a lady's man as much as Martha claims he is, maybe it wouldn't hurt to have a female with you."

"I thought I was the detective," he said. "I've been doing fine on my own."

"Wasn't I a help on the last case?" I asked.

"Sure, but, that was directly related to you. You don't know who Edward Herman is. He could be dangerous."

"Oh, don't worry. I know Krav Maga. I can defend myself."

Sterling looked at me with amusement. His arms were not crossed anymore and there was a small smile on his face.

"What am I going to do with you?"

"You can take me along to help."

"Fine." He gave an exaggerated sigh and stood up.

"Great!" I put my mittens on. "Let's go."

As we walked out of the station, Sterling got a call.

"Sterling Matthews."

Sterling listened for a bit and then said, "So nothing huh? Keep trying."

He shut off his phone and sighed.

"Forensic hasn't found anything useful so far. No fingerprints, no footprints. It seems like someone had taken care to clean the place—and any evidence along with it. Even the floor is clean and properly washed."

"What? Whoever was there tried to clean around the body?"

Sterling nodded and unlocked the door of his car. "Yup. The killer made an effort to clean up the evidence, or at least the floor, the door handles, things like that. The killer must've cleaned whatever he or she touched, which doesn't seem to be much at this point."

I got in the car and Sterling started the engine. He turned and looked me in the eye.

"Are you sure Nick didn't have anything to do with this?"

"No way he could've done it." I shook my head. "Nick is definitely not a killer."

"Seems a bit odd that he'd sleep through the whole murdering and cleaning up process."

"That's Nick. When he's asleep, he's asleep."

Nick could be oblivious to his surroundings. I guess you could say he was a little self-involved sometimes. Narcissism was expected of a movie star, I supposed, but I didn't excuse him because of that. It drove me crazy.

"So are you guys back together now?" Sterling asked

"No," I said. "Of course not."

I didn't want to have this conversation, but I guessed we had to. We were on the road together for the next half hour. And I did owe Sterling an explanation.

"He came to town with a ring, saying that he wanted to propose. It's what you wanted, right?"

I bit my lip.

"It was," I said slowly. "But that was before I saw you again and…"

"So I made things complicated."

"No! I'm just confused because Nick and I broke up not too long ago, and you and I are pretty new. It's my fault. I mean, I should have taken things slow with us, not that I don't want to be with you, because I do…"

Sterling didn't respond for a while. He kept

looking straight ahead. Soon, we were out of Hart-field and surrounded by snowy fields.

"It's not your fault," he finally said. "I have to admit that it was upsetting to me at first. The old Sterling probably would've shut you out, but I want to change. Hell, the way I communicate was one of the reasons I got divorced. So I want to be open with you; I want to let you know that I understand."

"You do?"

He nodded. "It's hard. I'm sure you had very strong feelings for him and it doesn't just shut off like that. But I also know that you feel strongly for me. So I'm not taking myself out of the race. If he's willing to fight for you, I'm going to fight harder."

"Sterling..." I looked at him, but he kept looking at the road. His eyes looked sad, but his expression was full of determination.

"I appreciate it," I said.

"I figured that if you were really set on marrying the guy, you'd decide right away and tell me, right?"

"I would," I admitted.

"So is there anything you want to tell me?"

"No. I'm not together with Nick. However, since he has to stay in town until the investigation ends, he is staying at my house—in a separate room, of course."

A dark cloud passed over his eyes, but he shook it

away. "You haven't said yes to him, which means that the chances are still in my favor."

I'd never had two guys compete for me before. It was nice enough to be pursued by one guy that you love, but two?

However, when you loved two guys, it made you doubt the love you had for each of them, which was why I needed more time.

Did I want to live an international, jetsetting, but chaotic lifestyle with Nick, or did I want to settle down in my hometown with my first love? Each of them captured a different side of me and I wasn't sure which side I was in favor of yet.

We didn't talk about it again during the rest of the car ride. Instead, we prepared the questions we'd ask. Sterling would play the bad cop, while I would be the good cop and flirt if necessary. I let my red hair down and applied red lipstick. A bit of mascara made my green eyes pop.

When we reached the farm, we were ready.

*S*terling pulled up in front of little gray house at the farm. We rang the doorbell, but nobody answered. We peeked into the windows and saw no one. It was so quiet.

"He must be working in the farm," I said.

We trekked across the snow-covered field to the big red barn. The two doors were closed, and we knocked and waited.

No one answered and we knocked again.

"Anyone there?" I called. "Mr. Herman?"

When there was still no response, I pulled the door open.

The smell of cow manure hit us with full force and we plugged our noses.

"Pee-yew," Sterling said.

"Nothing's more revolting than this," I said.

Inside, dozens of cows formed two long rows. They were hooked up to tubes and contraptions that mechanically milked them. The cows looked miserable and who could blame them? I would be if I were caged and pumped full of hormones so I could lactate for another species' benefit. And to be trapped in a place where you were forced to smell your own stink all day? No thank you.

A man was at the end of the barn. He was far enough away to be only a dark figure. His features emerged the closer he walked to us.

"Are you Edward Herman?" asked Sterling.

"Who's asking?" he said in a cross voice.

The man wore a puffy black down coat over corduroy overalls. He was around sixty, but still lean and tall. Wrinkles lined his dry, chapped skin, but you could tell he used to be a handsome man by his strong bone structure and bright hazel eyes.

"I'm detective Sterling Matthews and this is my partner, Emma. Are you Edward Herman?"

When Edward Herman saw me, he gave me an appreciative smile and a quick once-over.

"Yes," he said. "Sure stinks in here, huh? But don't worry. You'll get used to the smell in a minute. Then you won't smell anything."

"I only pray," Sterling said dryly.

"So what can I do you for?" Edward asked us.

"We're here to ask you a few questions."

Edward took a second look at me. "You look familiar. Have we met?"

I smiled and shook my head. "I don't think so."

"I'm sure I've seen you before." He paused. "Are you on TV?"

How strange that Edward Herman, the dairy farmer, would recognize me out of everyone in town. I could usually run my errands in town without attracting a second look.

"Actually, I'm a singer."

"Emma...Emma Wild?" Recognition struck his face. "Oh, I know you. I mean, I know someone who's a big fan of yours."

"Really?" I said.

"I'd love to get an autograph."

Sterling cleared his throat. This wasn't the time for a fan meeting. He told him we were here about Martha's murder. Edward's face fell.

"Good grief!" Edward exclaimed. "A knitting needle?"

"When was the last time you saw Martha Owens?" Sterling asked.

"We'd broken up months ago. I think Martha drove down to visit me to return a sweater of mine. That was about a month ago."

Sterling raised an eyebrow. "She drove all the way down here just to give you a sweater?"

"Well, I think it was just an excuse. I think she

wanted to see me, not that she'd ever admit it. But actions speak louder than words, and I had a feeling she wanted to get back together."

"But you didn't want to?" I asked.

Edward leaned against the rail over one of his cows. He stroked the cow's head.

"No, that relationship was not...ideal."

"Now, what were all the screaming fights between you two about?" Sterling said.

Edward was taken aback by the question. He looked at Sterling and narrowed his eyes, but he answered the question anyway.

"We did used to fight, which was why we broke up. Martha was a bit paranoid and had trust issues. It was because her husband used to cheat on her."

"So you never cheated on Martha?"

Edward balked. "What's this about? Am I a suspect?"

"I'm sorry," I said. "My partner's just doing his job by questioning anyone in connection with her. Anything you know would help us with the case."

Edward regarded Sterling again, but when he looked at me, he softened. "No, I never cheated on Martha. I liked her a lot. I always liked strong women. But all the accusations were getting to me. I couldn't live with her, so I ended it."

"Do you happen to drive a pickup truck?" Sterling asked. "You must since you live on a farm."

"Yes. It's behind the barn. Why?"

"Someone spotted your truck parked in front of Martha's inn on New Year's Eve."

"Why that's impossible—" Edward stopped himself from saying anything else.

"What?" Sterling said. "Where were you that night?"

"I was here," Edward said. "I mean, in my house."

"Alone?" asked Sterling.

Edward opened his mouth but did not answer.

"Was there someone here with you on New Year's Eve?" Sterling repeated with impatience.

"If you have a witness, that would clear you," I said.

Edward relented and nodded. "Yes, there was someone here. But I'm not at liberty to say who."

"Why not?"

"Because." Edward gritted his teeth. "She's married."

We were silent for a moment.

Sterling wasn't rattled. He pressed on.

"So you never cheated on Martha, but you have the morals to get involved with a married woman, huh?"

Edward sighed. "They're not in love. They're only together for the children."

"Who is it?" Sterling asked.

Edward closed his eyes and shook his head.

"I assure you that we're not here to get involved in your personal life," I said. "If you tell us who she is, we will just get her statement privately."

"You promise not to tell her husband?" Edward said.

"As long as you're innocent," Sterling said, "there's no reason to expose your relationship."

Edward breathed hard and rubbed his temples. "All right. If you must know. She's the mayor's wife."

I suppressed a gasp. Mayor Richard Champ's wife, Eleanor, the perfect Stepford wife?

"She has three children," Edward said, "so it's imperative that no one else knows about this. She'll kill me when she finds out that I told you. Richard and Eleanor haven't been in love for years, and he was away for the holidays. Richard doesn't know, so let's just keep it that way. But heck, I wouldn't be surprised if he was cheating himself. They're only together because of his public image as a family man."

He trailed off, looking embarrassed.

"Did Mrs. Champ stay the night?" Sterling asked.

Edward nodded. "Yes."

"We'll speak to her shortly to confirm," Sterling said.

"Can you tell us anything else you know about Martha?" I asked. "Did she have any enemies? Was there anyone else she had disagreements with?"

"Well, it was hard for most people to get along with Martha. She often complained about the women who used to come over and knit. She also complained a lot about her son and they fought often."

"Did they?" I was intrigued. "What about?"

"Martha was quite bossy with him. Telling him what to do all the time and treating him like a baby. Even I was tired of it. There was always something that she wanted him to do, so he never felt good enough. I sympathized with the guy. No wonder he moved out, but it took him long enough. He was living with her until he was thirty! But now I hear he's found a girlfriend and Martha hates her. She was calling her all sorts of names when I last saw her. She always expected Cal to take over running the inn, but he refused. Works as a mechanic now. Good riddance. Otherwise he'd end up a Norman Bates."

"Did they ever get violent with each other?" I asked.

"Not as far as I know," Edward said. "But I wouldn't be surprised if he just snapped one day."

CHAPTER 8

$\mathcal{B}$y the time we drove back into Hartfield, the sun had already set behind us. Sterling got a last minute call. His partner was asking for help on a separate drug case so we decided to part ways until tomorrow.

When Sterling dropped me off in front of the house, he walked me to the door despite my protests.

"Were you disappointed that it wasn't the dairy farmer?" Sterling asked.

"I thought it could be," I said.

"At least we're another step closer. Another one off my list."

"I just want this case shut already."

"It must mean that you're eager to get Nick out of the house," Sterling said. "Once we catch the murderer, he's free to go. Then I'll have you to myself."

Sterling came closer, wanting to kiss me. I did want to kiss him—his scent was intoxicating—but given that Nick was inside, it didn't seem like a respectful thing to do. I quickly pecked him on the cheek.

"I'll see you tomorrow," I said. Before I could push open the door, I paused and turned around. "Do you really think it could be matricide?"

"I've seen some weird stuff in my career," Sterling said. "I wouldn't be surprised."

"Get some rest," I said.

"Sure. I'll call this mayor's wife in the morning. Come by around ten."

"Sure."

When I entered the house, Nick was walking down the stairs.

"How was your day?" he asked. By the look on his face, I could tell that he had seen Sterling walking me to the door from the top window.

"Fine." I felt guilty, like I was going behind his back.

But I reminded myself that I didn't owe Nick, or Sterling for that matter, anything. I was the one doing Nick a favor by letting him stay at my parents' place while the investigation was under way.

I told him what had happened at the dairy farm and what Edward had said about Martha's son.

"So you think Cal might be the killer?" he said.

"I don't know. But he did seem highly emotional when he saw her body. Maybe it was an act."

"I met Cal once," Nick said. "He joined us for dinner on Christmas Eve. I had just gotten into town and was starving, so when Martha offered some food, I figured I'd eat with them before I set off to see you that evening. Cal was there, but he didn't know who I was. I just said that I was visiting from the states and here to see some friends later that evening."

"How did they behave toward each other?" I asked.

"Martha babied him. Told him to eat this and that, and he groaned when she did that. She even put food on his plate when she thought he wasn't eating enough of a certain dish. He was embarrassed about that, but not angry. We chatted a bit about soccer. He seemed pleasant enough. But he did get agitated a few times throughout the course of the meal when Martha put him down."

"What kind of things would she say?" I asked.

"She'd criticize his hair, his clothes, and his posture, things like that. She'd compare him to me, telling him he should cut his hair like mine, or dress like me. I didn't think it was out of the ordinary. Isn't that what most moms do?"

"And that's why you got along with Martha," I said. "The difference is, she probably doted on you."

Nick had a way with women. His mom also spoiled him a bit too and babied him. Unlike Martha, however, his mom never put him down. Instead, she thought nothing and no one was good enough for him, which meant she didn't approve of me. I was the one she put down. She was too polite to do this outright, but I could tell by the way she looked at my outfit or asked me about my education, which was strange because Nick never went to college either. Nick always said I shouldn't take it personally because she never approved of any girl he dated, but still.

"She kept hinting that he should be working at the inn again," Nick said, "But he'd just groan and change the subject."

"What else do you know about him?" I asked.

"He works as a mechanic. Martha kept badgering for him to quit his job and work at the inn, saying how if he did, business wouldn't be down. She sure did lay a lot of guilt on him. He ate fairly fast and seemed like he was in a hurry to get out of there."

"So eating dinner with her was just a duty to him," I said.

Nick nodded. "Probably. If I was being treated that way, I'd be fed up as well."

"Fortunately, everyone worships the ground you walk on," I teased.

"Well, not everyone." He walked closer and put his hands around my waist.

He pulled me in closer until his nose touched my cheek. Nick smelled amazing too. While Sterling smelled like the ocean, Nick smelled woody, like the forest.

"Dinner's ready," Dad called. He walked out from the living room and saw us. I jumped away from Nick.

"Oh, I'm sorry. Didn't mean to interrupt."

Dad turned and walked right back into the kitchen.

"That was awkward," I said to Nick.

He wasn't as fazed. Nick was always cool, never letting anything ruffle him. He was never at a lack for confidence, a trait I'd always admired.

"Listen, Emma. Why don't I help you?"

"Help me set the table?"

"With the case. I know I'm not a detective, but I am an actor. We study character and we are more conscious of human behavior than psychologists because we embody different personalities. Knowing the motives of a character is the key to acting. Plus, I already know Cal Owens. I can talk to him for you."

"Oh, that's nice of you, but—"

I did promise Sterling that we'd work together. He wouldn't be so happy to have another amateur sleuth tagging along with him, especially not my ex-boyfriend.

"Come on, Emma. I'm cooped up all day reading bad movie scripts. Let me help you. I can go talk to Cal and draw him out for you."

I raised my eyebrows at Nick. I wasn't sure how well he could read people. Sometimes I felt like he took people at face value. He liked everyone, probably because he was used to people liking him. He certainly hadn't been able to read me and my discontent during the relationship for the last few months of our relationship.

But he was a talented actor. His ability to embody characters was more than impressive. Maybe he did have the ability to figure out a person's motives. It was his job.

Maybe he had more in common with Sterling than I realized.

"What would you say to him?" I asked.

"You know me. I can make friends with anyone. I'll ask him to have a beer, talk about his mom, and see what he says."

I considered this. Nick certainly had a charm that could make most people open up. Even Martha liked him. It wouldn't hurt to give it a try.

"All right," I said.

Nick hugged me and kissed me on the top of my head since I was so short.

I was nervous. Sterling wasn't going to like this.

CHAPTER 9

In the morning, Nick and I set off for Sterling's office at the police station. Although the walk was only ten minutes, it was so cold because of a nasty snowstorm that we both couldn't take the sharp wind cutting our skin. We were lucky enough to hail a cab and we jumped in and huddled each other for warmth.

"We're supposed to get six inches of snow by tonight." Nick sighed. "I wish we could go skiing."

We went skiing every year, just the two of us. We'd ski in different resorts around the world—Switzerland, British Columbia, France. If we were still together, we would've gone to Aspen this month. Nick was practically a pro, while I was still trying to make it down the bunny slopes on a snowboard without falling on my rump.

"I feel bad that you're stuck in this town," I said. "And, you know, suspected of murder."

Nick groaned. "Say it loud enough for everyone to hear."

Then he leaned forward to address the cab driver with a smile. "I'm not a murderer."

"I sure hope not," the cabbie said.

"Sure I could be living it up somewhere," Nick whispered to me, "but I want to be with you. If that means being suspected of murder, so be it."

He had his arm around me, even though the heat of the cab had long warmed us up.

"You know, Nick. Have you ever considered that you might only want to marry me because of the chase? I know that men enjoy the chase, but once they get what they want, they get bored. How would I know that you really mean it?"

Nick frowned. "Emma, have I ever flaked on you before?"

I thought about it. "No."

"So why don't you trust me?"

Nick had never lied or cheated, but the truth was I expected him to because he had beautiful women surrounding him all the time.

"Because you're...Nick Doyle," I finally said.

"And you're Emma Wild. It took losing you to realize what I had, and I'd be stupid to risk losing you again."

"But I want to have children someday," I said. "Maybe not immediately but within the next five years. If I do, I want to take some time off from music. You're so busy with your career. I hardly even see you as your live-in girlfriend, so I don't know, Nick. I'm not sure if you're ready for such a big commitment. And I also don't want to hold you back from your career."

Nick shook his head. "Emma, you're so stubborn. What do I have to do to show you that I'm willing to do what it takes? I don't have to work back to back. I don't need to prove myself anymore. Maybe when we first started going out, I wasn't ready for marriage, but I'm in my thirties now. I do want to have kids someday too. When you left I realized what a big hole you left. I'm ready now."

I was silent for a moment. I thought about the family life we'd lead, about how much more the paparazzi would hound us.

"We'll figure it out together," said Nick. "Who knows, maybe in a few years, my popularity will take a dive. Nobody might care. Would you still love me then?"

The cab pulled up at the station. I didn't know what to say to Nick. Maybe he did mean it, but he also had a way with words. Sterling, on the other hand, was solid. He always meant what he said. The problem with him was getting him to say it.

We went in and I knocked on Sterling's door. He was happy to see me, but his face fell when he saw Nick.

"What's he doing here?" Sterling asked.

"He wanted to help."

"How?" Sterling said. "He's a murder suspect."

"Am I really still a suspect?" Nick said.

"Yes," Sterling said.

"He's spoken to Cal before," I explained to Sterling. "So Cal knows him already. It might be a good idea for him to take him out to lunch and have a long chat."

"I wouldn't be talking to him as a detective," Nick added. "I'd be talking to him as a friend. Plus, I have a way of getting people to reveal information."

Nick smiled in his self-assured way that some people thought charming and others thought egotistical. Sterling was in the latter category. He scowled.

"I'm not sure you're up for this type of field work," Sterling said.

"Come on," said Nick. "I've jumped off seven story buildings. Danger's my middle name."

"Is it?" Sterling asked dryly.

"No. It's actually Emmett."

Sterling sighed, unamused.

"I had a chat with the mayor's wife," he said. "It's true. They're having an affair. Edward Herman's off the hook."

"Okay," I said. "So what do we know about Cal Owens?"

"I checked and he doesn't own a pickup truck. He owns a silver Honda civic. That said, he does have a record for beating a guy to a pulp in a bar fight when he was in college. He had to pay $5000 and do community service to avoid jail time."

"So he does have a history of aggression," I stated.

"That's a surprise," said Nick. "He didn't seem the type to get into fights. In fact, I thought he was a complete pushover."

"It's always the quiet ones," said Sterling.

"So should we all go pay this guy a visit at the car shop?" I said.

"I want to talk to Cal alone first," said Nick.

Sterling opened his mouth to protest, but I cut in.

"If it doesn't work, you can always interrogate Cal after," I said.

"I'm not an Oscar nominated actor for nothing," said Nick. "Plus, I'm very good at improv and adapting to different situations."

Sterling let out a big sigh. "Fine. But I'm giving you the questions to ask. This guy is our closest lead. He may not own a pickup truck, but he works in a car shop—maybe he has access to one. Are you even sure you can get him to go to lunch?"

"Trust me," said Nick. "He won't be able to say no."

"I guess your charm works on guys and girls," Sterling said.

"It's a power I only use for good," said Nick.

Sterling shook his head. "Let's just get this over with."

We drove Nick around the corner from Cal's car shop and dropped him off. After we watched him walk in, we parked on the street and waited at the restaurant nearby. If all went to plan, Nick would have lunch in here with Cal soon. We picked a booth where Sterling had his back to the other tables so that Cal wouldn't recognize him.

In the meantime, we ordered lunch. Sterling ordered a cheeseburger while I resorted to a Caesar salad. Lately, I'd been packing on the pounds. Living at home meant eating all of Dad's finest dishes and desserts. Nearly every morning I ate his famous oatmeal cookie pancakes. I had been snacking on his homemade brownie S'mores like crazy that week. The man could start his own comfort food restaurant. I wouldn't mind all the weight gain if it didn't all go to my stomach. My job required that I wore these slinky dresses so I had to start eating healthy and exercising again.

It did make me sad to think that I couldn't stay in Hartfield much longer. My manager, Rod, would soon get over his weeklong hangover and call me at a moment's notice to tell me about some booking for a magazine interview or talk show appearance or other to promote my third album. It was going to be released soon and I had to do the rounds later in the month.

While my first music video was in the can, I had to shoot the video for my second single, but I didn't know where that would take place yet. It was all tiring but fun. For some, it was a fantasy life, but for me it was getting back to reality. Fantasy was staying in my hometown and settling down with family. As much as I loved travelling, I was a homebody at heart.

As if he could read my thoughts, Sterling asked, "So how long are you planning on staying in Hartfield?"

"I know I can't stay in my parents' house forever," I said. "Maybe I'll move back to New York."

"Oh." Sterling looked disappointed.

"For work," I said quickly. "I'm based there for work. It's not too far from Hartfield."

Sterling played with the handle of his coffee mug. "You didn't exactly visit often before."

"I know. But that was because I was scared of running into you all those years."

He gazed into my eyes with tenderness. Thick lashes framed those stormy gray eyes.

"Well you don't need to be anymore." He looked down at his coffee.

Last month, I was single and feeling as if I had failed at love. Now I had two strong prospects to choose from and I didn't want to mess it up. Could I really see myself settling in Hartfield with Sterling? Making him coffee in the mornings as he went off to work and helping him with cases on the side while I composed songs at home? I could. Being a stepmom to his little girls sounded nice as well. I could see myself taking a hiatus as I raised children for a while. Now that I was heading into my thirties, my priorities were changing.

But I also knew I couldn't stop myself from working for long. I loved singing and making music too much to give it up completely. In an ideal world, I would be able to do both. It would probably be difficult for Sterling to get too much time off. If I kept up my career, there would be months when I wouldn't be able to see him because I'd be touring.

"I'll support you in whatever you do," said Sterling. "If that means traveling to New York on the weekends or taking time off to follow you halfway around the world to visit you, I'll do it. I'll always give you the freedom to do what you want."

I smiled. Sterling was the type to sacrifice anything for the people he loved. I squeezed his hand on the table in appreciation.

"I know you would," I said.

He knew how much of a worrywart I was, but he didn't press on the issue any further. I didn't want to think about it either and I was glad when our food arrived so I could perform an action to dig myself out of my slew of nagging thoughts.

Just then, Nick entered with Cal. Cal looked deflated and lifeless, and Nick was trying to cheer him up.

"Don't look back," I whispered to Sterling before I took a bite of my salad.

Cal slid into the booth next to ours and sat with his back to Sterling. Nick spoke loud enough for us to hear.

"Lunch is on me," Nick was saying.

"That's nice of you," said Cal.

"It's the least I could do," said Nick. "I'm just sorry about your loss. Your mom was really gracious and hospitable when I was staying at her inn. How are you doing, anyway?"

Cal sat with his shoulders hunched. He spoke in a listless voice. "I'm okay, considering."

"She treated me like a son," Nick said. "She was nice, wasn't she? Nicer than people think."

Cal nodded slowly. "People do find her unbearable, but she's misunderstood."

He began to cry. I couldn't tell at first, but his whimpers got louder. Nick handed him a tissue, then clapped him on the shoulder.

"Let it out, buddy."

Cal blew his nose out loud. The waitress and the folks at the counter turned to look at him.

"I miss her," Cal said.

"I know." Nick nodded sympathetically. "Do you need help with anything? Are the funeral arrangements taken care of?"

"My dad and his family are flying in from Vancouver tomorrow. They're going to take care of it."

"You don't have any other relatives in this town?"

Cal shook his head. "No. Mom was an only child, and both my grandparents have passed."

"Wow," said Nick. "I guess she was pretty lonely when you moved out, huh?"

"She didn't take it well," said Cal. "She doesn't have too many friends."

"What about all those knitting group ladies?"

Cal blew his nose again. He had stopped crying.

"No. Mom used to complain about how they were all using her for her space. She didn't like them, but

Mom didn't like anyone. I think she only kept them around because their company was better than no company."

"Why did you move out?"

"I was getting too old to live with her," said Cal. "I needed my own life."

"Did you feel guilty at all?"

"Of course, but Mom always made me feel guilty about everything so I got used to it. It didn't affect me the way it would to others."

"What are you going to do about the inn?"

Cal shrugged. "I don't know what we'll do with it yet. We'll probably sell it."

"So you don't want to live at the inn, then?"

"No. My fiancée would never allow it."

"I didn't know you were engaged," said Nick.

"Oh, just recently."

"Congratulations."

"Thanks."

"Did your mom know about your engagement?"

There was a slight pause. "No. She didn't approve of Jasmina. My fiancée is, well, Muslim. My mom was not so...evolved, so she ignored her completely."

"I see," Nick said. "Is that why your fiancée doesn't want to live at the inn?"

"No," said Cal. "Well, she thinks that the inn is spooky. You know, haunted."

Nick chuckled. "I keep hearing that. What do you think?"

"Well, I don't know. Sometimes I do think there are some dark spirits festering in that house. I know that my great grandfather shot himself in the attic."

"Wow."

"And once I was going through the records of the inn and found out that two children had died there in the early 1900s." Cal paused. "It sounds crazy, but sometimes I did think that I could hear children giggling in the corridors."

Nick shuddered. "But you never saw them, did you?"

"Nope," said Cal. "And I never want to. I do wonder if the dark spirits had anything to do with mother's death."

Nick leaned in. "You mean, you think that a ghost killed your mother?"

They were interrupted by the waitress, who came by with their drinks and burgers.

"I don't know," said Cal. "But it makes sense, doesn't it?"

"Er, I'm not sure..."

"I know it does sound a little crazy, but there's no other way to explain it."

"When was the last time you saw her?" Nick asked.

"The last time I saw you. For dinner on Christmas Eve. I wanted to visit her on New Year's Eve too, but I had already spent Christmas dinner without Jasmina and left her at home. I wasn't going to abandon her on New Year's too."

Cal sounded defensive. Maybe he was guilty for being a bad son, unless he was guilty for other reasons.

"So you spent New Year's Eve with your fiancée?"

"Yeah. We just sat at home and watched TV. Had dinner, you know." Cal lowered his voice. "So, on that night, you really didn't hear anything? See anything suspicious?"

Nick shook his head before biting into his bacon burger. "I was out like a light. Wish I did though. I did hear from someone else that a pickup truck was spotted outside of the inn."

"What?" Cal exclaimed. "Do the police know?"

"Of course they do." Nick looked at him closely. "Any idea who it could be?"

"A pickup truck?" Cal did some biting and munching of his own. "Why, no. Oh, it could be Edward Herman. He must have a pickup truck."

"No, it wasn't him," said Nick. "He had an alibi."

"Oh." More silence and chewing. "Then I don't know."

I saw Nick looking at him intensely. He said nothing more. For a while, they ate their lunch and we finished ours and then sat there and waited until they left.

CHAPTER 11

The three of us met back at the car. The snowstorm had stopped, but it left a thick layer of snow on Sterling's car that took some time for him to scrape off.

"What do you guys think?" Nick asked when he got back into the car.

Sterling started the engine. "Something's definitely weird. Ghosts? That's what he could come up with?"

"But the guy would be a damn good actor if he could just cry on command like that," Nick said.

"Maybe he's just a crazy hysteric," said Sterling.

"He did sound a little defensive when you asked him where he was on New Year's Eve," I said. "Maybe he wasn't faking. Maybe he was crying out of guilt."

"When I first questioned him," said Sterling, "he

was also shaking and crying a lot. At the time I thought he was upset about his mother, but now with all this ghost talk, I do question his mental well being."

Sterling was way too logical sometimes. I changed the subject.

"Let's go question the fiancée."

"You and I will go," said Sterling. "If Nick comes, it'll be too distracting."

Nick grinned. "Why? Because I'm an international sex symbol?"

"Please," Sterling sneered. "You're just not needed. I'm dropping you at the Wild house."

"Fine," said Nick. "But if you ask me, it's not Cal."

"And how would you know that?" said Sterling.

"It's a little thing called instinct."

Sterling snorted. "We'll see."

"Let's make a bet," said Nick. "If I'm right, Emma belongs with me."

My mouth hung open. "Nick! Don't drag me into this. I'm not something that you can just bet on."

"I agree," said Sterling. "Have some respect, Nick. Besides, Cal is definitely involved. I don't even have to look at his face to know that guilt is written all over it."

"And how would you know that?" Nick asked.

"It's a little thing called years of experience."

After we dropped Nick off, Sterling and I went

straight to the apartment building where Cal lived with his girlfriend. The concierge let us in after Sterling showed him his badge. Fortunately, Jasmina was home when we knocked.

"Yes?" She poked her head out the crack of the door.

She was pretty, with dark eyes lined with black eyeliner, dewy dark skin and shiny long black hair. No wonder Cal would rather live with her than with his mother.

"I'm detective Sterling and this is my partner, Emma. We're here to ask you some questions about your fiancé."

Jasmina frowned. "Fiancé? How did you know that we were engaged?

"Can we please come in?" I asked.

She stared at me for a second. "Do I know you?"

Then recognition flashed in her eyes. "Oh, you look exactly like Emma Wild, the singer."

"I get that a lot," I said.

"And didn't you say your name is Emma too?'

"A coincidence." I smiled.

She opened the door and let us in.

"I'm sorry about the mess," she said. "I would've cleaned if I knew I would have company."

The apartment was spotless. I didn't know what mess she was referring to. The living room was spacious with huge windows facing a park. She sat down on a beige sofa while Sterling sat on the couch. I remained standing.

"Where were you on New Year's Eve?" Sterling began.

"Here," she said. "In this apartment."

"And where was Cal Owens?"

"Here, with me."

"At any point, did he leave this apartment?" Sterling asked.

"No. We were here the entire evening. We ate dinner, watched the countdown, then went to sleep. What's this about?"

"Have you ever visited his mother, Martha Owens?"

Jasmina's face twitched, or was I just imagining things?

"I did see her about a month ago, but not since."

"And what did you think of her?"

Jasmina paused. "Is this about her murder?"

Sterling nodded.

"Well, she wasn't exactly happy to see me. She didn't approve of me, because of my...race. I didn't stay long."

"And you hadn't seen her since?" I asked.

She shook her head.

"What was Cal's relationship like with his mother?" asked Sterling.

"Are you here because you suspect Cal of killing his own mother?"

"We'll be asking the questions," said Sterling.

Jasmine looked agitated and shot him a dirty look, but she answered anyway.

"His mother was a little overbearing, but Cal would never hurt her. He would never hurt a fly."

"The same Cal Owens who broke a man's nose in a bar fight?"

"That was ages ago," said Jasmina.

"So you knew about that?"

"Yes. He was in college, and drunk. He was young back then. It doesn't mean that he's a murderer. Like I said, Cal was with me all night. He loves his mother. He would never do anything like that."

I paced in the living room behind the couch Sterling was sitting on, observing the apartment. I looked out the window, down into the parking lot. A vehicle stuck out to me, but I didn't want to interrupt yet. There was something else that intrigued me as well.

"Are you a knitter?" I asked Jasmina.

She had a knitting bag beside the sofa. It looked like she was starting a scarf with cable stitching.

"Yes," Jasmina said. "Is that a crime too?"

I didn't say anything. She sounded defensive, but she had every right to be.

Just then, there were footsteps down the hallway.

The door opened and Cal burst in and slammed the door behind him.

"Jasmina!" he said. "They know about the pickup truck. We have to get rid of it."

He was panting because he'd been running and in such a daze that he didn't notice Sterling and me sitting at the side of the living room.

"So you do drive a pickup truck," Sterling said, standing up.

When Cal saw us, his face turned pale. He opened his mouth, but nothing came out.

"It was you, wasn't it?" Sterling said. "You went to visit your mom on New Year's Eve, but a simple visit turned into an argument and you killed your mother in the midst of it. Then you covered it up by wiping your fingerprints from the knitting needle, cleaned the place up and ran."

Cal sat down and began to cry again. I'd never seen a man cry so much in my life.

"It was me," Cal said. "I did it. I killed my mother."

CHAPTER 12

Nobody said anything for a moment. Cal was crying on the floor and everyone froze, watching him break down.

"It was an accident," said Cal. "We got into an argument. I felt bad about leaving her alone on New Year's Eve, but when I got there, she was angry."

"And you stabbed her?" I asked.

Sterling took out a pair of handcuffs and went over to handcuff Cal, but I stopped him.

"I'm still not convinced it is Cal," I said.

"But he just confessed," said Sterling.

"Yes, but what was Jasmina doing there on New Year's Eve?"

Jasmina looked shocked. Sounds came out of her mouth, but she couldn't speak.

"It was your pickup truck, wasn't it?" I said. "And

your scarf that I found in the bottom of Martha's trash can in the kitchen. You went with Cal to Martha's inn, and gave her a present, but Martha didn't want it, did she? She insulted you, and you reached for the needle and struck her in the chest. Then you cleaned away the evidence, didn't you?"

Jasmina began to sob herself. "Yes, it was me. Cal was just trying to cover for me. I killed Martha."

"Jasmina didn't mean to do it!" Cal exclaimed. "We had both been drinking, and she doesn't handle her liquor well. When my mom lunged at her, she was only trying to defend herself."

Jasmina hung her head and buried her face in her palms. We waited until she calmed down and then she spoke.

"Cal and I have been together for two years. Martha had never accepted me. She just wanted to control Cal and keep him chained to her side. I was sick and tired watching her emasculate him. She just saw me as a threat, but I tried to get along with her for Cal's sake. On New Year's Eve we hadn't planned on visiting her, but at the last minute, we felt bad for leaving her alone. Cal's car was in the shop, so we took my truck."

"Why do you have a pickup truck anyway?" asked Sterling.

"It was my dad's," said Jasmina. "He passed away last year and left it to me. I thought that New Year's

Eve might be a good time to talk to Martha again, so she would give us the blessing to get married. The new year was a time to put past disagreements behind us. Cal valued her approval and I guess I did too. I brought along a scarf I knitted, because I knew that she appreciated homemade knits. If she didn't want it, she could've at least donated it to the sick children along with the things that she made. But no, Martha had to get nasty about it. She spat on my scarf and threw it in the trash! She called me horrible racist names and attacked me, my family, and my religion. Then she called Cal a traitor, calling him a loser for resorting to being with someone like me..."

Jasmina continued to sob and Cal stumbled over to hug her.

"It was all too much for me to take," she said between the tears. "Martha was getting aggressive, yelling and coming closer and in my tipsy state, I thought she was going to kill me, so I grabbed the closest thing I could find and—"

She sobbed into Cal's chest. Cal stroked her head and whispered, "It's okay, it's okay."

"Why didn't you just come forward?" said Sterling. "You would've had a much lighter sentence."

"We got scared," said Cal. "I didn't want Jasmina in jail. We wanted to get married and start a life together. So I told her that we should clean up and nobody would know."

"But you tried to blame it on the dairy farmer," I said.

"It was stupid," said Cal, "but we were desperate. I never liked that bastard Herman anyway. He laid his hands on my mother."

"But *ghosts*, for Pete's sake," Sterling exclaimed. "You tried to blame your mother's murder on ghosts."

"That house *is* haunted," said Jasmina. "I'll never step foot in it again."

"I'm sure that the evil spirits had something to do with what happened," said Cal.

"All that negativity swirling in there," said Jasmina, shaking her head. "I'm sure that I was possessed somehow, momentarily."

Sterling made a phone call to the police station.

When he hung up, he looked them both in the eyes. "The good news is, at least you can plead for insanity."

CHAPTER 13

"So I was right," Nick said. "Cal didn't do it. I win."

"Wrong," said Sterling. "Cal wasn't innocent. He tried to help his fiancée cover up her murder. He's just as guilty. Looks like I win."

Sterling had dropped me off at home and Nick came out to get the scoop.

"What did I tell you guys?" I fumed. "I'm not to be bet on and claimed."

"Oh," Sterling said. "Sorry."

"How did you know that the scarf in the trash was Jasmina's?" asked Nick.

"It was the same color and the same stitching as the material on Jasmina's throw on the couch. She was also in the middle of knitting another scarf with the same pattern. Adding in the fact that she loved to clean, I just knew it was her."

"Brilliant," said Nick.

Nick and Sterling both looked at me with such adoration that I blushed.

"I'm just glad this is all over," I said. "It's so sad. They just wanted to get married."

Sterling shook his head. "An unfortunate event. Anger is a dangerous thing, more dangerous than any firearm."

"I hope her sentence is not too harsh," I said. "Poor thing. I'm sure it was hard to have been the recipient of racism, especially coming from your own fiancé's mother."

"Still, that's no excuse for murdering someone," said Nick.

"Yes," I agreed. "It's just an all-round horrible situation."

"You never actually thought I killed Martha, did you?" Nick asked Sterling.

"No," Sterling replied. "I wanted you behind bars, but my instinct ultimately told me no."

"I guess we both have pretty strong instincts."

They turned to me again, looking at me with a mixture of adoration and expectation. I was used to being looked at by thousands in a stadium or millions on TV, but these two men made feel like shrinking into myself.

"It's been a long day," I said. "Thanks for everything, Sterling."

He leaned in and kissed me on the cheek goodnight.

I was glad that he was gracious enough to shake hands with Nick.

"And how long will you remain in town?" Sterling asked.

Nick rubbed the back of his neck. "Well, I got a call from my agent earlier this afternoon. The studio wanted to reshoot some fighting scenes in Morocco, so I'll have to ship out in a couple of days."

"I see," said Sterling.

I didn't say anything. I didn't expect Nick to leave so soon. I was hoping for more time to make a decision.

"You'll miss me, won't you?" Nick teased Sterling, grinning.

"Hmm," Sterling said. "Well, I suppose the question is, will Emma be going with you?"

They turned to me for the third time and I took a deep breath.

"I know it's not fair that I haven't made up my mind, and I'm sure you're eager to know so that you can move on with your lives. If I had to choose right now, I'd pick, well, no one. I want some time alone to figure some stuff out. You know I do have feelings for the both of you, but I'm causing more pain by delaying this decision, so I just want you to be happy. If you can be with another girl who is one hundred percent sure about you, I won't get in the way."

Sterling frowned. "Are you sure that's what you want?"

"It is," I said. "It's been so chaotic this holiday season. I'd just like to spend some time with my family and figure out my next career move, settle down a bit before I make any important life decisions."

"I'm willing to wait for your decision," said Nick. "As long as Sherlock here doesn't try to put the moves on you while I'm away."

Sterling shot him a look. "I'm willing to give Emma the space, just as long as you don't bombard her with calls."

"Fine," said Nick. "It's fair if we both give Emma some space while I'm gone for the month so that she has the clarity to come to her senses and pick me."

Sterling rolled his eyes. "Oh, please."

All things considered, Nick and Sterling were handling this very well. In the movies, when two guys were fighting over a girl, they often got violent. These two actually considered me and my feelings over what they really wanted. This was about to make my decision even harder.

"I appreciate it," I said to both of them. "I think a month will be long enough. By the time Nick finishes his reshoot, I'll let both of you know. In the meanwhile, I won't be in contact with either of you."

"You can count on me," Sterling said, staring Nick down.

"I won't call, I swear." Nick met Sterling's gaze and held it.

"Thanks for being so great about this," I said.

Nick came downstairs with his leather duffel bag, ready to go.

"We'll miss you, dear." Mom gave Nick a hug.

"Can't wait for *Dead and Alive 2*," said Dad. "Opening day, I'll be in that theater."

"Thanks Mr. Wild." Nick grinned.

My parents went into the kitchen to leave us alone. Mom gave me an encouraging smile.

"This is it," said Nick.

"Have fun in Morocco," I said. "Don't break anything, like last time."

Nick had sprained his ankle during an action scene when he shot the film months ago. I had been worried to death. He was lucky he didn't break any bones. For this film, he had to jump from one building to the next, parachute, and fight from day to night. It would be physically draining.

Nick noticed the worry on my face.

"I'll be fine," he said. "I'm like a cat. I always land on my feet."

"Okay," I said dubiously.

"Just know that I'll be thinking of you," he said. "Even if I can't call you, or hear your voice. I'll just watch videos of you online singing."

"No!" I laughed. "Don't. And don't read the YouTube comments. They are so mean."

His cab was here. Nick put on his wool coat and I hugged him. He smelled like someone I'd miss already. I'd missed him before and I knew I'd miss him again.

He held me in the embrace but tilted his head back to look at me.

"But seriously," he said. "I'll be thinking of you. I'll imagine you next to me and talk to you out loud."

"I hope you don't do that in front of the crew."

Before I could stop him, he kissed me on the lips. It was an all consuming, all devouring kiss, the same kind that had left me breathless many times before.

"Now you'll have to think about me too," he said when he pulled away.

"Nick..." I began to scold. But he looked so adorable that I didn't.

I opened the door. I watched him get into the cab. He waved from the back as the cab drove off, just like in the movies. I stood in the middle of the street, waving back, feeling a pang in my heart.

The street was calm, the snow was fresh, and the wind grazed my cheeks. I hugged myself in my oversized knitted sweater as I walked back to the house.

It was the new year.

Time to start anew.

With no boys around me, I could focus on my own life and figure out what was really important.

Despite all the flurry of emotions running through me, I was looking forward to that little piece of freedom.

RECIPE 1: MARTHA'S BLUEBERRY SCONES

Ingredients:

- 4 cups all-purpose flour
- 1 1/2 cups fresh or frozen blueberries (if frozen, don't thaw to avoid discoloring batter)
- 2 eggs
- 6 tbsp sugar
- 3/4 cup + 2 tbsp milk
- 4 1/2 tsp baking powder
- 1/2 tsp salt
- 1/2 cup + 2 tsp cold butter

Combine flour, sugar, baking powder and salt; cut in butter until mixture resembles coarse crumbs.

In another bowl, whisk eggs and 3/4 cup milk. Add to dry ingredients just until moistened. Turn onto a lightly floured surface and gently knead in the blueberries.

Divide dough in half. Pat each portion into an 8-inch circle. Cut each circle into 8 wedges. Place on greased baking sheets. Brush with milk.

Bake for 15-20 minutes at 375 degrees F or until tops are golden brown. Makes 16 scones.

RECIPE 2: DAD'S BROWNIE S'MORES

Ingredients:
- 1 package brownie mix
- 1 1/2 cups miniature marshmallows
- 6 graham crackers
- 8 bars milk chocolate, coarsely chopped

Preheat oven to 350 degrees F (175 degrees C). Prepare brownie mix according to the box directions and spread into a greased 9x13 pan.

Break the graham cracks into 1-inch pieces into a medium bowl along with the marshmallows and milk chocolate. Set aside.

Bake brownies for 15 minutes. Remove and sprinkle the s'more mixture on top. Bake for an additional 15-20 minutes, or until a toothpick inserted in

the center comes out clean. Allow brownies to cool
before cutting into squares.

RECIPE 3: DAD'S OATMEAL COOKIE PANCAKES

Ingredients:
- 1 cup all-purpose flour
- 1 cup old fashioned oats
- 2 large eggs
- 2 really ripe bananas, mashed
- 1/2 cup brown sugar
- 2 tsp baking powder
- 1/2 tsp baking soda
- 1 tsp ground cinnamon
- 1/4 cup (2 ounces) chopped walnuts
- 3/4 cup sour cream
- 3/4 cup whole milk
- 3/4 cup raisins
- 1/2 stick butter + 1/4 cup melted butter
- 1 tsp vanilla extract
- Honey or maple syrup for drizzling

Mix dry ingredients (oats, flour, sugar, baking powder, baking soda, cinnamon, walnuts) in a bowl.

In another bowl, mix the sour cream, whole milk, eggs, and vanilla. Whisk this into the dry ingredients until combined, then fold in mashed bananas and raisins. Stir in melted butter.

Heat pan on medium and brush with melted butter. Cook pancakes (around 1/3 cup each) until bubbles form on top. Then turn. Cakes will cook in 2 minutes on each side. Serve with honey or maple syrup drizzled on top.

To keep pancakes warm, cover with a piece of foil.

BOOK 3: DEATH OF A SNOWMAN

CHAPTER 1

*T*he children were gone. Almost without a trace, if it hadn't been for the handwritten note dangling from one of the "hands" of the snowman to inform us that they had indeed been taken. At least I heard rumors of this note—a ransom note probably—that the police had removed before the crowd gathered.

The town square was a media circus. The townspeople should've been at home eating their dinners, but curiosity got the best of them and they gathered at the scene of the crime to see the newly infamous snowman. It had been made by the abducted children, mayor Richard Champ's daughter Zoe, six, and son Joseph, four, for the contest.

Even though the snowman section of the town square was sectioned off by police tape, everyone stood around and snapped pictures of this sinister looking snowman. Its carrot nose had been taken from its rightful spot on the face and inserted into one of the branch "hands". The branch had been repositioned at a higher angle, holding the carrot in such a way that it looked like a knife, ready to stab at whoever got in its way.

The other "hand" had held the note, which had disappeared into the hands of the police.

"How dreadful," said an old lady in the crowd to her friend. "Those poor children."

"What kind of monster would do this?" her friend exclaimed. "And to make a joke out of it?"

"A sick, twisted game." A man in his fifties shook his head at no one in particular.

The snowman did look menacing with its squinty pebble eyes, hollow nose and cruel snarl. I zoned in on it with my camera phone and snapped a few pictures. The whole thing intrigued me. I had to help the case in any way that I could, especially now that I was friends with the mayor's wife, Eleanor.

All around me, the townspeople of Hartfield muttered their grievances with the kidnapping and the distasteful way the kidnapper flaunted it in our faces. It was such a big ordeal that reporters and news crews came all the way from Toronto to report it.

My very pregnant sister, Mirabelle, put her arm

around me and squeezed my shoulder with reassurance.

"Who knew this town could be so dangerous?" she said. "Child abductors now?"

She stroked her belly to soothe herself. There had been a couple of murders in Hartfield recently, but when children were involved in a crime, it was beyond fear and anger. There was outrage.

The crowd was shushed by a news crew producer. The camera turned on, the light flashing in the attractive brunette reporter's freshly made up face. I pulled my coat hood up to stay incognito within the crowd in case the camera panned my way.

"Police are still on a wild goose chase to find the mayor's two missing children in Hartfield, Ontario. They went missing in the middle of the Snowman Festival earlier this afternoon, here in the town square at Hartfield. The children were taken after they had completed their snowman for the Snowman Building Competition. Police are questioning everyone in connection with the children and the festival contest. If you have information, please contact the police. A ransom note had been left in the hands of the snowman, threatening the lives of the children, although police will not be releasing the official contents of the note as of this moment..."

Up until the kidnapping, Hartfield had been a fun place for me to be, even though the holidays were over. The locals and tourists alike looked forward to the Annual Snowman Festival that took place every January. It was something that started twenty-five years ago to cure the winter blues. The time between New Year's Day and Valentine's Day was usually boring, if not depressing, in the cold weather and the festival was a way to get people excited again.

I had been looking forward to the festival too, since I'd missed the last five Snowman Festivals due to work. It was always something I used to enjoy as a child. There were contests, performances, plenty of food, and free stuff given out by people dressed up like snowmen.

I used to enter the snowman-building contest with Mirabelle all the time, and once we even won second prize, which was a fancy four-slice toaster that my father thoroughly appreciated.

It was nice to be back in the town where I grew up. When I was eighteen, I set off for New York to be a singer. After a few years of singing at open mics, my career finally took off. Now, I was what you would consider to be a celebrity, although I still felt a little strange about it sometimes. For the most part, I was used to the paparazzi, adoring fans, and nosy journalists. It was all part of the game. What was real to me was my family and my little Canadian hometown.

My third album was about to be released on Valentine's Day, and I had been AWOL from the usual promotional stuff, even though my manager, Rod, the guy who had discovered me, was calling me up and bugging me like crazy now that he had finally gotten over his holiday haze of binge drinking and general gluttony.

I wanted to take a break from the industry, but taking this long of a break wasn't my style. I was usually quite the workaholic, touring and promoting all the time, but getting by unnoticed in Hartfield had been a nice change.

However, over a week ago, the mayor found out who I was and that I was in town. I had been in Hartfield since December, but I supposed he didn't know who I was and wouldn't have cared if it wasn't for the fact that his wife, Eleanor, was a big fan of my music. She suggested the idea of making January 18th Emma Wild Day in Hartfield. This was certainly wild. Sure, winning Grammys and topping the album charts were accomplishments, but getting my own *day*? This was something else.

The funny thing was that most people in town didn't have a clue who I was—mainly because half the population was over the age of fifty—but Eleanor explained that Emma Wild Day would attract more tourists, which would boost the town's economy. I loved this town and I wanted to help in any way that I could, so how could I have said no?

The inauguration of Emma Wild Day took place a few days before the Snowman Festival. It wasn't a huge celebration. I just went on the stage to receive a plaque, shook hands with the mayor and posed for photo ops. He made a lovely speech about my career and how much I had contributed to the music industry. I was sure that Eleanor wrote most of the speech for him, but it was still rather touching.

Only local reporters knew about the surprise event and who broke the news before the major outlets did, so the paparazzi didn't have time to descend. I told the reporters the lie that I would be traveling to promote my third album soon so that media types wouldn't come and harass me in town after the fact.

So it had been a quiet but lovely affair. My family members were in the audience, as well as a group of about a hundred fans I didn't know I had in town. I signed autographs and there were plenty of coffee and snacks for everyone, catered by my sister's Chocoholic Cafe. My fans here weren't as zealous or crazy as the fans in New York or the ones I met backstage at my concerts. Hartfield was a quiet Canadian town, and Canadians were too cool to care much about most things.

I was relieved because I was used to being

photographed whenever I stepped out of my apartment in Manhattan, but here, I got to chat with fans about the most random things. I probably spent about half an hour talking to one lady about scrapbooking. It was just that kind of town.

The only glitch in the day was when I spotted Sterling Matthews lurking somewhere in the crowd. Usually I would've been happy to see him, but he was with someone else—a pretty brunette with a ponytail and wearing a burnt orange jacket. It wasn't his ex-wife because I'd seen photos of her and she was blonde.

Was Sterling on a date? He only passed through the crowd with her, avoiding my direction and any kind of acknowledgement.

But that was supposed to be the deal. Sterling had agreed that he wouldn't contact me for the month until I made up my mind between him and my ex Nick Doyle.

Nick was in Morocco reshooting scenes for an action movie and I hadn't heard from him either. I did see a picture of him in the papers recently. He was laughing with his cute female co-star. Rumors were spreading like wildfire about the heat and chemistry between the two of them, but I tried not to give them a second thought. Rumors were rumors. He'd been linked to every woman he'd starred in a movie with, and I'd been linked to every bachelor—and a couple of married men—I was photographed standing next to, so I knew that it was all a bunch of baloney.

I hoped.

Still, between Nick's rumored new love and Sterling's apparent date, there was the chance that I didn't have to decide anymore. Maybe they'd both moved on.

As hurt as I was, I couldn't blame them entirely. It probably didn't feel too great when the one you loved couldn't decide between you and another man. Maybe I had expected too much for them to be understanding.

The thing was, I had come to a decision about who I wanted to be with only a week after Nick left for Morocco. It took a while for me to get used to the idea and accept the decision. Now I wondered if it was too late.

On the bright side, taking the time to be alone in the past month gave me the chance to assess my career—and my life. I wrote a bunch of new songs. They were much happier, optimistic songs. Some of them weren't even about heartbreak or romantic love, which was a huge departure for me, since I was that singer who always crooned about being unlucky in love.

I was done with singing depressing songs. They

were still nice songs and people really liked them, but I didn't want the songs to translate into my real life anymore. I wrote new songs about the love of family, of friends, of life in general. I took it as a sign that I was heading into a better phase in my life as I headed into my thirties. No longer would I depend on a man for my happiness and self-esteem. I had the strength to create my own happiness as long as I was surrounded by loving, supportive people. A relationship was only the icing on top of a rich, delicious cake.

After celebrating Emma Wild Day, I felt utterly ready to take on the world again. No more hiding out from the press or even people in town. I vowed to do more charity work this year and give back rather than fret over my love life. I wanted to meet new people, take on new projects and develop deeper relationships with my fans.

Things had been going well until the kidnapping happened. The children had probably been taken when I was on stage singing at the Snowman Festival. It had been a surprise performance with only three songs in my set.

The festival was a popular event. I had kept an eye on the snowman building contest because that was my favorite activity. All the built snowmen were behind my little audience, so it was just close enough that I could make out the outlines of the people who were busy building, but too far to see who they were exactly.

I had already met little Zoe and Joseph on Emma Wild Day. They were absolutely adorable children, so when I saw them building their snowman, I glanced back at them a few times. By the end of my set however, I thought I saw them talking to someone: a man, too thin to be the mayor. Then the man left and they continued on building the snowman.

After my set was over, I changed into my normal clothes and walked around the festival. I checked out all the snowmen that the contestants had built—the children were nowhere to be seen. I had thought this was because they had finished their snowman early and Eleanor had taken them to get ice cream or something before the judging began. At the time, their snowman hadn't had its nose repositioned nor had a ransom note tied to one "hand."

That would happen later, after Eleanor became frantic because the children were nowhere to be found when the festival was over.

I wondered who this man was, the man who had been talking to the children. It was as if he knew them. And was I the only one who had seen him?

CHAPTER 2

$\mathcal{I}$ tried calling Sterling right after we found out that the mayor's children had been kidnapped, but his phone was off. He must've been busy working on the case. I wanted to tell him about what I had seen from the stage, even if it wasn't much to go on. I left a couple of messages saying that I wanted to meet, but I fell asleep before he called back and left a message saying that he would be working all night.

I wanted to visit Sterling at the office first thing in the morning. As I walked out the door, Rod, my manager, called. I sighed, but I answered it anyway. At least it was something to do as I walked to the station, and I had been avoiding his calls for the past couple of days.

"Well, well, well," he said. "I thought you were dead."

"Is that why they have a day named after me now?" I joked.

"You're very impressed with yourself these days, aren't you?"

"Aren't I always?"

"Are you really still stuck in that little nowhere town?" Rod yawned.

He was one of the coolest managers around, having been a rock star himself in his twenties. He quit around my age though, claiming that he did so in order to save his own life. Any more of the rock and roll lifestyle and he would've been dead face down in a toilet bowl. Knowing how he lived now at the age of fifty-eight, I believed him.

"Yes," I replied. "Things were pretty calm around here until these children got kidnapped."

"Children, yeah, what a shame." Rod yawned again, not sounding the least bit interested. He was a New Yorker, after all. "Tell me, what's the deal with this Snowman Festival anyway?"

"What do you mean?"

"What's there to celebrate? Is Santa Claus, Cupid and the Easter Bunny not enough for you people?"

I chuckled. "Well, it's based on this Hartfield legend. Our founder, Henry Hartfield was said to have been guided to this town by a snowman after he wandered off from a group of explorers."

"What? You mean he met a man covered in snow?"

"No. A real snowman, a man made completely out of snow. I know it sounds ridiculous, but that's how the story goes. It was over a hundred years ago, and Henry Hartfield was rumored to be addicted to opium, so it's probably a bunch of crap."

Rod exploded into laughter. "Of all the ridiculous stories I've heard in the world, I have to live until I have one foot in the grave to hear about a town founded by a magical snowman?"

"This is why I don't go around telling people this story," I said. "January twenty-first is Henry Hartfield's birthday, but it has always been Snowman Day by default. Kind of like Santa overshadowing Jesus."

"Or the Easter bunny overshadowing Jesus, again. That Jesus can't get a break."

Rod kept laughing until I could practically hear the tears dripping from his eyes.

"All right, all right, I know you called me for something other than a ridiculous history lesson."

When the laughing subsided, Rod got down to business. "All the talk shows are calling. So are the journalists. You did the cover shoot for Rolling Stone ages ago but you still haven't confirmed for the interview. The magazine's out in February for God's sake. Work with me here."

"I'm sorry," I said. "I've been taking some personal weeks; you know that."

"Months is more like it. Your record company's getting annoyed. They're questioning if you're doing your promotional duties. It's not looking good. Oh, and *New Woman* called. They want you on the cover."

"Really?" I wrinkled my nose. I wasn't thrilled about the idea of being on a cover with my tiny boobs pushed all the way to my neck with two pushup bras, and being surrounded by headlines with references to sex and vaginas. Once was enough.

"I know," said Rod. "I told them no, that you're all booked up. Which you are. You have two talk show appearances next week."

"What? I do?"

"Yes, I told you ages ago. Now, you're booked for a flight to LAX on—"

"I can't!" I said. "It's crazy here. As I told you, these children are kidnapped and I have to help solve the case."

"But, honey, they have detectives for that."

"I know, but I can help—"

"Darling, you're more Nancy Sinatra than Nancy Drew. You have a job to fulfill, responsibilities, and my ass on the line."

"I know, but hopefully I'll crack the case in a

couple of days. I think I only have a couple days anyway before the children are murdered so it's not like I have a choice."

"Murdered? That's tacky."

"Rod? I have to go now. I'm at the station."

"Emma—"

I hung up. I had been in a rush earlier to get to the station, but now that I was there, I hesitated.

What if Sterling didn't want to see me? And did I want to see him? I'd had no contact with Sterling or Nick for over three weeks now, and to tell you the truth, it had been peaceful. I spent all my time with my parents, with Mirabelle, and a couple of girl-friends. We had a few girls' nights and even a sleep-over once and it felt like old times. But I had to face the music sometime; there was no avoiding Sterling. I had to tell him about what I saw on stage. I took a deep breath and pushed the doors open.

CHAPTER 3

*E*ver since Emma Wild Day, some of the guys at the police station were aware of who I was now. Before I was just the crazy chick that was always following Sterling around on cases.

However, Sterling would never talk about his love life to his colleagues. He was just that private.

When I came in, the guys greeted me with more enthusiasm than I'd received in the past. I flashed them a smile and told them I was here to see Sterling. Some of their eyes lingered on me, even though I was in a puffy winter coat. I did make an effort with hair and makeup that day. I hadn't officially seen Sterling for three weeks, after all.

His office door was wide open, but before I went in, I peeked through his office's big glass window.

Sterling looked like he hadn't slept all night. He had dark circles under his eyes and a thick five o'clock shadow that made him look more rugged than ever. His dark hair was perfectly messed up and the light of his grey eyes had dimmed from their usual brightness.

I poked my head in the door. "Hey."

He looked up, slightly startled by the sight of me.

"Emma, hi. What are you doing here?"

Smiling seemed to take all his energy, but he smiled nonetheless. In his stressed out state, I appreciated the effort.

"How's it going with the case?" I asked eagerly.

"It's been hectic," he said.

"What have you done so far?"

"I've been talking to the mayor's family to get leads."

I sat down on the chair across from his desk. "So what have you found? Have you received further communication from the kidnapper?"

"No." Sterling looked deflated. "Nothing. Oh, and congratulations on Emma Wild Day. I wanted to call you, but, you know."

His voice trailed off. I wished it were the right moment to tell him that I wanted to be with him, but we were in the middle of a kidnapping case. It wasn't exactly a romantic moment to break the news. Plus, maybe he was dating someone else. It wasn't the right time to have this conversation yet.

"Did you find any leads?" I asked.

"The mayor does have a few enemies. Political competitors for this year's election for example. And it took hours for Champ to admit this, but a few years before he was elected, he took part in a money laundering scheme that had been unsuccessful. Now he thinks that the same guys he was in business with are out to get him."

"Wow," I said. "So you're tracking all these leads?"

"Yup. My new partner's out questioning Stewart Branson, the mayor's biggest competition for reelection, and I'm about to head out to tail one of the money laundering guys."

"What about the mayor's wife?" I asked. "She could have enemies too."

"We already thought of that." A female voice came from behind me.

I turned around in my chair. It was the brunette I saw with Sterling on Emma Wild Day.

"I'm Detective Sandra Palmer." She stepped into the room. "Sterling's new partner."

I took her outstretched hand and shook it.

"Emma Wild, nice to meet you."

She gave me a quick once-over, and I thought I detected a sneer.

"So you're our local celebrity."

Even though I was used to being judged and criticized by the public, I still felt self-conscious from time to time and this was one of those times. I was wearing a white cashmere sweater and cream-colored pants. With makeup on and hair in waves that could only come from a curling iron, I felt extra girly.

In contrast, Sandra was a barefaced beauty wearing a dark pantsuit. Sterling might not have gotten much sleep, but Sandra looked refreshed. She had her dark brown hair tied back into a neat bun. With her big brown eyes, olive skin, and the fullest lips I'd ever seen, she was definitely pretty. Gorgeous, in fact. Although she was in a boring pantsuit, I could tell that she had a good figure.

My heart sank. I met beautiful women all the time, but not one to work 24/7 with Sterling.

"I didn't know Sterling had a new partner," I said. "What happened to Philip?"

Sterling cleared his throat. Was he nervous?

"He got engaged and relocated to Ottawa, where his fiancée lives."

"Yes," Sandra answered. "I heard about this opening from Toronto and I applied and got it through recommendations from my superiors. I always wanted to be a detective, so I didn't mind moving to a small town if I could fast-track and become one. So here I am."

"Great." I smiled. "Congratulations. How is the case going?"

"I'm sorry, but the information is confidential. I know that you're Sterling's friend, but it's classified."

"I see," I said slowly, "but I wanted to help. Actually I have some information to give you."

Sandra raised an eyebrow. "Oh? Sure, whatever info you have would help if you know anything."

"Well, first of all, I thought that Edward Herman, the dairy farmer, could be a suspect. Sterling and I discovered that he was, well, *connected* with the mayor's wife."

"I know the story," Sandra said, sounding unimpressed. "Sterling told me about your little run-in with Edward and how he was having an affair with Eleanor Champ."

She let out an amused laugh.

"We got one of our boys on him, in fact," Sterling added quickly.

"Yes," said Sandra. "Thanks, Emma, but we've got it covered. Edward seems to be going about his daily routine, and our guy has nothing to report other than the fact that he'd been calling Eleanor Champ at least two times a day to check in on her, so I think he's off the list. Anybody else that you suspect?"

Her constantly arching eyebrow was beginning to annoy me. It was like a question mark to challenge answers out of me that she knew I didn't have. Plus she looked at me like I was some sort of bimbo.

"I did see the children when I was performing on stage," I said, mustering as much confidence and certainly as I could. I set up the scene for them, of how far they were and what I noticed. "I saw a man talk to them."

Sterling frowned. "Who?"

"Well, I couldn't tell since they were so far, but I remember looking at him, wondering if he was the mayor, but quickly decided he wasn't because he was thinner."

"What color hair did he have?" Sandra asked. "How tall was he?"

"I'm sorry. They were so far away that I couldn't distinguish any features."

"So is there anything more you can tell us about him then?" asked Sandra.

"All I know was that a man talked to them. I saw them while I was singing, so I wasn't paying complete attention. The next time I glanced their way, the children were gone and it was the end of my set."

"But it could've been anybody," said Sandra. "Our team is interviewing all the witnesses they can find. If they saw someone, they would surely let us know. I mean, there were plenty of people at the festival."

"That's the thing," I said. "I think if he was a stranger, wouldn't somebody notice him? What if the guy was someone the children already know? Maybe he's a friend of the family."

"Are you sure that the person was even a man?" Sandra's eyebrow arched again.

I thought about it. "Whoever it was had short hair, so it's a possibility that it could be a woman, yes."

"It's really very little to go on," Sandra said. "It could've been anybody. Maybe just a friendly neighbour or something. You didn't actually see the man take the children, right?"

I hated to admit it, but Sandra was right. Maybe it was nothing.

"I just thought you might want to know this bit of info," I said. "It seemed strange that the children would be gone just moments after the man left."

"Well, thanks for taking the time." Sandra smiled condescendingly. "We'll continue to interview people at the festival and see if anyone else has a more detailed description of this man."

She stared at me, as if waiting for me to go. My gaze reverted to Sterling, who said nothing and only put on a strained smile in the midst of the tension.

My eyes fell to a ziplock bag on the table. There was a piece of paper inside.

"Is that the ransom note?"

Before they could answer, I jumped up to read it.

It was written in a funny cursive writing, sloppy, like a child's.

"The twisted sunlight of morning's path; to the land of turmoil in the night's dead; children's laughter echoes hollow..."

"Please!" Sandra's pretty face twisted into a less pretty scowl. "This is classified information."

She grabbed the note from the desk.

"I'm good at solving cases," I said. "Let me help."

Sterling spoke up for me. "Yes, Emma has a knack for this. She can be an asset."

Sandra shot him a look. "This is against police regulations. You can have your badge suspended for divulging information to the public. We have plenty of boys on the case, and Sterling and I have plenty of experience. Let us professionals handle it."

"I just have this hunch that the kidnapper is close to the family. Whoever he is probably knows the children—"

Sandra raised an arm and cut me off. "Now of course this kidnapper knows who the children are. They're famous. Maybe celebrities don't have the perspective that we civilians do. The mayor's family is in the public eye. Everybody knows who they are." She sighed impatiently. "Celebrity or not, you can't just waltz into our office and start pointing fingers. We have a system in place and we are working as hard as we can. We have no time to waste on the silly musings of an outsider."

I looked at Sterling, but he looked defeated. He didn't defend me again.

Sandra's arm pointed to the door and I went out.

I turned around and tried one more time, "I just think—"

The door slammed in my face.

CHAPTER 4

The nerve of that woman. I stormed out of the station, absolutely livid, and headed straight to Mirabelle's cafe.

The lineup for coffee and chocolate wasn't as long as it usually was, and Mirabelle was behind the counter helping another barista make the drinks. When I came in, she saw how upset I was and waved me back to her office. We were sisters; we could communicate without speaking.

I plopped down on her blue beanie chair at the corner of her office and told her all that had transpired at the station with Sterling and Sandra.

"She sounds so rude," Mirabelle exclaimed. "Slamming a door in your face. I know they're under a lot of stress, but that's uncalled for."

She got up and took out a box from her freezer.

After fumbling around back there, she slid me a red velvet cupcake on a plate with a plastic fork.

"This is absolute amazing. You have to try this."

"Thanks Mirabelle," I said.

I dug into the cupcake, straight for the centre. The cheesecake filling oozed out. I shoved half of the thing in my mouth and felt better immediately. It would've been better if it was warm, but you couldn't go wrong with a red velvet cupcake.

"Don't let her get to you," she said. "Maybe it's not personal. She might be the high-strung type."

But I couldn't help thinking that Sterling and Sandra looked like they would make a good couple. They were both detectives and gorgeous. Sandra was the smart type. I had always been terrible at school. I never studied and only thrived in music class and art class.

What had I been thinking when I wanted to follow Sterling to college at eighteen? No wonder he wanted to break up with me then. He knew I wasn't the smart type. They probably had plenty more in common. Plus they'd be working together all the time and who knew what would happen when they spent a lot of time together.

When I expressed all this to Mirabelle she gave me a quizzical look.

"That's funny," she said dryly. "I can't believe you're

actually jealous. You're one of the most popular singers right now. Your face is on more covers of magazines than mine is in the picture frames at my house. Men are practically drooling over you. Not to mention there are two very hot men fighting over you right now, and one happens to be the hottest movie star of our time. Plus you're gorgeous. Don't you know that?"

I shook my head. "That's just makeup. And some designer clothes and a gay hairdresser who's really good with a hairbrush."

"You're just crazy." Mirabelle shook her head. "You write your own songs and your albums have sold millions. For God's sake, no wonder the lady detective slammed the door in your face. Now that I think about it, I'd slam a door in your face too."

That didn't cheer me up. I was still sullen, even with the cupcake all gone.

"When you were with Nick, he was probably working morning to night with hot actresses, right?"

"Right," I mumbled.

"And he didn't cheat on you. He wants to marry you."

"You're right." I nodded, trying to convince myself. "It's just a bunch of silly fears. But...she wore a pantsuit, and has a badge and a gun and everything."

"So?"

"She's a real detective," I said. "I'm just some silly wannabe. I don't even know how to use a gun."

"Look, you solved, what, two murder cases now? You're intuitive and have a knack for this kind of thing. Intuition can come in handy more than logic sometimes, right?"

"I suppose," I said. "I just want to help on this case, but she's shutting me out. I guess she's just being professional."

"If you can't work with Sterling, why not do it on your own? You're wasting time stuffing yourself with my baked goods, even if they are the best in town."

"Why are you always right?" I sighed and smiled. Mirabelle's pep talk and a cupcake did wonders for my spirit. "Those kids have to be found. I hope they're all right. I met them, and they're lovely. Sterling and Sandra might be going in one direction, but they don't have everyone covered." I thought about the case a bit more. "It could be someone closer than they think. Once I read about this kidnapping case in Connecticut where a little boy got kidnapped. It turned out that it was the gardener who was fired over some dead geraniums and he wanted to get revenge on the parents."

"And what happened?" asked Mirabelle. "Was the boy okay?"

"Unfortunately he locked the boy in a car trunk

for too long. Since it was a particularly hot summer, the trunk was overheated and the boy died."

"Wow. I hope the guy got what he deserved."

"Two life sentences," I said. "The thing is, I'm not sure if this kidnapping is about money. The ransom note didn't say anything about money. It was just sort of...cruel."

I told Mirabelle what the note said. The handwriting on the note was scrawled by someone who wanted to disguise his or her writing. It looked like it had been written with the left hand so that it would be hard to analyze.

"I wonder what the motive is," Mirabelle said. "It does sounds like someone wants to torture the parents."

"Exactly," I said. "Whoever this is wants the mayor or his wife to suffer. Or both, but who would go out of their way to be this cruel? The dairy farmer is out. Plus, when I did speak to him, it sounded like he genuinely cared for Eleanor, so I don't think he would do this to her, even if he wanted to get back at the mayor."

"I don't even think the mayor's all that rich," said Mirabelle. "He's only a small town mayor. He may live in a better house now, but he used to live in a house the same as ours a few years ago."

"Right, which is why I do think this crime is more personal. But who would really want to hurt him? It could be the money-laundering people, I suppose. But if it's them, Sterling's team would surely dig up something. But I can't ask him because I don't want to get him in trouble."

"Is it him?" Mirabelle asked softly. "Did you choose Sterling?"

I hesitated to answer, but I was dying to tell someone. "Yes. I thought about it long and hard. I choose Sterling."

Mirabelle grinned. "I knew it."

"He was always the one who got away. I do love Nick, I really do. Heck, once I was madly obsessed with him. But my life wasn't going in the direction I wanted with him. I'm not sure that he would cut back on the work and travel if we did marry. He's just too in demand. What if he falls back into his old patterns? Meanwhile, Sterling's always been a rock. I need that kind of security right now."

"It's hard to forget your first love." Mirabelle nodded in sympathy.

"Right. I've always wondered, 'what if?'"

I looked at Mirabelle's huge baby bump.

"I mean, I'm not sure if I'm quite ready for kids yet, but I'd like the option. Soon."

"I hear you," said Mirabelle. "But sometimes I envy you and your life. You get to travel around, meet all these interesting people. And what do I get to do?"

"Eat chocolate and drink coffee all day," I teased. "What torture."

"So you want to quit your celebrity lifestyle and come back here?"

"No. I can't stop singing. I'll just have to slow down my career. I've already accomplished what I wanted. I'll just have to keep challenging myself musically. But I can do that here too. I can buy a house and build my own studio. Why not? Sure, I'll have to tour and promote, but that's only sometimes. It's not going to kill me if I appear on fewer covers of magazines."

"But what if Nick wants that too? Buying a house and settling down with you?"

"He said he wants his career to slow down," I said. "But I don't know. I feel like Sterling is a more sensible choice."

"Which one is better in bed?" Mirabelle smiled slyly.

"Mirabelle!" I exclaimed. "I'm not going to talk about that with you."

CHAPTER 5

*O*nce I picked myself up from my moment of self-pity, I decided to pay Eleanor Champ a visit at her house. If Sandra didn't want me on the case, I would go around her. It wasn't hard to arrange a meeting to see Eleanor because she was a big fan of mine. We had talked quite a bit after the Emma Wild Day ceremony, and we got along really well.

I took a taxi to the Champ estate. The house-keeper opened the door. She was a short stout lady wearing a grey apron that matched her knotty hair. When she saw me, she narrowed her eyes, all the wrinkles crinkling on her face like a road map.

"I'm here to see Mrs. Champ?"

"Who's inquiring?" she asked sharply.

"Emma Wild," I said. "I'm a friend."

"Stay here." She closed the door in my face.

What was with all the doors slamming in my face today? It reminded me of the early days of my career when I used to visit record companies with my demo.

I heard her taking her sweet time trudging up the stairs while I waited outside in the winter cold. By the time I began to worry whether I was getting frostbite, the door opened, and the sour housekeeper appeared once again.

"She's upstairs," she barked. "First room to your left."

"Okay," I said. "Thanks."

I walked up quickly, eager to get away from her.

Eleanor was sitting in a library room looking perfectly composed and beautiful. She wore a baby blue sweater, a knee-length corduroy skirt and tan leather boots. With her immaculate ivory skin and blonde hair, she looked very well kept for someone in her early fifties. All the walls were lined with books. Sunlight streamed from the window, lighting her from behind and giving her a golden aura. She was drinking her tea when she saw me, and had I not known better I would've thought that she was just enjoying a quiet morning to herself.

"Ah, Emma."

She stood up to greet me, but I signalled that it was okay for her to sit. I closed the door behind me, and sat in the chair next to her.

"Would you like some tea?" She gestured the empty cup and saucer on the tea tray next to the pot.

Her lips were smiling, but her eyes weren't. They were red, probably from hours of crying last night and this morning.

"I'll help myself," I said. "How are you holding up?"

For a second, Eleanor couldn't speak. Then I noticed her lower lip quivering before she pressed her lips together. She was trying not to cry.

"I trust the police are doing all they can," she finally said.

"Yes," I agreed.

I sure hoped Sterling and his new partner were getting somewhere.

"I just don't know what this person would want," she said. "They're not asking for money. Yet."

She teared up and sobbed. I stood up and put my arm around her shoulders.

"They'll turn up," I said, trying to sound convincing.

"I'm such a bad mother," she said. "Maybe this is God punishing me."

"That's not true. I've seen you with your kids and you're a great mother. Those kids love you."

She continued to sob and I passed her a napkin from the tea tray.

"Whoever took them is out to get me for all that I've done. I'm a terrible wife and a terrible mother."

I didn't know whether to bring it up, but now it felt appropriate.

"Eleanor, you can't torture yourself like this. I know about your...affair."

Her blue eyes grew wide. "You know?"

I nodded. "With Edward Herman, the dairy farmer, yes."

She buried her face in the napkin and made a sound that was between a laugh and a cry.

"How humiliating," she said. "Does the whole town know?"

"No. Not at all. I only know because I was questioning him for a murder case. Remember the woman who owned the inn? Edward used to date her."

"Oh. And you suspected him of murder. I remember the police calling me about his alibi. So you were with the detective?"

"Yes. I helped with the case."

"That's impressive," she said.

"Thanks. Well, I wanted to help you with this case too. I know that the police are doing all they can to go after all the leads in connection with the mayor—where is Richard anyway?"

"I'm not sure," she said. "He might've gone to his office to work."

"Does Richard know about Edward?" I asked.

"I don't know. If he did, he probably wouldn't even care. He probably has his own mistress, or two. I wouldn't know or care either. All he really cares about is his political career. Wants to move to Toronto and be the mayor there in the near future."

"Is that something you want to do?"

"I thought I did. Before I met Edward." Her voice got quiet. "I wish Edward were here."

"Why don't you just get a divorce?"

"And have two failed marriages?" She let out a bitter laugh.

Looking at Eleanor in that pristine room, in that big fancy house with servants, I supposed she was the type to keep up appearances.

"But you do love Edward?"

"Yes," she said. "Even if he is a dairy farmer. But I wanted to wait until the kids are grown to leave Richard. Richard and I have a good understanding anyhow."

"How is Richard with the children?"

Eleanor turned pink, or was it just my imagination?

"He loves them, of course. He's worried to bits."

"Does he know who would take them?"

"He does suspect some of the men he used to be in business with, so I'm praying that they catch them soon."

"But do you think it might be somebody else?" I watched her carefully.

Eleanor sighed. "I don't know. I wish I did. All I know is that I've sinned and I'm being punished. I just hope that God doesn't take it out on the children. The thing is, at the festival, I left them. It was my fault. I left the kids on their own while I stood by Richard's side to work the festival and greet the visitors."

She began to sob loudly.

"Oh, Eleanor, it's not your fault. It was planned. There was a note, so this person was waiting for a chance to take them."

"But who? And why would the kids go so easily?"

"That's why I suspect that it might be someone your family is close to."

Her teary eyes grew wide again. "You think?"

"It's what I'm trying to figure out," I said. "How many people are working or living in this house?"

"Well, there's me, Richard, Joseph and Zoe, our housekeepers Joanne and her husband Henry. They cook and Henry also tends to the garden."

"That's everyone?" I asked. "Are there people who come here often?

"Sometimes my eldest son Matthew comes to stay," she said. "He's eighteen and going to Callen University, so he usually lives on campus. There's also our babysitter Isla, who works part-time."

"I see."

"Do you really suspect someone in this house? I just can't imagine any one of them being involved in this!"

"I wouldn't rule it out," I said.

"But I trust them," Eleanor said.

"All of them?"

"Why, yes. Joanne and Henry like the kids. Joanne was taking care of the kids for a while, but she had back trouble so we hired Isla. She's been working with us for a couple of years, and she's great with them. There's no reason why any of them would want to kidnap my poor Joseph and Zoe."

"I'm not accusing anyone," I said. "I just want to know all the facts. Be aware of your surroundings is what my bodyguard always tells me. It could be someone in connection with the people who work for you as well. We just don't know so we have to be careful."

Eleanor took a deep breath. "Okay."

"Please tell me about the babysitter."

"Isla? I found her through a nanny agency. She had good recommendations from the previous families she'd worked for."

"So she doesn't live here," I asked.

"No. She picks the kids up from school and takes them home, feeds them and plays with them. She's studying literature at the same university as Matthew actually."

"Oh, are they friends?" I asked.

"No. Matthew studies History. I thought that he and Isla would make a cute couple, but Matthew told me that she's a, well, lesbian."

"Really?"

"Yes, but I'm quite forward thinking about these sorts of things. Richard doesn't know of course. I'm not sure how he would feel about it."

"Oh, does Richard not approve of gays and lesbians?"

Eleanor frowned. "Unfortunately not. This is a conservative town, as you know. Richard is against gay marriage."

"I'm not sure how well he'd do in Toronto then."

"Yes, well, Richard knows how to turn on his charm in public."

"Does he ever rant about his stance against gay marriage in this house?" I asked.

Eleanor thought about it and she turned even pinker with embarrassment. "Maybe. I hope he didn't offend Isla. She's really good with the kids and they adore her."

"What about Joanne and her husband? I haven't met her husband yet."

"They're lovely too. Henry does odd jobs around the house and works in the garden. He's a sweetheart.

They'd been living in the house before we even moved in here. I guess you could say that they came with the place. They have their own section, adjacent to the garage. This house is very old and it has servants' quarters. But the good thing about their room is that they have their privacy."

"And you think they always enjoy working for your family?"

"I think so," Eleanor said. "They're lovely to me and the children, but I guess Richard can be a bit gruff and demanding. But he works so much and he's out of the house most of the time that they don't mind. I'd call them my friends."

"Are they well paid?" I asked.

Eleanor gave me an incredulous look. "I sure hope so. Sure Richard got his assistant to order them some thoughtless presents for Christmas. He gave Joanne a new vacuum and Henry a new rake. Richard thought it was funny, but I felt like the gifts were insulting, so I baked them cookies and got them gift certificates to go shopping at the mall."

"And your son—he's the son you had with your first husband, right?"

"Yes. He's all grown. Time goes by so fast. Can you believe it? His father lives in Calgary and Matthew is close to him. Luckily he likes the school he's in here so he's closer to me. Otherwise he'd be in Calgary and I'd never see him."

"Why? Does he not get along with his stepfather?"

"They get along okay. Don't speak much, but it's all right."

"I'm starting to get the picture that not a lot of people get along with your husband."

Eleanor laughed that same bitter laugh. "Yes. Well, he's not the easiest person to get along with. But he's powerful and he's got charisma, which was what attracted me to him in the first place, I suppose."

Speaking of the devil, Richard Champ's voice boomed from downstairs.

"Eleanor? Eleanor! Where are you?"

I jumped up and opened the door to the library and stuck my head out to the staircase.

Mayor Richard Champ was stomping up the stairs right at me.

CHAPTER 6

Joanne followed Richard Champ up the stairs, lecturing him for stomping on the carpet that she had just cleaned. Richard ignored her and kept calling Eleanor's name. He was waving a piece of paper around. His round face was flushed red and he was panting from running. When he saw me, he stopped and took a deep breath.

"Emma, hello."

"Is everything okay?" I asked.

"Where's Eleanor?"

"Right here." Eleanor appeared looking frightened. "What is it?"

"The bastards!" Richard waved the paper around. "Found this at my office."

He showed us the note.

Place $50,000 in a brown bag inside the mailbox in front of the Canoe Creek today at 6pm. The big one will take it. Any interference and the little one's gonna get it.

The ransom note was a lot less poetic this time. The Canoe Creek was a canoe rental place just outside of town near the lake. It was closed at this time of the year so the canoes were strapped and locked in and the place was more or less abandoned.

"I knew they wanted money," said Richard.

"What are we going to do?" Eleanor said.

"I already called the police. Once I get my hands on this guy, I'm sure he'll live to regret it. Just wait!"

The mayor paced in the hallway with a murderous look in his eyes. The police were on their way, which meant that Sterling, Sandra, or both, might show up. I dreaded the thought of meeting Sandra again so soon.

The news of the ransom note threw off my theory that the kidnapper was out for personal revenge. This was a disappointment, but I still had to keep up the investigation on my end to cover what Sandra wanted to ignore.

The note had been delivered. There was no handwriting this time; the writing was printed from a computer. The police would want to analyze the paper, the font, and the type of printer used to print it.

And what would I do? The only thing I could do

—talk to the other people in the house. I went downstairs to find Joanne. As unpleasant as she was, I had to talk to her. When I got into the living room, I looked through the glass windows and saw the gardener shovelling snow in the backyard. It must've been Henry, Joanne's husband.

Could he have been the man I saw talking to the kids that day at the festival?

I stepped outside the glass windows to talk to him.

"Hello," I said. "I'm Emma, Eleanor's friend."

The man looked up at me and smiled. He was missing one of his front teeth, and his pale skin was as dry and wrinkly as his wife's, but his eyes were hazel and kind.

I made small talk. "It's cold outside today, huh?"

"Sure," he said. "But I'm not looking forward to this ice storm this weekend. I think I'll stay in then."

He chuckled. It was odd that he was in such good humour when his employers' children were missing.

"Yes," I said. "I hope those children are all right, wherever they are."

The smile remained on his face. "Little Zoe and Joseph, yes."

Henry didn't look too concerned that the children had been kidnapped. I thought they were supposed to be close.

"I have faith that they'll be back," Henry said, still

smiling. "That's why I'm continuing my work, preparing the backyard for them to play in. Sure was a heavy snowfall yesterday."

"I suppose that's an optimistic way of looking at it," I said. "But aren't you concerned that maybe they are in real danger?"

The smile stayed on Henry's face. I was beginning to think that he was a bit out of it.

"If they are, what can we do? Worrying will only make it worse. The most that I can do is imagine that they're safe and sound and back here."

I thought that there was something that we could do: find out who did it. Henry and I must've had very different life philosophies.

"Any idea who would do such a thing?" I asked innocently.

He shook his head. "Beats me. But I'd rather not focus on this. I want to focus on the image that they're safe and sound."

"Yes." From the way his face looked with his permanent grin, I was starting to think that there was something mentally wrong with him. Still, I pressed on with my questions.

"How do you like working for the mayor? Must be a privilege, huh?"

"He's a bright man. He gets the work done in this town."

"What about at home? Is he a good father?"

Henry hesitated. I thought I saw his eyes dim. "The kids are lucky to have so many people working in the house and looking after them."

I nodded. This wasn't getting anywhere. Henry wasn't forthcoming with information. I had to go in another direction.

"When was the last time you saw the children?" I asked.

"Before they went to the Snowman Festival yesterday. Joanne was helping them with their hats and mittens."

"So the babysitter wasn't here to help?"

"Isla doesn't work on Sundays."

"I see. So you didn't go to the Snowman Festival?"

"Me? No. Had to paint the garage. Mr. Champ also wanted the toolshed to be cleaned."

"Wow, he works you hard, huh? Even during the festival, when you could be having fun?"

Henry shrugged. "Well, it's not an official holiday. Plus the festival's really for young people anyway. Working's good for an old man like me. Keeps the spirit young."

"So your wife didn't go either?"

"Oh no. Joanne, she doesn't like big crowds."

Henry was piling the snow up high and I didn't know what else to ask. All I knew was that they were both home when the others were out. Could they have done it? Henry seemed a bit slow, but could he have a crazy side stemming from his apparent mental illness?

When I went back inside, I heard yelling coming from upstairs.

I quickly snuck back up.

It was a male's voice that was shouting. An angry voice. It wasn't the mayor's because it wasn't as deep. I listened.

"Oh, so now that they're asking for money, you care?"

The door to the library was open, but I couldn't risk looking in without being seen.

"What are you implying?" the mayor bellowed.

"I don't think you give two shits about your kids," said the man. "You're more upset now that they're asking for your campaign funds. You weren't this upset when they were merely going to be murdered."

"Stop it, Matthew!" Eleanor cried. "Of course Richard cares about the children. He's just doing the best he can."

Eleanor was sobbing. It must've been her first son doing all the yelling.

"No, you stop, Mom. I don't know why you're defending him and making all these excuses for him when you know what he's like. Everybody knows. Hell, I know that you don't love each other, so why are you even here, Mom? So you can have all this?

Well, the kids are gone. What are you going to do now?"

"Matthew, I know you're upset. Everybody is, but we have to pull together. The police are doing all they can. We have to keep together."

Matthew only stomped his feet and stormed out. I scurried behind the door so that he didn't see me. I listened to him charge down the stairs and slam the front door shut.

When I slipped out of the crack between the wall and the opened door, I rounded the corner and ran into Joanne at the bottom of the staircase. I almost gasped at the sight of her staring back at me with her narrowed eyes.

CHAPTER 7

"*A*re you still here?" she asked.

"Yes," I said. Blood rose to my cheeks from getting caught. I had to get better at my spying skills. "I was just going to say goodbye to Eleanor, but seeing as there's all this commotion..."

"You're not a reporter, are you?"

"No, no, of course not. I'm a musician."

She gave me a once-over. "Musician? What kind of music?"

"I sing. My style of music is contemporary blues and soul."

"I don't listen to music," she said.

"Right."

Who didn't listen to music?

"Got those journalists snooping around here all day yesterday, with their cameras and tape recorders.

I had to shoo them away with my broom. Now the police are coming, wanting their coffee and donuts."

"Er, yes. They can be quite a nuisance. When are they coming exactly?"

"Any minute now."

I'd better question her fast if I wanted to get out before Sandra showed up.

"So that was some commotion now, with Matthew. Do they argue like this often?"

Joanne looked at me, then nodded. I could tell she wanted someone to vent to about the goings-on of the house. Now that I'd spoken to Henry, I figured that she had no one else to talk to about this sort of thing.

"Yeah, well, don't mind him, them two men never got along in this house."

"It must be extra upsetting for Matthew to have his siblings go missing. But why would he accuse the mayor of not caring?

"I don't blame Matthew really. Richard's always berating everyone around him. The kids, his wife, even us. Poor Henry. He must've called Henry a retard about a million times. Can you believe that?"

"That's terrible."

"He even calls me a lazy cow when I don't have the food ready on time."

"How do you stand it?" I asked.

"I don't know," she said grimly. "He attacks Henry

of being mentally ill, but you know who's really ill? The mayor. He has two different personalities. To the public he's charming, loveable, all jokes and all smiles. If we're lucky, he's like that here when he's had a good day at work. But when he's cross, watch out. Luckily he works a lot. Ignores his kids really. Only uses them to pose for photo ops. Like at the Snowman Festival."

"Oh, were you there?"

"Yes," she said. "I mean, only passing by on my way home from the grocery store. I saw the kids on stage when the mayor was making a speech."

"I see. Well, who do you suspect kidnapped the kids?"

"Who knows?" she said. "Maybe it's those friends that he goes drinking with. Maybe he shows his true colors to them. I don't know where he goes with them. The wife doesn't ask."

"It must be such negative work environment here."

"Everybody else is nice," she said. "We all get along. Just the mayor is the bad egg. I suppose it's because he's a politician. After blood and power. They're all the same."

"What about the babysitter, Isla? How does she like working here?"

"Seems like a nice girl," she said. "Likes the kids. Doesn't like the mayor either, although she doesn't interact with him as much as we have to."

"So she's not coming in today, is she?"

"Why would she? The kids are gone. She's out of a job if they come back. God help them. Isla needs the work too."

"Why? Is she in financial trouble?"

"All I know is her father's unemployed and she's been working hard. And the mayor stiffed her on her Christmas bonus this year. University aint cheap and I think she's deep in student loans."

Before I could inquire further, the doorbell rang.

"Oh, they're here. Ate all the donuts last time, so none for them today."

Joanne bustled out to get the door.

I followed, wondering if I could slip out the back. Before I could even budge, Joanne threw the door open.

"What are you doing here?" Sandra asked, her dark eyes burning into mine.

CHAPTER 8

Sterling stepped in behind her, along with two other policemen. Did they really need that many policemen to look at a note?

"Hi." I flashed my biggest smile to deflect Sandra's scowl. She didn't smile back.

"Hi, Emma." Sterling wore an amused expression. "I guess I shouldn't be surprised to see you here."

"Didn't I warn you about getting mixed up with official police business?" Sandra asked bluntly.

"I'm here to see Eleanor," I said innocently. "She's my friend. Is it a crime to visit a friend?"

Richard and Eleanor came down the stairs to greet the police. Richard's face was still red with anger, and Eleanor looked like she had been crying again.

I told Eleanor that I'd give them their privacy and would be going now. I could feel Sandra's eyes burning a hole into me as I walked past her.

When I went out the door, Sterling came out after me.

"Emma, wait."

He closed the door and grabbed my wrist.

"I'm sorry about my partner," he said.

"Yeah, well, it's not your fault, I guess."

"Everyone's on edge because of the case."

"I get it."

"I apologize for any rudeness on her part."

"You can't apologize for someone else, but I appreciate it. Any progress on the case?"

He shook his head, but I couldn't tell if it was because he didn't make any progress or if he just didn't want to tell me.

"That's okay if you can't tell me," I said. "How's your new partner working out anyway?"

"She's efficient. Of course I'd much rather be working with you. She is a bit hot tempered, so sometimes it helps with the suspects. I get to be the good cop for once, if you can believe it."

"I believe it." I smiled.

Sterling smiled back, but his expression dropped into an even more serious one. He put his hands on my shoulders.

"Listen, Emma, I know you like to do detective work, but this is a serious case. The people we are investigating are criminals. I don't want you snooping around and getting mixed up with something dangerous on your own, okay?"

"But Sterling—"

"Please." Sterling looked deeply into my eyes.

I looked back into Sterling's warm grey eyes. I wished he would put his strong arms around me to hug me and kiss me. I was tempted to initiate it, but this wasn't the time.

"I'm not getting mixed up with those guys," I said. "Don't worry."

It was the truth. I wasn't investigating other politicians and con artists. I was looking more into babysitters and housekeepers. But it would've sounded too silly to tell him. I would've if I'd had more proof.

I could've been completely off track as well.

Still, I wished I could work with Sterling like old times. Must that Sandra be around all the time?

"Let's talk when this is all over," Sterling said.

His look let me know that he was ready to hear my answer: whether I was choosing Nick or him.

"Okay." I smiled and he smiled back. I wondered if he could tell that I'd already chosen him.

I stood still, hoping that Sterling would lean in

and kiss me. He only looked at my lips, considering it. I felt heat all over my body from his intense gaze.

"Sterling?" Sandra stuck her head out.

She blinked at us.

"So talk later?" Sterling said.

"Sure. Good luck with the case."

I watched Sterling walk back inside.

I knew I shouldn't take Sandra's nasty attitude so personally, but I couldn't help but wonder if this was the way things were going to be. Why did she find me to be such a nuisance? Maybe she had a little crush on Sterling. I saw the way she looked at him just now, as if he was her possession. And were they in fact on a date when I saw them at my ceremony, or was that just Sterling being nice and showing her around the town because she was new?

Maybe she was simply a hot-tempered cop. I didn't like the fact that Sterling made excuses for her behavior, but he was a gracious guy. He wouldn't slag her off behind her back, and I didn't expect him to.

As much as I ached to be with him, everybody was so worked up about the case and so was I. I just needed a bit more confidence in my own skills.

So far it sounded like everyone could be a suspect. Joanne obviously had issues with the family, but as a kidnapper, she wouldn't be spilling all her grievances on me, would she? Henry had mental issues, but was he crazy? Was his overly optimistic attitude a facade for a nasty dark side? Matthew sounded like he hated the mayor and resented his mother. Could he have kidnapped the kids to get back at them somehow? He was certainly angry. And what about Isla? Not accepted for being a lesbian in the Champ house, and full of financial burden, she had plenty of motive to make some quick cash as well.

As I thought about this, Mirabelle called me.

"So, part of the note sounded familiar," she said. "And I couldn't figure out why. Then I finally realized that it's from a Harold Winken poem. It's not very famous, but Winken was a local poet. Well, he grew up in Hartfield in the 1940s anyway. Then he traveled, had a sort of tramp lifestyle."

"Never heard of him," I said. "What is the poem?"

"All his poems are untitled, so they take the first line from each poem. This one's called 'At the Wake of Dusk, A Swallow called'. I found it in our library. It's actually an old book of mom's."

"Are you still at mom's house?" I asked.

"No, I went back to my house, but I have the book with me, so come over."

"Great, I'm waving down a cab, so I'll see you in five minutes."

When I got to Mirabelle's house, we dissected the poem.

"I think this poem is saying that life is transient

and that we should love each other unconditionally," I said.

"Weird for someone who is threatening to kill little kids."

"Whoever it is is well read," I said.

"A poetry lover."

Something struck me. "Their babysitter is studying English Lit. Plus she had a day off when the kids were kidnapped."

"What, you think she's holding them ransom for tuition money or something?"

"Could be a possibility. Can I use your computer?"

"Sure," Mirabelle passed me her laptop on the coffee table.

"Let's see. *Isla Waterstone*."

I typed the baby-sitter's name in Google to see what would pop up. The first two were links to another Isla Waterstone, an amateur figure skater from Iowa. The third link was the nanny. It was her profile page from Callen University's website. She was the secretary of C.U.' S Charity Association. Under her bio, it said that she loved road trips, video games and poetry slams. No picture.

"Well it is someone who knows their poetry," said Mirabelle. "But does that make her a kidnapper?"

"I'll have to find out. I wonder where she is now. I want to talk to her. Chances are she's in class. But who would know which class?"

I searched Isla on Facebook. I found her out of a dozen of other Isla Waterstones when I saw the name of her school in connection with one profile. Isla's profile picture was of the back of her head. She was standing over the lake. She had short brown hair, and seemed to be dressed very boyishly in a white hoodie and black leather jacket.

If I'd only seen her from the back this way in real life, I would've assumed that she was a guy. Perhaps she had been the "man" I saw at the festival?

She kept a huge portion of her profile private, but I was able to learn some basic facts about her.

She was in a relationship with a girl named Camille Frankfurt.

I went to Camille Frankfurt's page. Her profile was a lot more active. She was a trainer at the Hartfield Community Centre gym and her posts were mostly fitness tips, inspirational quotes and nutrition advice. Under her musical likes, my fan page was there.

"Look at you," Mirabelle said. "You have two million fans? That number's doubled since the last time I checked."

I chuckled. "I know; I'm popular."

"So she's a fan of yours. Are you going to to talk to her?

"Yes," I said. "Maybe she knows where Isla is right now."

"Here." Mirabelle gave me her keys. "Take my car."

"Thanks."

"Try not to get into too much trouble.

"I'll try," I said.

CHAPTER 9

I drove Mirabelle's adorable navy Mini Cooper to the community centre. The parking lot was full, probably because of all the seniors who enjoyed swimming during the day.

A middle-aged receptionist with hair like a beehive sat at the front desk. She smiled at me when I came in.

"Hello," I said. "I was wondering if I could see Camille Frankfurt?"

"Do you have a membership?" she asked.

"No."

"I'm afraid you need a membership for access to the gym."

"Oh, I don't need access. I'm not here to work out. I just wanted to talk to her."

"In that case, she is in the gym training someone

at the moment. I don't know when she has a break, so you can go right on in and ask her."

"Thanks."

I used to go to the centre a lot as a child. Swimming was my favorite activity. I probably never even stepped into the gym more than twice growing up. Even now, I'd do yoga, Pilates and Zumba—anything other than being in a gym with all those sweaty machines. I just hated the smell of human sweat and mechanical machinery. Now that I was a celebrity, however, there was no avoiding gyms, or trainers, for too long, and I had to face the unpleasant odors more times than I could bear on some weeks when I had to be especially fit for a photo shoot or something.

The dreaded smell hit me when I walked past the pool and went into the gym portion of the building. There was also a squash court and a basketball court at the centre.

As I expected, the gym contained mostly retired seniors. I spotted Camille helping a man who appeared to be an octogenarian with leg lifts. Camille looked just like her profile picture except that a red headband held her blond hair away from her face and she wore red track pants to match. At the sight of her, I knew why she looked so familiar. I had shaken hands with her during Emma Wild Day.

When she saw me, her jaw dropped. She had been holding up the old man's leg, and she dropped it as she stood up and jumped in excitement. I cringed, hoping that a bone didn't crack.

"Emma Wild?" Camille squealed.

"Hi, Camille."

"Wow, I can't believe you know who I am."

"Of course," I said. "I remember meeting you at the meet and greet."

"There must've been hundreds of people there."

"Well, I did look you up before I came," I admitted.

"Are you here to work out?"

"I'm here to talk to you actually. If you have a moment."

"Me?" She abruptly turned to her client. "Let's take five, Bernie."

Bernie panted and stayed on the ground. With a weak arm, he felt the ground for his bottle of water.

"Is there a place more private where we can talk?" I asked.

"Sure. We can go to the squash court. It's hardly ever booked at this time of day."

We left the gym, and left Bernie to his well-deserved break.

There were no seats in the squash court and we had to stand. Camille was still looking at me the way fans looked at celebrities—not quite believing that we were made of flesh and bones.

"I thought you were out of town," she said. "I

read that you were going to start promoting your third album. I can't wait for its release, by the way!"

"Thanks. I'll be sure to send you a signed copy."

"Really? That would be so great. You're really the nicest."

"No problem. I'm sorry to cut into your time at work. I just wanted to ask whether you knew Isla Waterstone."

Camille face dropped. "Oh. Isla? Sure, she's my girlfriend. At least, I thought she was. I'm not sure how we stand right now. She hasn't been returning my calls lately."

I frowned. "You mean you're broken up?"

"I don't know. That's the weird part. We used to talk all the time, and I tried to reach out to her when I found out that the kids she was babysitting were kidnapped, but she seems to be avoiding me. Why? Are you looking for her too?"

I nodded. "I'm a friend of Eleanor Champ's. I wanted to talk to Isla to see if she knew anything to help with the case."

"I wish I could tell you. I even went around to her dad's house yesterday, but he was so drunk and didn't seem to know his own whereabouts, never mind hers."

"Does she do this often? Disappear and flake out every so often?"

"No, I don't think so," said Camille. "Well, we've

only been dating for six months, but I thought we had a serious thing going on, you know? I mean, I hope she's alive. Unless she broke up with me and didn't want to break the news to me. In that case, I don't care if she's alive or not."

"Strange," I said.

"I think she's just avoiding me. If she wanted to break up, she should just do so. I hate it when people are dishonest. But I should've seen it coming. She'd been acting weird for a couple of weeks before. She'd be taking calls during our dates and would leave to go to the other room. When she came back, she'd act all weird when I'd ask who she was talking to."

"How many times has this happened?"

"Well, three times. I remember that the last time was when she was waiting out the front of the community centre when I was getting off work. She had been on the phone and got off in a hurry, saying something about helping a classmate. But she's not the best liar. She blinks a lot when she lies. And she seemed distracted. I thought it was because the holidays were over and she was readjusting back to her school schedule, but I don't know."

"That's really odd," I said. "Would she be in school right now?"

"I think so," she said. "I swear, if I find out she's been cheating on me..."

Camille took a deep breath.

"What class would she have right now?" I asked.

"I think she has Modern Poetry. It ends at four. At the Peterson Building."

"Oh, speaking of poetry, does she like Harold Winken by any chance?"

"Like it?" Camille laughed. "The girl is obsessed with Winken."

CHAPTER 10

As I drove the Mini Cooper out of Hartfield to Callen University, which was about thirty minutes away, I went over all I knew about Isla Waterstone.

She was definitely secretive online. There were no face shots of her online, not even in Camille's albums. Camille had explained that Isla hated having her photo taken and would block out her face with her arm if a camera so much as came near her.

She apparently loved the kids, but she was in debt. Plus she hated the mayor and had been acting strange and M.I.A. with Camille. And the Harold Winken obsession? It was not looking good for our girl Isla.

I called Eleanor.

"Do you happen to have a picture of Isla?" I asked.

"Sure, I have some pictures of her with the kids. Why do you need them?"

"I'm just curious to know what she looks like."

"Okay," she agreed. "Whatever I can do to help. I just really hope it's not her, because she's a sweet girl."

"If you can send me a photo as soon as possible, that would be great."

"If I can find it on my phone, I can forward one to you right away."

"Thanks," I said. "How is everything going? Did the police find anything yet?"

"Well, they are still looking for this old enemy of Richard's, but I don't know. We haven't heard anything back yet."

"That's too bad."

"Do you really think Isla is a suspect?"

"We'll see," I said vaguely. "But isn't it odd that she hasn't been around since the kidnapping, not even to comfort you?"

"Odd? Well, now that you mention it. I suppose, but I assumed she was busy with school. I've been so worried that I haven't thought about Isla not being around. You're right; it would've been nice if she called. I thought we were close."

"Hmm, well. Did you know that she's a big fan of Harold Winken?"

"Oh, the poet? Yes. She's a huge fan. She was always quoting him to us, so much so that I started reading Winken. Matthew and Joanne have taken to his poetry too, and I didn't think they were the poetry type. Even Henry has been quoting Winken. We have all his poetry collections. The house is Winken mad."

"Really?"

Damn. There went my argument against Isla. But at least it did prove that it was someone close to the family.

"How many people outside of your family know that your household is crazy about Winken?"

"Plenty, I suppose. Why?"

"Are you aware that a portion of the first ransom note is from a Winken poem?"

"No. Really?"

"Yes." I recited the lines to her.

"Oh my God." Eleanor gasped. "I didn't know. I mean, we do have dinner guests here sometimes, so maybe there are people who do know. I really didn't think it could be my staff."

"Well, we don't know anything yet," I assured her. "However, I'm trying to find out more about Isla. When was the last time she came into work?"

"The day before the Snowman Festival."

"Did she act unusual at all?"

"No. Well, she was a bit stressed, but she was talking about a project she was working on for school, so she had her reasons."

"Hmm, okay. Thanks."

I hung up. The only thing to do was to find her and talk to her. Why was she M.I.A. with her girl-friend? Was that really her way of breaking up with her girlfriend, or was she merely busy with school? Or could there have been some other explanation — like planning a big kidnapping plot against the employer she hated so she could pay off her student debts?

I pulled up to the school. Now that people were aware of who I was in this town, staying incognito was a luxury. But I really wanted to be a good spy. Usually my bright red hair was a dead giveaway so it was tied back into a bun and covered with a black beanie hat. I was dressed in my spying outfit of black pants and a black turtleneck sweater. My face was completely bare, so pale that I looked like a snowman myself. You wouldn't believe how much hair and makeup could transform a girl. Given enough of a makeup artist's magic, I had the theory that most women could look like celebrities. That was why I tried not to take the title too seriously. Like anything, it came with perks and downsides.

Eleanor sent me a picture with a clear shot of Isla's face. She was with the kids. They had built a castle out of foam blocks in the living room and Isla was kneeling between the two of them, smiling.

I pulled up to the building that Camille mentioned and checked the time. I was early because sometimes class let out early. At least that was what people who had gone to university have told me. I'd never gone to college, forgoing school in favor of a music career. I didn't regret it for the most part, although seeing all the college students walking around with their books and chatting together in groups made me long for the experience.

Not that I was ever a huge fan of being in school. I hated high school. But I admit I did have a chip on my shoulder for missing college, because it was the experience most people had. I'd missed the fun parties and clubs. And friends my age who were normal. Even sitting in a lecture would've been fun once in a while. Maybe.

Now that I was there, I did like the feel of a campus. The buildings were brown and old. I bet it smelled old too. It was quite a contrast to sleek hotels and big stadiums. Or the hole-in-the-wall bars where I sang when I was first starting my music career.

Maybe some part of me did want to go to university even when I was young—maybe it wasn't about following Sterling as I'd always believed. Part of it was probably that I did long for the normal experience that others got to have. Although the other part of me, the part who wanted to sing and be on stage, was a lot louder. So loud that I listened and followed it. Then I actually got what I wanted. My career exploded. I couldn't regret my decision, right? How many other girls were struggling to be singers? I struggled and I made it. That was something to be proud of. I knew that after awhile I would've gotten tired of the campus life and would've been aching to go out and sing.

After waiting for another ten minutes in the car, students began streaming out the front doors. I watched for the face in Eleanor's photograph.

In the photo, Isla was dressed in a black T-shirt, jeans, and black Converse sneakers. She had a short boyish haircut, a round face, and a thin but fit frame. What if I missed her if she was wearing a hat or a hood or something? I tried to carefully look at each face, but it was a strain, sitting in that car, to try to look at everyone. And I was also trying not to look too eager.

The students weren't too quick to move because the weather was nice today. The air was still and the snow was fresh and crunchy on the ground—not too much slush yet, except in the gutters. The students stood in circles, chatting away, and many smoked and tried to look cool.

It made me think of Nick. Nick used to smoke, right around the time I met him. On our second date

I told him that I didn't like men who smoked, but on the third time we went out, he showed me his patch and told me that he vowed to quit. And he did. It was hard when he had to do a film when he had to smoke, but he used herbal cigarettes.

It was sweet how he quit for me. I did love him, but I couldn't be with both Nick and Sterling. Of course, Nick wouldn't be single for long. Girls were always buzzing around him like bees to honey. Maybe that was part of the reason I chose Sterling too: the insecurity that I would lose Nick and that I was replaceable by the bevy of Hollywood girls who came onto the scene every day.

Finally Isla came out. She was wearing black jeans, the same black Converse sneakers, and a puffy navy winter jacket. She could've been mistaken for boy, although a very pretty one.

Isla walked towards one crowd of smokers and lit up. She smoked and chatted with them for a bit, laughing and in a good mood. I wanted to wait until she was alone to approach her in case I got recognized by a bunch of college kids, but the crowd lingered.

Then something interesting happened. A petite girl with long curly blond hair came up behind Isla. They separated from the crowd and kissed. They were all over each other in front of that school. Camille was right. Isla was cheating on her. Or dumped her. But it did seem like she had a thing for blondes.

They began walking, and I didn't know whether to drive on, or get out and follow them. It didn't matter because Isla stopped in the middle of the sidewalk and answered the phone. She signalled to the blond girl that it was a private call and that she had to go. She quickly kissed her goodbye and turned the corner. I quickly restarted the car and followed her around the corner.

I pulled up to the curb and waited to see what she would do next. I couldn't decide whether to get out, follow her and try to listen in on the conversation, or to continue to tail her in my car. I was more comfortable in my car. There were way too many people around to stay incognito for long.

I didn't have to decide because Isla took out her keys and unlocked her Jeep. The old Jeep was black and looked like it was from the 80s. Where did Isla have to go that was so important? Although one little mystery was solved—whether she was cheating on Camille or not—there were plenty of other reasons why I still suspected her.

So I followed her. I made sure to stay two to three cars behind her so that she wouldn't catch me. Whenever I was in L.A. and driving around, I could always tell who was tailing me. The paparazzi, however, didn't know a thing about being inconspicuous.

She drove off, back in the direction of Hartfield.

I was disappointed when she pulled into the parking lot of a supermarket. This was her important errand? Maybe she wasn't the kidnapper; maybe she was just a normal college girl after all. I could still go in and ask her questions, but I didn't want her to know that I'd been following her. She was probably going home so I figured that I'd wait and follow her to her house. If she had anything suspicious going on at her house, I'd be more apt to find out. What if her father was in on it? He didn't exactly sound like a first-class citizen. Anything was possible.

Sterling had told me that this was what detective work was like sometimes, all the waiting around in cars. Frankly, it wasn't that exciting. Nick played a spy in his action movie, *Alive or Dead*. That looked a lot more exciting. Spying was only fun in the movies. Plus, Nick had been super sexy in that role.

The sun set while I waited. It sure got dark fast in January. I was beginning to feel sleepy.

Isla finally came out with three plastic bags of groceries. She placed them in the back of the car and then drove off.

As I drove after her, my phone rang. It was Sterling. "Emma, hey."

"What's up?"

"What are you up to?" he asked casually, or trying to sound casual.

"I'm just grocery shopping," I said.

"You? Grocery shopping? Shouldn't you have an assistant for that?"

"No. But in New York, my housekeeper did it."

"Okay, well, I know that you know about the new ransom note," he said.

"The one about the money?" I asked.

"Yes. And I just have this feeling that you are going to get involved somehow."

I hadn't planned out what to do yet, but he was right: I was planning on going to the Canoe Creek later, but I had been hoping that I would figure out who did it before it came to that so there wouldn't need to be a big showdown.

"What do you mean?" I asked innocently.

"You know what I mean. I just wanted to warn you because we've got a lot of undercover guys covering the whole thing. We have the Canoe Creek bugged and everything. There'll be guns. It'll be too dangerous for you."

"Guns? But you know the kidnapper will be with the kids."

"We're going to be careful, but if this guy is armed, it's a possibility. That's just a worst-case scenario, but I don't want you to be in a dangerous situation like that. The guns are just for protection, and we might not use them, especially if the kids are involved, but if this guy is armed and dangerous, we are prepared. And I think we figured out part of his plan. We discovered that there's a hidden section in the Canoe Creek after talking to a historian about the place. There used to be a hidden speakeasy in the basement and there's a passage out that leads to the forest. So I think this guy will use this tunnel tonight."

"Really? Wow. That's crazy."

"Yes. So we're stationed around the area in the forest where the tunnel leads to."

"Just tread lightly," I said. "Remember those kids."

"Promise me that you won't get involved. We have plenty of men on this case. Please promise me."

I couldn't do that.

"Sterling, I think we're breaking up. Can't hear you."

"Emma..."

I hung up.

Isla's Jeep was still in my sight, but we weren't in Hartfield. We were going further out north, into the woods. Isla lived in Hartfield. Where would she go?

As we made our way farther up and the cars became scarce on the road, I turned my headlights off. As long as I stayed close enough to Isla, I could still see enough of the road.

She kept going, driving right up into the woods. I'd been up to this neck of the woods once. My high school friend Jennifer's family had a cabin up here, and I used to come here with her on some weekends.

What was Isla doing near these cabins?

She pulled up to a moderately sized cabin. We were surrounded by trees. The moon was out and it was a spooky place to be. I parked a good distance away from her. Thankfully Mirabelle's car was dark and blended in. There was no time to hide the car. Isla was moving fast.

I got out and followed her. Each step crunched the snow. It sounded extra loud in the silence.

She approached the cabin and I saw Isla drop the bag of groceries on the porch and walk away. Then she pulled out her phone and began texting. This was odd. I got closer, and Isla walked away, back into her car and I heard her drive off.

I prayed that she didn't see my car on her way out.

When she was gone, I waited. There were shadows moving in the light of the cabin windows.

The most bizarre sight greeted me when the door of the cabin opened. I gasped.

CHAPTER 11

It was one of the costumes from the Snowman Festival. There had been at least six of those guys running around at the festival. But this snowman was in a cabin in the middle of the night.

I also heard kids' voices. Could they be the mayor's kids? When the door closed, I inched closer. The porch light seemed to be automatic, so I went to one of the side windows.

Slowly I inched up and peeked into one of them. It was Zoe and Joseph! They were jumping up and down because of the food. The snowman put a felt hand into the bag and got out some candies. The kids actually looked happy.

So this was where they were? Kidnapped by a

crazy person dressed like a snowman? It could've been anyone.

Isla was involved, but was she the mastermind? She had dropped off the food, so she definitely knew what she was doing. The question was, who was in that snowman suit?

Maybe it was one of her friends and she was paying them off.

At least the kids weren't hurt in any way. I began to back away slowly. I took out my phone to tell Sterling where I was and what I found out.

But suddenly a face appeared before me.

I almost screamed.

"So you've been the one following me around. I knew I wasn't being paranoid."

Isla looked at me in the moonlight with one eyebrow raised.

I jumped back, arms up and ready to fight. It was the Krav Maga training.

"Wow, take it easy." Isla jumped back herself. "I don't want to fight. Who are you?"

"I'm a friend of Eleanor's."

Her eyes grew wide.

"Really?"

"You might want to tell me what you're doing with these kidnapped kids."

I talked a mean talk, but I was actually very

scared. What if Isla had a gun? She did kidnap these kids after all.

"I know it looks bad, but..."

She stuttered, nervous, and I realized that I had the upper hand.

"Keep talking or I'll call the police," I said roughly.

"Okay, okay. I was just helping. I didn't actually kidnap the kids. I found out about it, and I was talked into helping. I mean, it was for the mayor's own good. He treats his children like shit. He treats everyone like shit. But I didn't know it was going to go this far, with the money and everything. I just wanted to make sure that the kids were okay and well-taken care of."

"That's why you brought them the food?" I looked at her, still not completely trusting the story. "How much are you getting out of this?"

"I don't know," she said. "Like I said, I didn't know that there would be money involved. It wasn't even my plan."

"Then whose was it? Who's the guy in the suit?"

"Please don't tell the police," Isla begged. "God, it wasn't supposed to get this serious."

"How is kidnapping not serious?" I asked. "If you tell me, I'll try to help you, but the police are on your trail. They will find out."

Her eyes got even wider. "No, please don't. I'm on

a scholarship. I can't be a criminal." Isla began to cry. "I can't deal with any more pressure these days."

"Do you have any idea how serious this is? There are dozens of armed policemen ready to take the kidnapper down. We have to put a stop to this."

"Okay, okay I'll tell you."

She let out a big sigh.

When Isla told me the name of the kidnapper, I wasn't completely surprised. Why hadn't I realized it sooner? Of course. No wonder the snowman suit was required.

"I really didn't think it would go this far," Isla said. "As far as I knew, it was supposed to be a prank to retaliate against the mayor."

"Yes, but Eleanor is in absolute panic."

"I just feel awful. Of course she would be. It's so stupid of me. I just wanted to make sure the kids were okay."

"Don't worry," I said, "Now just go tell your snowman to call the thing off."

When we headed back to the house, we noticed all the lights were off. We heard an engine start. A car was driving away!

"Oh no!" Isla cried. "They've gone to the Canoe Creek."

"I didn't know there was another car."

"It's rented," said Isla. "Just for the occasion. It was parked on the other side of the house."

"I see," I said. "Let's go stop them. Otherwise, you'll be in big trouble. I'll take the kids to the police and I won't mention your name if I can avoid it. If you'll just help me now."

Isla nodded.

"Come on," I said. "Let's drive."

She got into the passenger side of my car.

"Tell me the best way to go to Canoe Creek," I said.

She gave me the directions and told me what the plan was.

"Zoe has been instructed to take the money from the mailbox at the Canoe Creek. Then she would go back into the Canoe Creek. There's a secret passage in there. There used to be a speakeasy in the basement, and there's a tunnel connected to the speakeasy from the forest in case the patrons needed to sneak out."

"And this little girl is going to do this? Wouldn't she be scared?"

"Well, Zoe is a tough little girl. She's very bright, and was taught what to do as a sort of game. She was supposed to be dropped off in the woods, get the money, go into the Canoe Creek, and head straight into the tunnel."

"You know what?" I said to her. "The police know about your plan. They're going to catch them right at the tunnel's entry in the forrest. And the men will be armed."

"Oh no." Isla exclaimed. "I'm so stupid for not talking them out of this. Now the kids are really in danger too."

I looked ahead in the darkness. "I don't see their car."

"Their headlights could be off." She sighed. "It could be too late. They could be there already."

CHAPTER 12

As we continued to the Canoe Creek, I tried calling Sterling. He didn't answer and I had to leave a message telling him who the kidnapper was.

I was afraid that they would do something drastic to seriously hurt the kidnapper in the snowman suit.

When we drove up, the place looked dead. Not a sound. The police must've been hiding. The situation was beginning to scare me. I checked my watch. It was almost six.

I couldn't believe that the kidnapper would actually be driving in that snowman suit.

"I tried on the costume once," Isla said. "Just the head. You can actually see through the eye holes quite easily, and there are sound holes for the ears and around the neck, so it's not that bad."

"Still, it takes dedication. Let's just hope that your friend gets out of this unscathed. The mayor must've put the money in the box already."

Then we saw her. Zoe came out of the woods and ran to the mailbox. Gingerly, she stuck her hands into the box and pulled out a thick envelope. $50,000 in bills wasn't as much as you would think.

"Do you know where the end of the tunnel is?" I asked Isla.

"Yes," she said. "But, I wouldn't know how to get there by car because it's in the woods."

"Are they going back to the cabin after?"

"Yes."

Just then, we saw a couple of cops run into the Canoe Creek with guns in their holsters.

I looked at Isla accusingly. "I can't believe you guys would let the kids be in this situation. They're going to be scared to death."

"I know. I'm sorry. But what can we do?"

"Is the snowman armed?" I asked.

"I don't think so. Wait, maybe he is. They do keep a spare gun in the cabin."

"If they so much as catch a glimpse of a gun, what if they fire?"

Once we got into the woods, we became quiet. I was scared because I knew there were armed policemen all around us. Isla continued to lead the way.

We ran, and I tripped over a branch and fell on my knees.

"*Oufff!*"

"Are you okay?" Isla whispered.

"Fine." I grimaced.

We kept going, until we saw a glint of metal under the moonlight: the rented car. Then we saw the snowman, its face white underneath the moonlight. Joseph, the little boy, sat in the passenger seat.

"Just crazy," I muttered.

We approached and saw a shadow sprint before us.

"It must be a cop," I said. "They must've seen the car too."

"They're surrounding him."

"We gotta go stop them."

We ran to the car just as Zoe ran out of the tunnel and jumped into the car.

I saw a few of the men in the shadows, armed with guns.

Isla gasped. "Stop them!"

The snowman hugged the boy close.

One of the men was Sterling. I could tell by the way his hair fell in the back of his head, its specific swirl.

"Sterling!"

He looked back at me.

"Emma, what are you doing here? This is not the time."

"I know who the kidnapper is!"

"Who?"

"It's Matthew, Eleanor's son. He's not a dangerous criminal. Hold your fire."

Just then, the snowman drove off, but the police fired anyway, aiming at the tires so that the car sputtered and deflated.

"Oh my god." Isla cried at the sound of the gunfires.

"Stop!" Sterling cried to the men on his team.

Sandra appeared on the scene. She was in her pantsuit with a black coat over it.

Isla called out to the car, to Matthew. "They know it's you. Just give it up, move slowly and you'll be fine."

He did. It was a funny sight: a snowman coming out of the car. The men surrounded him and got him into handcuffs.

"Okay, but please don't take off this costume," Matthew said. "I don't want the kids to know that it's me."

I supposed he was like a person in character at Disneyland. Taking off the costume might've been traumatizing to the kids.

"This is absolutely ludicrous," Sandra said.

The police took Matthew away. The kids came out and hugged Isla.

"Where's the Snowman going?" Joseph asked. "He said we were playing a scavenger hunt."

"Is Matthew in trouble?" Zoe asked.

Isla frowned. "How did you know it was Matthew?"

Zoe rolled her eyes. "Of course I knew it was him. I'm not a baby you know. I also know that there's no such thing as Santa Claus either."

"Yes there is," Joseph insisted.

"No, Joseph. The presents are really from mom and dad. I told you already."

Tears formed in Joseph's eyes. "No, they're from Santa," he wailed.

Sterling turned to me. "How did you know that it was Matthew?"

"It's a long story," I said.

Sandra came back to our group. "Come on, let's go to the station. Tom, can you bring the children back to their parents?"

The officer on the scene nodded.

"Can I go with them?" Isla asked. "I want to explain my part in this to Eleanor."

"Just let her go," I said to Sandra and Sterling. "She helped me get here. She's not going anywhere."

CHAPTER 13

"Just say it," Sterling said.

He was driving and Miss Pantsuit was sitting beside him. I was in the backseat, feeling like a criminal with these two cops up in front.

"Say what?" I asked innocently.

"I told you so."

I grinned. "But it would be too easy."

He sighed. "We should've listened to you, okay? We should've scooped out who was close to the family too. We did find out that the ink and printer from the second note was printed on the same type of printer that the Champ family owned, so we did start thinking like you then."

Sandra turned back and looked at me rather coldly. "How did you figure it out?"

"It was rather difficult," I said diplomatically. "There wasn't a lot to go on. All I knew was that I saw someone talking to the kids at the festival. I was sure it was a guy. Isla told me everything. It was actually Matthew, telling the kids to meet a snowman at the snow cone stand after they finish building their snowman. He was going to have surprise presents for them. So the kids hurried to finish up their snowman for the contest so they could get their gifts. By the time they did, Matthew was in his snowman costume."

I told him about having my suspicions towards Henry, Joanne and Isla, and ultimately decided that Isla had the strongest motives, so I followed her. Surprisingly, she led me to Matthew.

"But what was Matthew's motive?" Sterling asked.

"He never got along with the mayor. In fact he hated him, hated how he verbally abused the kids, his mom, and the staff."

"Did he physically abuse them?" Sterling asked with concern.

"Not as far as I know."

"Because we'd book him for that."

"Matthew just wanted some revenge. He wanted to see the mayor get worked up. Matthew didn't seem to be pleased with his mother either, because she'd stayed with him for superficial reasons. Since Isla hated the mayor too, Matthew managed to convince her to help him buy food and run errands so the kids were well taken care of in the cabin. Oh, and they'd been staying at a cabin by the way. It's actually the Champ family cabin. Matthew thought that because he was dressed like the snowman, the kids wouldn't recognize him."

"I'm sorry for not listening to you," said Sterling. He nudged Sandra.

She cleared her throat. "Yes. Good job, Wild."

Sterling nudged Sandra again. "And sorry for slamming a door in your face. I tend to do that under high stress situations."

"Apology accepted," I said. Although I was pretty certain Sandra still hated my guts and we wouldn't be BFFs any time soon.

"It's going to be a crazy night," Sterling said. "Lots of action at the police station. The mayor will be furious."

"But knowing the mayor," I said, "he probably wouldn't want word to spread that it was Matthew. He would want to keep his reputation of having a perfect family."

"Yes," Sterling said. "He'll probably spin it as a family joke gone wrong. Too bad it's not anytime close to April Fool's Day. Anyway, I'm sure he'll come up with some excuse to save face. Was Matthew after money as well?"

"I don't know. But when he saw that the mayor

wasn't as affected by the ransom note as he'd hoped, he introduced the money element. That really got the mayor riled up."

Sterling shook his head. "Some people are just horrible."

"Big cities or small towns, political families are just the same anywhere, aren't they?" Sandra said.

We drove on for a while, out of the woods and back to Hartfield. I yawned. It had been a long day and I was starving. I'd barely eaten lunch. Being an amateur spy really took a toll on your body.

"I'll drop you home first," Sterling said.

"Great," I murmured before closing my eyes involuntarily.

By the time he pulled up to the Wild house, I was practically asleep. When Sterling opened the door on my side, my vision of him was blurred.

"I'm going to walk her up," he told Sandra.

I yawned and stretched in the back seat. Sterling looked at me as if I were an adorable kitten.

"Be quick," Sandra said. "Because we have to go to the station ASAP."

Sterling helped me out of the car. He held me by putting an arm around my shoulders as we walked up the stairs. I was still a bit groggy, but I exaggerated my sleepiness so that I could feel Sterling's arm around me. By the time we reached the top step of the porch, I felt like I'd melted into his arms.

In the month that we were apart, I had missed him terribly, and I hadn't wanted to admit to myself just how much I did.

I wanted to tell him that I chose him, but Sandra was in the car, glaring at us. Why was she concerned with our business? I really did think that she had a thing for Sterling.

To piss her off, I could've leaned in for that kiss, but it didn't feel right. A kiss had to be pure and full of love, not performed to spite someone.

"Have a good night then." Instead I gave Sterling my warmest smile and went inside.

CHAPTER 14

Early next morning, I went to Eleanor Champ's house again. We'd agreed to a brunch date. Joanne led me to the dining room to see her.

Eleanor's eyes were once again swollen when I came in.

She gave me a tight hug and I patted her back. When she pulled back, I could breathe again. She pointed to a chair.

"Please, sit."

I did, letting her compose herself a bit.

Brunch was already prepared—salmon quiche with Greek salad. A bottle of red wine was opened as well. Eleanor had already helped herself to a glass.

"How is everything?" I asked.

"I'm just glad that the kids are all right."

The kids could be heard running down the stairs and into the living room. Zoe was chasing Joseph around and Joseph was laughing with delight.

"Usually I'd tell them to quiet down, but I'm just so happy that they're safe that they can do whatever they want at this point."

"I'm glad," I said. "So how are Matthew and Richard handling all this?"

"Richard doesn't plan on pressing charges. He's furious as hell, but at least he's not doing anything to harm Matthew, as long as Matthew does community service hours for the next three months. And, well, Matthew decided to transfer schools to be with his father in Calgary as soon as the semester is over."

"I'm sorry to hear that."

Eleanor sighed. "I don't want him to leave. But better that he leaves than to end up in jail and get a criminal record that could ruin his life, right?"

"He did try to extract $50,000 from the town mayor," I said. "He's lucky that he got off easy."

"Yes," Eleanor said. "He's my son and I love him, but if it were up to me, I *would* put him in jail for a few days to teach him a lesson. He'd be scared half to death. What hurts is that he knew his actions would hurt me too. I know he's acting out, but this was just so extreme. He'd always been an intense kid, very sensitive, but I didn't raise him to be cruel."

"Maybe it's the mayor who can be blamed for

that," I said. "So will your relationship change with Matthew?"

"Yes, but I also think my relationship will change the most with my husband. Matthew is right. I don't love Richard, and I'm not doing anybody any favors by being with him, least of all myself. I plan on getting a divorce in the coming months."

"Wow."

Eleanor sniffed. "Yes. I'm brave enough to do it this time."

She nodded, as if it was the fuel she needed to propel herself to believe it.

"Good for you," I said. "Why stay in a marriage if you're not happy?"

"Yes. It took me long enough to realize it. I always said I was staying for the kids, and to help Richard keep his image as a family man, but really, I'm scared. I'm scared not to have the security, scared of being divorced again, of being alone again."

I put a hand over her hand. She began to tear up again.

"Of course, I'll wait a bit. I want to make sure Matthew is safe from Richard's wrath. I'll divorce after the reelection. If he's reelected, great, if not, he doesn't need me anyway."

"You're strong," I said, looking her in the eyes.

She sniffed and laughed it off, embarrassed. "Thank you, Emma, for everything. I feel like such a fool, blubbering and crying around such a famous singer. But you're sweet. You're really a Hartfield girl. I'm proud that you're representing this town."

"No problem," I said.

She blew her nose into a tissue and then laughed.

"What happened to Isla?" I asked.

"She's fired. She was great, but it would've been unthinkable to keep her. Richard was tempted to press charges, but he wanted to hush her up as well. Poor girl. She has an unemployed, off-the-wagon father to take care of. I hope she finds a better job. I'd be happy to give her a recommendation, but if Richard ever gets wind of who she'll work for next, he'll want to talk to the family and destroy her in the little ways that he can."

"He's kind of scary, huh?"

Eleanor shrugged. "He's my husband."

CHAPTER 15

I was stuffed after brunch with Eleanor. At least things worked out in the end. No one was hurt, the kids were happy and healthy, and Eleanor seemed to be on track to living the life she wanted, even if she had to go through some obstacles first.

The first thing I did when I left her house was call Sterling. He didn't answer, but I left a message saying that I would be trying him at his office.

Now that this whole kidnapping fiasco was over, I had to face my own life—namely my love life. But I had it sorted out this time. I knew the man I wanted to spend the rest of my life with. He was my first love and I wanted him to be my last. I wondered if he had gotten any sleep last night. Either way, he could always benefit from a coffee or two. With me.

When I got to the station, the people working there looked at me in a new light. They had looks of admiration in their eyes, not unlike the fans I often met backstage at concerts.

"Good work, Miss Wild." An older officer approached me and shook my hand. "You saved everyone here a lot of grief."

"Thanks." I flashed a smile at everyone. "Good work yourselves, guys."

"Can I get an autograph?" A younger cop came up with a pad of paper. "My name is Steve."

"Sure, Steve." I wrote him a quick message and handed it back to him. He turned pink and grinned bashfully.

"I'm looking for Sterling. Is he in?"

"Yes," said the older officer. "In his office."

"Great."

I couldn't wait to see him. It was finally time.

When I got to his office I noticed that the curtains of the glass window were drawn closed. Even though they were never closed. I tried the door handle, but it was locked. I was about to knock when I noticed that there was a crack in the curtains and that I could peek through it. Something compelled me to look.

What I saw disturbed me. It was Sandra on top of Sterling in his chair. Her body was on his, pressing down on him hard. Her top was unbuttoned, showing ample cleavage.

I let out a gasp and felt a sinking feeling within me. Just when I was about to cry, anger took over and I pounded on the door.

SNOW CONE RECIPES

To make snow cones at home, you can buy a snow cone maker for under $20, or you can use a food processor to crush the ice.

Put the ice shavings in a cup or bowl. Now you can make different flavored syrups to drizzle and drench the ice.

Kool-Aid Snow Cones
- 1 cup water
- 2 cups granulated sugar
- 1 packaged Kool-Aid powder (any flavor)

Mix sugar and water in a saucepan and bring to a boil. Mixture should be clear. Stir in the drink mix until completely dissolved. Set aside to cool completely.

Drizzle over shaved ice with a spoon or from a squirt bottle.

Raspberry-Blueberry Snow Cones
- 3 cups blueberries
- 2 1/2 cups raspberries
- 1/2 cup sugar
- 1/2 water
- 8 cups shaved ice

This is a more sophisticated snow cone recipe with real fruit and fruit juice.

Coarsely mash 2 cups blueberries and 1 1/2 cups raspberries with water and sugar in a saucepan with a potato masher. Boil uncovered for 3 minutes, stirring occasionally. Pour mixture to a blender and blend until almost smooth. Pour it through a sieve into a bowl, discarding solids. Cool syrup, then chill in fridge loosely covered in plastic wrap, for about 1 hour.

Serve 3 tablespoons of syrup over 1 cup of shaved ice. Top with 1/4 cup remaining mixed berries. Makes 8 servings.

Mango Strawberry Snow Cones
- Ice
- 2 mangoes, peeled and chopped
- 1 pint strawberries

A quick and easy dessert. Fill a food processor with ice and process until the ice is fine. Add mangoes and strawberries and pulse to blend together. Serve in a dessert glass or dish. Garnish with a lime wedge if you wish and serve immediately.

BOOK 4: VALENTINE'S VICTIM

CHAPTER 1

"*C*ome on, Emma, it'll be fun."

My sister Mirabelle poked me in the ribs with her bony fingers.

"Ow, stop!" I cried.

I was lying on the couch still wearing my pyjamas in the middle of the day. Mom and Dad were at work, but I was taking an extended hiatus from my career as a singer...and celebrity. I was on strike. Eating ice cream, cupcakes and Doritos had been my full-time job for the past week.

"I don't even think you're in that much pain anymore," Mirabelle said. "I bet you're just using this as an excuse to eat more junk food."

"No," I said dramatically. "I'm really heartbroken. My life is this couch. Is there any more ice cream in the freezer?"

"I think there's only lemon sorbet."

"Boo. Sorbet sucks."

Mirabelle crossed her arms. "I just don't understand. This is a great opportunity for you to stuff your face with more sugary junk. And you get to be a judge. What's not to like?"

"People," I said. "I don't want to see people. Especially one particular person."

"I'll make sure he doesn't get on the premises."

We were referring to Detective Sterling Matthews. The bastard. I caught him making out with his partner Sandra at work a week ago. In his office too.

And to think I'd helped him solve a kidnapping case recently.

I covered my head with a blanket. Mirabelle yanked it down. Sometimes she was more like my mother than my older sister. She'd certainly been bossy growing up.

"The last time Sterling broke your heart, you went to New York and became famous. This time you're just going to sit around and do nothing while your phone rings off the hook?"

Everyone's been trying to get a hold of me, but I couldn't even bear the thought of checking who the messages were from or what they wanted. My manager Rod had been one of the more persistent callers, trying to pin me down for promotional duties for my third album. Representatives from my record company were probably peeved as well. And don't get me started on my PR team. I also knew that Sterling was trying to get in touch and I didn't want to hear from him.

A week ago, I had caught Sandra on top of him when I visited him at his office. When I pounded on the door, he opened up and was completely speechless.

"I see that you've really moved on," I had said coldly.

Sandra had smirked in the background while buttoning her shirt back up. I'd noticed that her bra was hot pink. With her hair down, she'd looked even sexier.

"Is this what you've been doing while we were apart?" I asked.

Sterling shook his head. "Emma, we were just..."

"I saw what you were doing. And it looked like you were enjoying it too."

"No!"

"No?" Sandra raised her ever-arching eyebrow. "It didn't seem that way to me."

"We were just, uh..."

I'd never heard Sterling stutter before. Completely silent and brooding, yes, but guilty and stuttering, no.

"There's lipstick all over your face," I pointed out.

Sterling just blinked at me, looking stupid with all that pink gunk smeared all around his lips. Some sounds came out of his mouth, but they weren't coherent words. I looked back at him with what was probably a hurt expression.

"I came here to tell you that I chose you," I snapped, "but you obviously chose someone else."

Sandra was smoothing her hair back into a neat bun and she smiled at me in her usual patronizing way. I'd never seen Sandra with makeup on before. She must've gotten gussied up once in a while to seduce Sterling. I wanted to smack both of them, but I resisted.

Instead, I turned on my heel and stormed out.

Sterling didn't even run out after me, so I figured there was nothing more he could say.

I guess I didn't know Sterling as well as I thought I did after all. We had been high school sweethearts until we graduated. Then he broke up with me, and I was crushed.

Long story short, I moved to New York, became a singer, dated a few famous and not-so-famous men, and then finally fell in love for the second time in my life with Nick Doyle, the movie star. We even lived together for four years, but we broke up because we were both working and traveling too much. I had wanted to get married, settle down and have children, and at the time Nick didn't.

This past Christmas, I had decided to take a break from recording and touring to spend time with my family. Here in Hartfield, my hometown in Ontario, I reconnected with Sterling again and we started seeing each other. I thought that we were returning to the passionate romance we used to have as teenagers.

But now I was starting to think that Sterling could have passionate romances with anyone. At least Nick only faked it with his leading ladies. Sure, he had dated his share of beauties before we were together, but he was always the monogamous type, despite how the press tried to portray him to be.

Sterling tried to get in touch with me the day after I caught him, but I was too sick to my stomach to see him and listen to his lame excuses. He even came around once, but I told my parents to tell him to scram.

While I avoided Sterling, I also managed to ignore my manager Rod and everybody else trying to book me for promotional appearances, interviews and performances for my third album release on Valentine's Day. I had responsibilities, and this was the first time in my life that I actively avoided them.

All I wanted to do was to hide. I'd spent most of my twenties in the music industry. I was only supposed to be taking a short break over the holidays, but I had extended it to February. Would this still be considered a quarter-life crisis if I was almost thirty?

Mirabelle poked me in the ribs again.

"You've got to go outside," she said. "Get some fresh air for God's sake."

"It's freezing outside," I said.

I knew I was being whiney, but I couldn't help it. I thought I was over being the vulnerable girl so sensitive to failed romances. My songs were all about heartbreak and I was sick of singing those songs. For my fourth album, I would record happier songs, reinvent myself. Right now, I just didn't feel up to it. I didn't feel up for anything.

Being a celebrity didn't make you immune to heartbreak. The industry was tough, love was tough, the whole world was tough and the safest I felt was inside my parents' home in Hartfield.

"Really, Emma." Mirabelle rolled her eyes. "It drives me crazy looking at you in that robe and those lame bunny slippers. Just get off your ass. Be one of the judges for the baking contest, get involved in something. It'll get you out of yourself, then you can go back to writing those happy songs that you were so excited about last week."

I grunted, then turned away from her on the couch.

"Also, do you want to throw me a baby shower?"

"A baby shower?" That got my attention. "You're

due next month and we haven't had a shower yet, that's right."

"So can you plan it?"

Gingerly, I sat upright. I'd been watching trashy reality TV shows all day and my brain and body both felt like mush.

"Of course I'll do it," I said with some excitement. "You're right. I have been dwelling on this whole Sterling thing too much. I definitely need to get out of this slump."

"I thought it would be good for you," Mirabelle said. "Since you don't want to go back to work yet and you don't even want to go outside, you need something to keep you busy."

"There are loads of cheesy baby shower games we can do," I said, the gears in my head turning. "It won't be one of those lame baby showers. It'll be fun and it'll have plenty of alcohol!"

"Great," said Mirabelle. "Except that I can't drink."

"It'll have plenty of apple juice!" I said.

"Now are you going to be a judge for this contest or what?" Mirabelle asked.

Hartfield was holding its third annual baking contest this weekend. Mirabelle, the owner the Chocoholic Cafe, which was the most popular cafe in town, was a sponsor of the event. The contest was open to all Hartfield residents except for professional bakers. The other two judges were one of the bakers who worked for Mirabelle, and another who worked in the supermarket's bakery section.

The contest lasted all weekend. The first round on Saturday required all the entrants to bring in cupcakes for a blind taste test. The best four entrants would move on to the next round, which required them to bake a cake on site on Sunday. The cakes were judged for taste, originality and presentation.

I did want to participate. My sister knew me well. It was exactly the kind of thing I wanted to do. I would've been more excited about it if I hadn't been in such a strange, hermetic mood lately. But Mirabelle was right—I had to take action to snap myself out of this depression. I couldn't let one guy get me down. Wasn't that what I sang about in one of my songs? I had to walk the walk.

"Right," I said, stretching my arms out. "I will be a judge for this baking contest. Count me in. Now if you'll excuse me, I'll be taking a long, hot shower."

"Atta girl," Mirabelle said. "Good idea. You were starting to develop some serious B.O."

Before I could make it up the stairs, the doorbell rang. I froze, afraid that it was Sterling.

CHAPTER 2

I made silent gestures to Mirabelle for her to get the door, but she simply shook her head, insisting that I do it.

I looked through the peephole. It was a guy who looked vaguely familiar. He wore chunky black glasses and was shivering in a hooded winter coat. Tentatively, I opened the door.

"Can I help you?" I asked.

"Hi, I'm Aaron Sanders, writer from *Rolling Stone*. I'm looking for Emma Wild?"

That was how I knew him. Shoot. A journalist in my home when I was in such a dishevelled state?

"I'm Emma Wild," I said.

Aaron gave me a quick once-over.

"Oh," he said. "Of course."

He flashed his own embarrassed smile. He probably had an image of me as a femme fatale, since the cover shoot for the magazine had been film noir-themed with lots of heavy shadows and sultry makeup.

"I look like crap without makeup," I said. "Print that if you want."

"No, you look beautiful," he said, mustering as much sincerity as he could.

"I don't mind," I said. "Maybe it'll make it easier for young girls who look up to me to know that. I hate it when they Photoshop me in pictures. But where are my manners? Come on in."

He stomped the snow off his boots on the Welcome mat and stepped in, still shivering. "I don't know if you remember me, but I interviewed you last year."

"Yes, of course I do. It was for that profile."

"It was pretty quick."

"I remember everyone who interviews me." I did too. At least their faces. Their names were much harder to recall. "Would you like some tea? And I think we have some homemade creamy zucchini soup if you're hungry."

"That would be great," Aaron said. "Sure is cozy in this town. It's a long way from Los Angeles."

"You're from L.A.? I love that city. I've been meaning to go back."

Aaron was so cold that it took him a while to take off his coat. What did you expect from a Californian? He was in his early thirties, with a slight bald patch. I had done a quick Q&A with him when I was doing a flurry of interviews in a hotel in Los Angeles a couple of years ago to promote my second album. He seemed okay. His write-up hadn't been so bad, but he didn't kiss my ass either. Some journalists were nice to your face, but wrote scathing things once they were back at their desks.

"I'm sorry to intrude on you in your home," he said. "But as you know, the issue with you on the cover is going to print in a couple of weeks and we still don't have an interview. Your manager said the best thing to do was to catch you down here. He said you weren't answering your phone."

"I have been sort of M.I.A.," I admitted. "I'm sorry about that. I'm recovering from...an illness."

"Oh. I'm sorry to hear that. Are you okay?"

"Yes. It was the flu." I faked a couple of coughs. "Almost over it. Sorry that you had to come all the way down here."

Aaron chuckled. "Canadians do apologize a lot, don't they?"

"Yes, we do," I said. "Sorry about that. I haven't been in the right state to talk to anyone, but I'm feeling much better now. Might be able to return to work soon too."

"I understand," he said. "I had the flu last year too. It was horrible. I thought I was going to die."

We went into the kitchen, where I put the kettle on for some tea. Mirabelle came in and introduced herself.

"So, are you staying somewhere in Hartfield, Aaron?" Mirabelle asked.

"Yes, I'm staying at the Sweet Dreams Inn."

The Sweet Dreams Inn was fit for a grandmother. It was all floral wallpaper, porcelain plates and crocheted afghans. It had been taken over by new management recently, by a Japanese couple in their late forties.

"Charming place," I said.

Except that it was rumored to be haunted, and the owner was murdered there by her son's girlfriend on New Year's Eve. But I didn't tell that to Aaron.

"Yes." Aaron chuckled. "Charm is the right word. I hope it's okay that I'll be following you around this weekend."

"Sure," I said.

I wasn't thrilled about it, but I supposed this was my punishment for not returning my manager's calls.

"What's a typical day like for you here?" asked Aaron.

"Well, since I'm feeling better now, I'm going to be throwing a baby shower for Mirabelle."

"Not just that," Mirabelle said. "She's judging the annual Hartfield baking contest this weekend."

Aaron smiled. "A baking contest?"

"Yes," I laughed. "Very quaint, I know. The first round is cupcakes."

"I can see why you like living here. You usually live in New York, right?"

"Yes."

"But you recently broke up with Nick Doyle. Was that why you moved?"

I laughed off his question. Part of my media training with my PR people was that whenever someone asked a personal question, you had to try to laugh it off as if it was the silliest thing ever you've ever heard.

"No, I still live in New York. Why wouldn't I? Hartfield is just where my family is."

"And what about Nick?" Aaron pressed. "How's he doing? Is it true that he'd been in Hartfield to visit you recently?"

I fake laughed again. Aaron was a nice guy—many journalists were—but it was his job to ask the questions the readers wanted to know the answers to, so I couldn't blame him. Not too much anyway.

"He's on a shoot right now in Morocco is what I know."

"We never got official word whether you were broken up or not."

I smiled sweetly. "I really can't talk about Nick. We have an agreement never to talk about each other to the press, to keep some semblance of privacy, you know?"

"So you are still together," Aaron said.

He had me cornered.

Were Nick and I together? I didn't know. Now that Sterling and I were over, I didn't know if Nick still wanted to be with me. Maybe there was truth in the rumor that he was cozying up with his co-star Chloe Vidal, the twenty-two-year-old blonde bombshell who was the latest It girl in Hollywood. Their photos were splashed all over the Internet. In one of them, they were having ice cream together on the streets of Morocco. I just hoped that Aaron wouldn't want to bring that up. I was barely over Sterling with Sandra.

"Oh, Aaron." I smiled mysteriously and shook my head in a teasing way. "You're just going to have to ask him. Anyway, you're from *Rolling Stone*, not *People*. Shouldn't we be talking about what really matters?"

"Politics?" He joked.

I mock rolled my eyes. "Of course not. The music."

This got the ball rolling on talking about my third album, about the producers I worked with, my vision and my influences. But as I spoke, I thought about what a pain it was going to be to have a journalist following me around in my hometown. It was my fault for taking the battery out of my cell phone. I could've given a phone interview if I would've known.

CHAPTER 3

After Aaron left, I breathed a sigh of relief. I'd dealt with worse, and he wasn't so bad, but I didn't like the feeling of being watched all the time. You'd think I'd be used to it by now.

"How exciting," Mirabelle said. "A *Rolling Stone* writer following you around."

I shrugged. "I wish he wouldn't."

"You've got nothing to hide."

"Except my personal life, which they always want to know about."

"What is going on anyway? I'm your sister and I don't even know. So are you going to get back together with Nick?"

I plopped back down on the couch and sighed.

"I don't know. He wrapped his film, but he hasn't

tried to get in touch or anything. Maybe that's over too."

"Do you want to be with Nick?"

I shrugged again, trying to look nonchalant about it. Sure I did, but he had probably moved on. Mirabelle could tell I didn't want to talk about it, so she changed the subject.

"Well, instead of choosing between boys, you get to choose between baked goods."

"You're probably right. The contest will be fun tomorrow. However, I've been packing on the pounds. I'll have to get back to my intense exercise regime soon."

I got up from the couch, feeling my stomach jiggle. Whenever I gained weight, it all went to my stomach. It was easier to hide under loose-fitting shirts, but my work required sexy, tight-fitting dresses.

"Sure is hard to be a celebrity," Mirabelle teased. "I've got to go home for dinner, but I'll pick you up tomorrow for the bake-off."

"Good night."

I went upstairs and took that long overdue shower and felt refreshed.

When I got out of the bathroom, I listened to some Ella Fitzgerald in my room and relaxed for a while.

After a week of incubation, trashy TV, heartbreak and boredom, my life was getting back its motion again. Things were speeding up all around me. The reporter, the bake-off, and the baby shower. Okay, so it wasn't exactly a lot. Not compared with my work life. Touring really took a toll on you. So did interviews and photo shoots and walking the red carpet. Not to mention getting chased by the paparazzi in your sweats.

I took out my notebook and started writing down ideas for Mirabelle's baby shower. I would invite only our closest female friends and hold it at this house. I'd make a banner that was a cutout of a baby-bottle with spilt milk. "Mirabelle's Baby Shower" would be written in the milk. There should be at least five baby shower games, like *who could suck the beer out of the baby bottle fastest* and *guess the mystery chocolate in a diaper taste test*.

Planning this baby shower excited me more than talk show appearances, awards parties and photo shoots that I was beginning to wonder when I'd ever want to go back to work.

By nature, I was simply a creative person. The celebrity thing was never really a goal. I had always wanted to sing and create. And now, I wanted to make the invitations to the shower by hand. I was pretty good at paper crafts, and I planned on making a pop-up card, where a baby would be springing out of a card shaped like an egg when the egg opened up.

In the back of my closet, I found my old box of craft supplies. There were construction paper, tape, stickers, doilies, goggly eyes and all sorts of other random knick-knacks that I had kept from when I used to do crafts when I was young. And by young, I meant up to my late teens.

Even now, I thought that if given a piece of paper and some scissors, I'd be happy for hours. I was a big kid at heart, which was why I wanted to have kids of my own soon.

In two hours, I managed to get eight invitations finished. I drew different expressions on each baby's face for a personal touch.

Mirabelle was going to have a son, but she wanted the shower to be gender-neutral. She didn't believe that only girls liked pink and boys liked blue. She wanted to be an open-minded parent and raise her son without conditioned gender preconceptions, so she didn't mind if we bought "girly" toys or pink things.

She felt this way because she had been a tomboy growing up but was reprimanded for liking boy's toys, which she thought had been unkind of my parents.

I wondered if I was going to have children of my own anytime soon. For a while there, I imagined myself marrying Sterling, settling down in Hartfield, being a stepmom to his two little girls, and having more kids of our own.

But now it looked like I would have to start at square one. I hadn't heard from Nick, even though his film shoot had wrapped. Maybe now that he was back in his Hollywood lifestyle of film shoots and press junkets, settling down with a family didn't matter as much as he claimed it did. My fears were probably realized: he had been chased me only when I had broken up with him. Playing hard to get—even though I wasn't playing—could get a guy to do crazy things sometimes. Maybe after some time away from me, he finally came to his senses.

I sighed as I made my ninth baby card. For now, I would just play with Mirabelle's baby and live the family life vicariously through her. She did the same thing with my celebrity lifestyle, enjoying the perks like attending parties with me sometimes and staying in posh hotels. Maybe I could just enjoy playing with a cute baby without all the work that came along with being a mother.

The thought cheered me up when the doorbell rang again. I hoped it wasn't Aaron, back with another load of questions about my love life.

I went downstairs, still wearing my fluffy purple robe and matching slippers. Nobody else was in the house. It was Friday, Mom and Dad's date night, when they wined and dined and enjoyed each other's company. It was sweet really. No wonder their marriage had lasted over thirty-five years.

I looked through the peephole again.

Yikes.

It was Sterling, looking really handsome even through the warped peephole.

"Emma," he said. "I know you're there. Can you please open up?"

"Just because I'm here doesn't mean I have to do anything," I said.

"Please, it's been a week. Can we talk?"

"Talk about what?" I said.

"About—you know what about."

I flung the door open, not even caring that my red hair was still wet, or that I wasn't wearing anything underneath my robe. Since Sterling was intruding on my time in my space, he would have to deal with it.

His eyes widened at the sight of me, and then he looked away when he found himself staring.

"May I come in?" he said.

"Fine. But you're not getting any tea or coffee."

He stepped in. His coat was covered with snowflakes and I resisted the urge to wipe them off, as I would have in the past.

Sterling sat on the couch, which made me avoid it. I sat on the sofa instead.

"So talk," I said.

"About last week," he started uncomfortably. "It isn't what you think. Sandra and I were not getting hot and heavy in the office all the time. That day, she closed the doors and the curtains and just sort of started kissing me."

"Out of nowhere, she started kissing you? Isn't that considered sexual harassment or something?"

"Yes, well, I admit I wasn't entirely innocent. I didn't exactly fight her off."

"Right. I noticed. You looked quite comfortable from what I could tell."

Sterling sighed. "I don't know what to say. This might sound really lame, but I was under a lot of stress that week."

"And you wanted to blow off some steam?"

"Sure, we get along and she flirts with me sometimes, and she is attractive, but I want to be with you. I have to admit it was difficult when I couldn't see you last month. It was a blow to the ego that you had to think about whether you wanted to be with me or your ex-boyfriend. I thought about it and I know that you're ultimately going to choose Nick. He was the one who left town."

"You said you were willing to give me the space. I had just gotten out of a breakup and I was confused."

"So was I," Sterling said. "I just felt rejected, and when Sandra was showing me attention, I was flattered. I know it's no excuse, but..."

He didn't know what else to say. This what was so aggravating about Sterling sometimes. He had a difficult time verbalizing how he felt. He was hurt because of the whole situation with Nick, and he took solace in the first brunette co-worker that shoved her cleavage in his face.

And I wasn't having it.

"Look Sterling, I know this was a difficult situation, but I'm looking for someone who wants to be with me and only me. You said that you did, but your actions say that you don't believe we have a chance. And I'm starting to think that we don't either. I'm looking for someone who's secure with himself and won't hook up with floozy co-workers if things are not going well in his relationship."

"Emma, I'm an idiot. I didn't think I had a chance."

"You said you were going to fight for me this time. But you never do." I shook my head. "No, I can't see us working out in the long-term. Being hurt by you once is enough."

Sterling's expression dimmed. "It's not as if Nick is innocent. You don't think he's with his co-star?"

I pressed my lips together and didn't answer.

"Just because you've never caught him, doesn't mean that he's been loyal."

I met Sterling's grey eyes. I couldn't believe that he would deflect this to Nick.

"This has nothing to do with Nick," I said. "Whatever he's doing doesn't concern me. I never said that we were together. Maybe he is with his co-star now, or maybe not. But when we were together, he was always faithful to me. I know that."

Nick just wasn't the type to cheat. Sure, other woman wanted him to, but he had been raised well. Nick was a mama's boy and treated women with respect.

Now that I thought about it, Sterling's parents divorced because his father had skipped out on the family to be with another woman. Did the apple fall far from the tree? Sterling was also divorced. Maybe he didn't know the first thing about how to make a marriage work.

I just couldn't risk giving up my career to be with someone who might not be worth it in the end.

"I'm sorry, Sterling. It's over. I hope you're happy with Sandra. I think you two have more in common anyway."

"Emma..."

I looked at him again expectantly, but he had nothing to add to that.

"I guess it was never meant to be anyway," Sterling finally said. "You have this huge career, and I'm just a small town detective. It was never going to work."

I nodded coldly. "It wasn't. You're right."

He stood up and made his way to the door. I sat where I was and watched him leave without another word.

When he left, I allowed myself to cry.

CHAPTER 4

*B*y the time Saturday rolled around, I was in a much better mood. If I weren't a judge, maybe I would've even entered the bake-off. Baking was relaxing, but I hadn't had much time to do that for the last few years. Once in a blue moon, Nick and I used to bake apple pies together in our New York apartment. In fact, Nick had done a lot of baking with his mother growing up, which I always thought was sweet.

The first round of the contest was in the early afternoon. The contestants brought their cupcakes to Hartfield High's gym, which was set up with tables, and the judges would just have to taste them and announce the four finalists. The rest of the day would be spent socializing and eating the rest of the cupcakes.

Mirabelle picked me up in front of the house. She was looking pretty classy in a black knitted dress under her black winter coat. We drove off to the high school. The reason the contest took place there was because they had a cooking classroom with six ovens that we could use for the Sunday portion of the contest when the finalists had to bake on the premises.

Aaron was already waiting for us in front of the high school when we pulled up. He was sipping from an extra large cup of coffee, from the Chocoholic Cafe no less. Mirabelle approved.

"What's that you have there?" she asked him.

"The Chocolate Americano," Aaron said. "I'd never had a Chocolate Americano before."

"It was Emma's invention," Mirabelle said proudly.

"Really?" It was the most impressed I'd ever seen Aaron. "This is amazing. Grammy winner and coffee genius."

"You just add some chocolate to it," I said. "No biggie. Adding chocolate to anything makes it better."

"Hence, the Chocoholic Cafe," said Mirabelle.

"Genius family," said Aaron.

The three of us went inside the gym, where many of the long tables were already full of cupcakes.

"We're going to try all these?" I exclaimed. There were at least forty contestants.

This was my first bake-off at Hartfield. They only started this tradition three years ago, and I'd missed every single one of them. Part of the reason I wanted to stay in town was probably to do stuff like this, which I never got to do anymore.

Aaron must've read my mind.

"No wonder you don't want to go back to New York," he joked.

When all the contestants sat down, Mirabelle went up to make her opening speech.

"Welcome to the third annual Hartfield Bake-off. It's a privilege to have you all here today. As you know, the winner receives a romantic getaway to Hawaii for two, courtesy of our sponsor, Sunstream Travel. You'll also get the coveted Chocoholic Cafe VIP card, which is good for one year's worth of free hot chocolate from my cafe."

The crowd cheered. She introduced the judges, and we each got up on stage. People snapped pictures, and a few people screamed my name, but this was a mild audience compared to my sold-out concerts. The pictures might end up in the town paper, although they could make their way to the tabloids and the Internet. I didn't mind too much, except the execs at my record company might be upset to see that I'd chosen cupcakes over promoting my new album.

The contestants were all of different ages, and there were almost as many males as females. I had assumed it was going to be mostly old ladies, but I was wrong. My dad wanted to enter, but he couldn't because there was a judge in the family, not to mention Mirabelle was also a sponsor.

Mirabelle announced that we would be doing our first round of blind taste tests soon. They had to start preparing their entries by cutting their cupcakes into four pieces, placing them on a tray and writing their entry number on the blank tag that they were given to put in front of the cupcake.

After that, we tried over forty cupcake samples. Not all at once of course. We each tried five at a time, and selected the two we liked the most within the five. That we did eight times until we had our top sixteen. Then the judges compared notes. The cupcakes that were favored by two or more of the judges got a pass into the top eight. If we disagreed, we had to try the ones the other judges picked and decide on the best ones collectively.

Once we had our top eight cupcakes, then we really got down to business in choosing the top four. Most of the cupcakes were delicious. Each judge had their preferences in regards to flavor. I loved red velvet, and the other judge, Mike, who was Mirabelle's baker, was an expert in anything chocolate. The third judge, Sylvia, preferred anything original. The lavender cupcake got her vote.

Some were dry, some were ultra light, some were heavy on cream, some were enormous and some were half the size of what cupcakes should be. In the end, we chose four great cupcakes: vanilla, strawberry, lavender, and chocolate Oreo. They didn't taste artificial, the frostings were rich and the cakes were moist but fluffy.

When we announced the winners, they went up the stage to receive their finalist ribbons.

Lena Mumson, a brunette in her thirties, looked very smug about the win. She had made the scrumptious lavender cupcakes with the lemon frosting.

Cherry Anderson, a pretty girl with honey blond corkscrew hair, had made the fresh-tasting strawberry cupcakes with fresh strawberries sticking out on top of the whipped cream frosting. She grinned from ear to ear as she bounced up the stage.

Demi Lauriston, a bottled blonde, had made the vanilla cupcake. She went up the stage carrying her youngest son in her arms. I gave the boy's little hand a high five when he passed by.

Larson Davies, a slightly tubby man in his mid-thirties, had made the chocolate Oreo cupcakes, to my surprise. He wore a soccer jersey and looked too athletic to be the baking type. His Oreo cupcakes were amazing. There was even a "surprise" melted Oreo at the bottom of the cupcake.

The four posed for a picture together after shaking our hands. Cherry had squealed when she shook my hand, saying that "Cornflower Blues" was a favorite song of hers and that she loved me. I gave her a hug.

"So that's our final four," Mirabelle said into the mic. "They'll be back tomorrow afternoon for the final cake bake-off. Remember, a romantic getaway to Hawaii is in the stakes, as well as free hot chocolate for a year! Now let's divide up the rest of the cupcakes and share them amongst the crowd. Let's party!"

After some mingling and pats on the backs, the finalists went home to prepare their recipes for tomorrow's contest. All except Lena, who stayed and mingled with the rest. Sylvia told me that Lena had won the top prize two years in a row and was gunning for the top prize this year as well. She sure looked confident as she chatted with friends in the crowd. It was if she knew she had it in the bag.

I couldn't take another bite of a cupcake for the day, so I worked the room, signing a few autographs here and there. It was fun to socialize a bit, since I hadn't talked to anyone aside from my family for a while, unless you counted Aaron...and Sterling.

The sting of imagining Sandra on top of Sterling making out passionately was slowly lessening. Soon, I might even forget it altogether. I hoped.

CHAPTER 5

The Sunday judging had gone off without a hitch. The contestants came in and baked their cakes in the cooking classroom. We tried them and announced the winner. The news crew from Hartfield's local TV channel was there to film the whole thing. They broadcasted snippets of the event throughout the evening news. I had to do a quick interview as well, talking briefly about my new album.

Unfortunately, another event made it onto the news later that evening: Lena Mumson's murder.

In the end, she did win—third year in a row.

After the contest ended at the school, Lena received her prize, the news crew left, and so did Aaron and everyone else.

It was already dark when we went outside. Once we reached the car, Mirabelle realized that she didn't have her car keys in her purse. We thought that she'd dropped them somewhere, so we unlocked the school door and retraced our steps back to the cooking classroom.

She found the keys on the ground. It was near the table where she'd placed her bag for the majority of the day.

We would've just gone home if I hadn't wanted to pee so badly. I made a quick dash to the girl's washroom. When I opened the door, however, I noticed a trail of blood coming from one of the stalls.

"Hello?" I called out.

I should've turned away, but curiosity got the best of me. The door of the stall was not locked and I nudged it open with one foot.

Then I saw it:

A dead body. Lena. She'd been stabbed in the stomach and she sat limp, slumped beside the toilet.

I screamed.

"Emma?" Mirabelle called from the hallway. "What's going on?"

She came in, but I pushed her out.

"You don't want to see this!" I exclaimed.

"What is it?"

"Lena! She's dead."

I described what I saw and told her to call the police. I was too shaken to hold a phone in my hand, so Mirabelle did the dialling and talking.

We went back outside and sat in Mirabelle's car as we waited for the police.

"I wonder if the killer's still inside," I muttered.

But it wasn't as if I wanted to find out.

"How could this happen?" Mirabelle asked.

"And when?" I thought about it. "Everybody left in the last hour. Lena must've left only half an hour ago. Who would just kill her when there were probably still people around?"

"It must've been someone who really hated Lena. Maybe it was done only in the heat of the moment."

"Right," I said. "It was right after she won, so do you think it could be one of the other contestants?"

"Oh my gosh. It might. I mean, there was no one else in the building except the news crew. And they had gone first. The school is locked. It couldn't be the other two judges. They came out to the cars with us."

"It had to be one of the other contestants then. I don't see why an outsider would come in and kill Lena in the high school washroom of all places. Someone must've been really sore about losing."

"Now who would want the top prize bad enough?" asked Mirabelle.

"Or hate Lena that much."

"Or resent losing one year's worth of hot chocolate at my cafe," Mirabelle joked. I was too horrified to laugh. "Come on. I'm trying to lighten you up."

"You didn't see the dead body," I said. "It was absolutely disgusting. So much blood."

I shivered.

Police car sirens sounded. I dreaded seeing Sterling. And Sandra. Sterling and Sandra together, recalling that scene where they were rubbing against each other at the office. But I took a deep breath. I was a strong woman. I could handle this.

Half a dozen policemen came out. Sterling was there, but Sandra wasn't, luckily. I wondered where she was, but I didn't ask. What did I care?

Sterling strode over to us in his casual clothes: a black wool coat, opened to reveal a gray sweater that matched his eyes. Why did he have to be so handsome?

"Good evening ladies," he said without a smile. Instead he had that smoldering look that I'd always found appealing. But no matter. If he wasn't going to smile, I wasn't going to smile back.

I knew I was being petty. What was there to smile about? There was a dead body in the ladies room.

"Hi Sterling." Mirabelle nodded at him just as coolly. I was glad to have my sister on my side, and literally by my side.

"What happened?"

I told Sterling about staying at the high school a bit later because we were looking for Mirabelle's keys. And then my discovery of the body in washroom.

The officer took down some notes and left. Sterling followed him to take a look at the scene.

Mirabelle and I were alone again. She wanted to go home, but something told me to stay. What if they found a clue or something? We could help solve the case.

"Oh, Emma. When I said to keep busy, I didn't mean with another murder case. Haven't you had enough?"

"Come on. They're hopeless at solving these things. They take way too long. I could help. What if this killer strikes again?"

Mirabelle's eyes grew wide. "No, don't get mixed up in this. What if the killer comes after you?"

The sun had set, and it was deadly dark around the school. We looked around.

"We'll be careful," I said, then gulped.

Our house had a security alarm turned on at night. Ever since I came back into town and Mom and Dad realized that I wasn't going anywhere after the holidays as expected, they got the alarm installed in case any crazy fans or reporters tried to sneak in. The town was generally free of paparazzi, but they had descended in the past when word got out that I was in Hartfield.

It must've been about forty minutes later that Sterling came back out.

"Well?" I stepped forward. "Did you find anything?"

Sterling looked impatient. I thought he was going to tell me to go home, but he revealed something.

"As a matter of fact, I did."

Sterling held up a ziplock bag with a small gold hairpin.

"This was in Lena's right hand."

Mirabelle and I both gasped. We both knew who it belonged to, and it wasn't Lena.

CHAPTER 6

*C*herry Anderson was the youngest contestant in the top four. She was in her last year of high school, so she knew the premises well. The gold hairpin belonged to her because her corkscrew hair was so unruly that she used a million of those pins to secure the hair in place and keep her curls out of her face.

"We found another in Lena's coat pocket," Sterling said. "Maybe they had been fighting and the pins fell out from Cherry's hair."

"Did you find strands of Cherry's hair in the bathroom?" I asked.

"We did find the type of hair as you described of Cherry's" Sterling said. "Two stalls over, curly blond hair. The washrooms were cleaned by a janitor this morning, although many people have probably been in and out of the bathroom from your crew. There's nobody else with long curly hair, is there?"

"No, Cherry's the only one," I said. "But it could just mean that she used the washroom recently."

"Cherry? A murderer?" Mirabelle shook her head. "She's one of the sweetest girls I know. Comes into my cafe all the time. She wouldn't murder Lena."

Cherry was very nice and smiled often. I remembered that she had been helpful to the other contestants as well, always lending them things, or offering to help if something went wrong. Maybe she thought it was only fair because she was familiar with cooking in those facilities because she went to Hartfield High.

Sterling's expression remained grave. "It doesn't look good. We'll have to take her in."

"There's just no way," Mirabelle said.

"The wound was pretty bad," I said. "You think Cherry really had the strength to do that?"

Sterling shrugged. "Anything's possible. Some people might look weak, but they're not. You just never know with people."

"Yes," I agreed, locking eyes with Sterling. "You just never know with people, do you?"

Sterling turned away.

"We don't have a weapon yet," he said.

"The contestants brought their own tools," Mirabelle said. "And after it was over, they packed up and took them home."

"Which is why we're going to go to Cherry Anderson's house and taking her knives in for testing. She might not have washed all of it off yet. There might still traces of Lena's DNA. Lena's knives were in her bag, still packed and untouched."

Mirabelle shook her head again. "Cherry," she muttered. "No, I just don't believe it."

"It's been a long day, ladies," Sterling said. "Drive home safely. We'll take it from here the rest of the night."

Just then, another car pulled up. A red Corvette. It was Sandra.

She got out in her prim dark coat that matched Sterling's. They should've been related, not dating.

"Come on, Emma, let's go." Mirabelle began unlocking the car.

"Oh, good evening," Sandra said. "Emma, fancy seeing you here. But you're always near the scene of a crime in Hartfield, aren't you?" She chuckled. "It's like that song of yours, 'Trouble Follows Me.'"

"I didn't know you were a fan," I said through gritted teeth.

"Who said I was?" Sandra stepped out of her car in heeled boots. Who wore boots to a crime scene? Did she think she was in a movie?

"Whatever," I said. "Good luck solving the case. You already have the wrong person, by the way."

Sandra's face fell, but she didn't respond. She

didn't even know what she was walking into. Having had the last word, I got in the car and Mirabelle drove off.

"Did you see her face?" Mirabelle laughed.

"I don't know what compelled me to say it. Maybe Cherry did do it, I don't know."

Mirabelle shook her head again. "She couldn't have, poor girl. I think you're absolutely right."

"So who did? One of the other contestants? There's Larson and Demi. Do you know anything about them?"

"Hmm." Mirabelle thought about it. "I do know that Demi and Lena had been hugely competitive in the past. In fact, they're pretty much rivals. They used to be best friends in high school, but they grew apart when they started getting more competitive. Last I heard, Lena was still jealous of Demi. Demi had it all—three kids, a husband, a dog, while Lena is still single in her mid thirties with a cat. Maybe Demi couldn't stand the fact that Lena was winning all these contests and going on fabulous vacations every year."

"Seems plausible." I said. "Although is Demi the killer type? She's a soccer mom. Would she be really that mad that Lena won a bake-off?"

"Before the bake-off, Demi was known as the town's best amateur baker. I mean, everyone would dive for her dessert stand whenever there's a fair."

"Oh, is she the one who made those lemon meringue pies that Mom loves so much?"

Mirabelle nodded. "She's the one."

"So she would be peeved to lose her reputation to Lena. Plus they fought over the same boy in high school or something. Maybe there's an even bigger grudge between them than we know."

"It sure doesn't sound good," I said. "Okay, what about Larson?"

"Don't know much about him. This is the first time that he has entered. He's big into sports, so I was surprised when he did enter, and he wasn't half bad either. That Oreo cupcake of his was killer, and his fudge cake? To die."

"You might want to rethink your choice of words," I said with a smile.

"Oh, sorry. Anyway, he used to date Lena for a few years, but they'd broken up last year and now they're both dating other people."

"Well, that sounds suspicious too," I said. "I mean, an ex-lover winning the top prize. And taking a new man on a fabulous vacation to Hawaii? Did he go on the vacations the previous two years?"

"I don't know," Mirabelle said. "We don't keep track once we give out the prizes. That's what the travel agency does. We could ask them."

"Great. Let's ask them first thing tomorrow. Although, we have to make sure that Cherry is innocent. Are you sure she doesn't have some sort of motive?"

"Let's see...she did want a job at my cafe," said Mirabelle. "But my staff was full. I told her I'd keep her in mind for the summer. She really wants to be a baker. She said she was planning on going to culinary school, so she's quite serious and ambitious about this. She told me she must've worked on two dozen recipes before developing and submitting the strawberry cupcakes. And she was also learning how to decorate cakes on her own. She wanted a part-time job so she could save up for college. I liked her and really wanted to help her."

"Wow," I said. "She does sound very determined. What if I was wrong? Maybe she did do it. She sounds like the competitive type. I'll have to look more into her too."

Mirabelle looked at me from the corner of her eye. "This is looking to be a very busy week for you."

"Certainly is," I said. "And I'm supposed to plan this baby shower in the midst of this murder case."

"I'm starting to think that you're staying in town so you can solve these mysteries. You're certainly not staying for Sterling, are you?"

"Oh, Mirabelle, I'm staying to spend more time with you."

"Uh huh."

"Plus, I think I deserve this break from the industry."

Mirabelle parked the car in front of our parents' house and turned off the engine. She faced me to listen to me.

"I think I'm burned out," I said. "Do I really want to be a famous singer forever? Just thinking about doing promotion for this third album is giving me anxiety."

"I didn't know that," Mirabelle said softly. "I thought you were just going through some relationship trouble."

"I thought so too, but I couldn't bring myself to answer Rod's calls about doing interviews. I think he's cancelling a lot of things for me and getting into trouble. But I just can't seem to face it. If I have to go on another talk show and make corny jokes, I swear..."

"Maybe you just want a long hiatus. Not quit."

I nodded. "Exactly. I was ready to start a family, but now I'm single again, so I guess that's what I've been upset about too. Plus there's this reporter following me around. I felt like I couldn't breathe today." I sighed. "I don't know what I want. Maybe I just need to have these distractions. Throw baby showers and do other things that I'm interested in."

"Like criminal investigation?"

"Yes."

"Fine," said Mirabelle. "I think you need this. I'll help you in any way that I can. After all, it is a contest that I'm sponsoring. I can't let the murderer get away with this."

"Okay. Tomorrow, we'll start, but first I'm going to go home and keep working on your baby shower to relax my mind a bit."

CHAPTER 7

"Hi, Emma."

I opened the door early Monday morning to see Aaron. Looking cheerful, he held a cup of coffee in each hand.

"Aaron, hi. I thought you were going back to Chicago. Don't you have a deadline?"

"I was," he said, coming inside without even being invited. "But I heard that someone was murdered last night and you were a witness?"

I took his coffee from the Chocoholic Cafe and thanked him. He sure was addicted to my sister's coffee. He had gotten me a chocolate latte, one of my favorite drinks.

"That's right," I said with hesitation. "But maybe I shouldn't be talking about it."

"I was at the cafe this morning, and I heard other

people gossiping about it. They said that you found the body."

"Oh no," I said. "How did word get around so fast? I mean, I thought investigations were supposed to stay confidential."

"It is a small town." Aaron shrugged. "I thought word always spread faster in small towns."

"I suppose." I sighed and took a long sip of my latte. Then I briefly explained what had transpired the night before.

"So, are you going to investigate?" Aaron asked.

"What do you mean?" I feigned ignorance.

"Well, I've asked around, and people here seem to know you more for solving murder and kidnapping cases than for being a singer. You've got quite a reputation here."

"I do?" I was surprised. Sure there'd been a write-up or two in the paper when I helped the mayor figure out who had kidnapped his kids last month, but I didn't know that people thought I was some sort of Miss Marple.

"Sure," Aaron said. "So, you're going help figure out who the murderer is, right?"

"Er. I don't know. I mean, I have to fly to Los Angeles soon to appear on a talk show."

"But we both know that you won't," Aaron said with a smile. "Look, I have an extensive background in journalism, sometimes investigative journalism. Maybe I can help."

I looked at him. He really didn't mean any harm. In fact, he looked excited by the prospect of working on a murder case. Maybe he was like me, bored with his daily routine and wanted to do something different.

"Fine," I said. "Can I trust you?"

"Yes, of course," he said. "I won't print anything sensitive in the article about this case."

"Can I have final approval of my article before it runs?"

"Okay" he said. "I have most of it written anyway."

"That was fast." Aaron sure was a professional.

"But I'm looking for something else to add," he said. "A different angle of you that no one else has seen before. An intelligent side."

I laughed. "Thanks a lot!"

Aaron chuckled too. "I'm sorry. I mean, celebrity interviews are always so, *blah*. It's more interesting when I stumble across someone with interests outside of the industry. So crime fascinates you. I can see that from some of the darker imagery in your lyrics, but the fact that you get to solve crimes in real life, well, that could be a real story."

"If we do solve the case, we don't have to write about it in detail, do we?"

"Well, why not?"

"Private investigators stay, well, private."

Aaron frowned. "So really, you just want to be a celebrity who moonlights as an amateur sleuth?"

I nodded. "Exactly. If people know that I'm good at this, they'll be cautious around me."

"Hmm, okay. Fine. We'll cut out the Nancy Drew angle then. But I still want to help you on this case."

I briefed him on everything Mirabelle and I had discussed about who the killer might be, and how we were visiting the travel agency that morning for information. But I told him that I needed help with the Cherry situation. She was being detained at the police station. Evidence was mounting against her, and maybe Aaron could go see what was happening. I certainly did not want to see that Sandra ever again.

"Okay, done," Aaron said. "Cherry Anderson...I'll see what I can dig up at the police station, and I'll find out more about her background."

"Great, thanks. We can meet back at the house later."

After Aaron had gone, Mirabelle came by to pick me up so that we could go to the agency.

"Charles is a friend of mine," she said, referring to the manager at Sunstream Travel. "So hopefully he'll let us know who Lena took on the vacations with her."

"By the way," I said, "I think we have a new ally."

I told her that Aaron was interested in helping us with the case.

"That's great," she said. "As long as we can trust him."

"He says I get final approval on the article, which is nice of him, because they never let me do that."

"Okay." There was doubt in her voice. "As long as he's more of an asset than a hindrance. I just don't trust these reporters. Remember that one woman who pretended she was your long lost BFF, then wrote the most hateful things about you? Horrible. And that other guy who kept trying to hit on you?"

I sighed. "I don't know Aaron that well, but he seems okay. Maybe I'm naive, but we do need the help. Sterling and Sandra are certainly not letting me in on anything, Sandra would make sure of it. I need all the help I can get. The murderer is still out there."

"Okay, okay, I'll trust you on this one."

Sunstream Travel was just off the main street. It was the go-to agency for anyone who wanted to book vacations in this town. While people usually booked vacations online these days, many people in Hartfield were still behind on the times and Sunstream's business was still healthy enough that they could afford to sponsor contests.

"How are you, Charles?" Mirabelle beamed at the man with the red hair and matching red beard sitting at the front desk.

"Mirabelle." He shook her hand. "Lovely to see you, as always. And here's the incomparable Emma Wild. My daughter loves your albums."

"Great," I said. "Always happy to have supporters."

"Sophie only had great things to say about you after meeting you on Emma Wild Day."

"It was nice meeting her too," I said, even though I didn't remember her exactly.

"What can I do for you ladies today?" he asked.

"We're wondering about the winner for the contest," Mirabelle said. "Now that Lena has, well, passed away, who gets the top prize?"

Charles made a scowl. "That's right. I haven't thought of that. A tragedy that something like that could happen. I certainly hope it wasn't over this Hawaii trip."

"Who knows what the motive was?" I said. "I suppose the winner is whoever the runner-up is."

Mirabelle looked at me. "Who is the runner-up anyway? I forgot."

"Let's see, Larson's triple fudge scored second highest, so I guess it was Larson."

"Just out of curiosity, who came third and forth?" asked Charles.

"Demi's strawberry shortcake was third. Cherry's black forest cake was last."

"Curious that Demi wasn't at least the runner-up,"

said Charles. "She's usually such a good baker. I always make a beeline for her bakery stand at every festival."

"Yes, she's talented," said Mirabelle. "Maybe she couldn't take the pressure of the competition. In the previous years, she'd been in the top two, almost winning, but losing out to Lena each time."

"It's a shame she won't be getting the vacation this year either," Charles said. "But we'll give it to Larson."

"But he's been on these vacations right?" Mirabelle asked casually. "Because he used to date Lena and she had won the previous times. Surely he's bored of them by now."

"Actually, Lena has never taken the vacation option," Charles said.

"What do you mean?" I asked.

"She always chose to take the cash equivalent, so we would just write her a cheque. I expected to write her a cheque this year as well."

"Wow," said Mirabelle. "Who wouldn't want to go to Hawaii?"

"Maybe she needed the money," said Charles.

"Well, we'll be on our way to tell Larson that he has won the free year's worth of hot chocolate," I said. "Would you like us to ask him whether he'll take the vacation or cash?"

"Sure," said Charles. He gave us his business card.

"Give him that and when he decides, he can call me here at Sunstream. It probably doesn't feel too great to win like this, so he can call me when he's ready."

"Yes," Mirabelle nodded. "It must be tough, even if she was an ex-girlfriend."

"Well, thanks for your help," I said. "I'll be sure to give Sophie a signed copy of my new album when it comes out."

"That would be great," said Charles. "She'll love that!"

"No problem. Oh and by the way, what is the cash value of the vacation?"

"To Hawaii for six nights, it's around $6700."

CHAPTER 8

"$6,700?" Mirabelle mused when we were outside. "That's some luxury vacation. What would she do with that money?"

I thought about it. "Who knows? Maybe she wants to save up for a bakery or something."

"I don't think so," Mirabelle said. "I overheard her talking to one of the judges. She doesn't want a bakery because it's too much work."

"That's right. I think she has her own online business or something and wouldn't have time for that."

"She's right," Mirabelle. "Thank God my cafe is doing well enough that I can hire people. In the first couple of years, I was working six or sometimes even seven days a week."

"You're lucky," I said. "You don't even have to do much these days."

"Hard work pays off. As you would know. Plus, our chocolate coffee mix is going to start selling in supermarkets next month."

"Congrats!" I said. "It's shaping up to be a great year for you. First the baby, then your own product line? That's really amazing. Oh, and this awesome baby shower that's coming your way."

"How's that going anyway?"

"Great."

"It's not murder-themed, I hope."

"Definitely not. It'll be very cute."

We drove to Larson's house. Mirabelle had his address from his contest application form. Like Lena, he also worked from home. Jobs in Hartfield were pretty limited, so there were some young entrepreneurs in town. Mirabelle said that Larson also had his own online business. He sold cell phone batteries online. It was so successful that it gave him the time to bake, which was what he wrote on his entry form anyway.

His house was a bungalow, fit for a bachelor. When we knocked, he greeted us in his bathrobe. Larson was in his mid to late thirties. Blond and losing his hair in the front, he had a slight beard and a beer belly.

He gave us a big smile and apologized for his attire.

"I wasn't expecting company," he said. "I'm so

embarrassed. I just took a shower, which is why I'm not dressed yet. To have Emma Wild in my house too. To what do I owe the honor?"

"We're here to congratulate you on your winnings," Mirabelle said brightly. "I know that under the circumstances, it's a bit difficult to get celebratory here, but you are the second place winner, and so..."

"Yes. I did hear about Lena. It's a real shame. I went over to speak to her boyfriend, Matt, this morning. She has no family here, so it's a tough burden on him with the funeral arrangements and everything."

"Oh, I'm sorry to hear that," I said. "Her parents have passed?"

"Yes," said Larson. "But we've been friends since we broke up, so I wanted to make sure that things were taken care of."

"That's kind of you," said Mirabelle. "Oh and what's that I smell? It's absolutely divine!"

Larson chuckled. "I've been working on my fudge cake recipe. It was passed down from my grandmother, but one of the judges said it was too sweet, so I've been trying to improve on it."

"It wasn't me," I said. "I loved the cake."

"Thank you."

Larson looked down at his robe. "I'm going to change. Would you like to stay here and share a piece of cake with me? It should be ready soon."

"Sure," said Mirabelle.

"Please sit anywhere in the kitchen."

The oven beeped. He put on oven mitts and took out the three cake pans. He turned them onto the racks to let them cool.

"I'll be right back." Larson disappeared up the stairs.

"What do you think?" Mirabelle whispered to me.

I shrugged. "I guess he's okay. Doesn't sound like he has a motive. Maybe we can just find out what Lena has done with the money."

"Okay." Mirabelle was interrupted by a tabby cat strolling along by her feet.

"Hey there," I cooed.

The adorable cat practically smiled. I'd never seen a cat so friendly.

"You are just the cutest." I squatted down to pet the cat. "Where did you come from?"

The cat cozied up to my ankles and purred.

Before long, Larson was stomping back down the stairs, dressed in a blue dress shirt, black pants and dress shoes. The cat disappeared as quickly as it came from the living room.

"You didn't have to get dressed up." Mirabelle laughed.

"Of course I do," Larson said. "A famous singer and the owner of the town's best cafe in my house? I have to look presentable! So, I won the prizes? A year's worth of hot chocolate, huh?"

"And a trip to Hawaii," Mirabelle added.

"But I guess you've been to these all-inclusive vacations with Lena in the past, so you're probably pretty used to it by now, huh?" I watched him carefully.

"Actually, Lena always used to take the cash," Larson said nonchalantly. "Not sure why. I always wanted to go on the vacations, but she just said she needed the money."

"Any idea what for?" I asked.

"Nope."

"Maybe she wanted to invest in something," Mirabelle suggested.

"Nothing I can think of," said Larson. "She makes a good living selling her handicrafts online. Although, I think she mentioned once about making a chari-table donation, but she wouldn't tell me what for."

Larson began spreading the fudge frosting over a layer of the cake on a cake stand. We watched, our mouths watering. It was hypnotizing to watch a cake being made. Even though Mirabelle worked with desserts, I could tell she was salivating as much as I was.

Larson's cake had been pretty delicious at the taste test. I might've even voted his the highest, since

I was such a big chocolate lover, but Lena won the judges over with originality with her caramel cheese-cake, which was just as good, but a bit too sweet for my liking.

He reached into the drawer for a knife to cut the cake. Then he walked back to the fresh cake on the counter. As the blade sliced through the three layers of cake and fudge, it reminded me of Lena's murder. We had to keep focused. We weren't here to enjoy ourselves but to solve a murder case, no matter how delicious and moist the cake looked.

"Here you go." Larson gave us each a huge slice.

"This is delicious," I said. I dug in with my fork and took a huge bite. "So, Larson, were you upset that you weren't able to go on those trips?"

Larson grimaced, but shrugged.

"Well, it was her winnings after all. I couldn't tell her what to do with it. It's not my place."

"But you were together for a while, no?" I asked.

"About four years," said Larson. "But we were too similar, and we both worked from home, which drove each other crazy. I mean, I loved her and thinks she was great as a friend, but we were more like room-mates who couldn't stand each other's bad habits after a while. Maybe it was a good thing that we didn't go on those resort vacations. We would've spent 24/7 together on those trips."

He chuckled. Was he chuckling out of nervousness? I thought I saw his hand shake as he lifted the fork from his own piece of cake.

"So who do you think would do this to Lena?" I asked.

"I thought they caught the killer, Cherry Anderson." He shook his head. "Kids these days."

Mirabelle frowned. "How do you know that?"

"I thought it was common knowledge," he said.

"Cherry's a minor," I said. "She wouldn't be reported on the news if she was taken in."

"I heard a bunch of ladies talking about it at the cafe this morning."

Mirabelle sighed. "This town. Does everyone know everything?"

"Yes, well, it's hard to keep a secret for too long here," said Larson. "I don't know much about Cherry. Do you think she did it?"

"No —" Mirabelle said.

"We don't know," I interrupted. "Anything's possible, right? What do you think?"

"Jealous aspiring baker killing a three-time baking champion? It could happen."

"What did you think of their interactions during the bake-off? Was there a lot of tension between them?"

"I don't know," said Larson. "I was so focused on

my own recipes that I didn't pay much attention. Cherry did give me some advice about the oven. She was nice, too nice, so that I suspected her of trying to sabotage my work."

"Did she?" Mirabelle asked.

"No, I don't think so. I just thought it was odd that she was so nice and helpful to everyone. Except to Lena, that is."

"Why is that?" I asked.

"Lena got grumpy whenever anyone got in her space, so she must've said something to Cherry. I didn't hear what she said, but her tone wasn't nice."

"How would you describe Lena as a person?" I asked.

"Lena, well...you had to know her to like her. She could be very competitive in certain atmospheres. But she was sweet as a kitten once you got to know her."

"Would you say that she had a lot of enemies?"

"Just whoever got in her path." Larson chuckled again. "But seriously. Sure, there are people who didn't like Lena. She stayed in her own bubble sometimes and didn't like to be disturbed. Heck, she wasn't even talking to me a lot when I made it to the top four with her."

"Why?" Mirabelle asked. "Is she that petty?"

"Like I said, she needed her focus to be the best.

There was nothing she liked better than being the best."

"What made you decide to enter the contest this year?" I asked.

"The love of baking," he said. "I've always baked too. That was one of the things I had in common with Lena."

"Would you say you were competitive with her?"

"No. I wasn't anyway. Lena's competitive with everyone."

"So when you entered, you just did it for fun?"

"Yes. In the past, I didn't enter because it was Lena's hobby and I didn't want to compete with her as a boyfriend. But now, why not? We had both moved on with new partners. I liked baking too. Why not have a friendly little competition?"

I smiled. "Yes. And you would finally be able to take a vacation with a girlfriend."

"For sure. Amy's great. We've been seeing each other for four months, but we're already pretty serious."

"Congrats," said Mirabelle. "And to stay friends with a ex too, that takes skill."

"When you live in a small town, you have to stay friends because there's no avoiding them."

Larson chuckled again.

I had asked all I needed to ask…for now. We finished our pieces of cake and thanked him. We gave him Charles's card from Sunstream Travel and passed on the message that he should call to redeem his vacation package.

"Fantastic," said Larson. "Thanks, girls. Come back anytime."

CHAPTER 9

"*T*hat was some cake," Mirabelle said. "I should commission him to bake some for the cafe."

"Let's figure out who the murderer is before we do that," I said.

"What, you think it's him?"

"I don't know," I said honestly. "I mean, he had the right answers for everything. The murderer is always someone you don't expect, right?"

"Except, you are suspecting him, so does that mean he's not guilty?"

"I still don't have the pieces yet," I said. "This money issue might give us a clue. What was Lena doing with it?"

"Suzy works at the bank. Why don't we ask her?"

Suzy was one of Mirabelle's best friends. She

came to one of our girls' sleepovers last month and we all had a great time catching up. She was married to her boss at the bank and would probably be able to help us.

"So let's go then," I said.

"It's lunchtime and I'm not hungry," Mirabelle said. "We shouldn't have had so much cake."

Mirabelle called Suzy and asked her if she was at work. Suzy had just been out grabbing a salad but met us back early at the bank. It was perfect timing because she was booked with appointments and meetings all afternoon.

We parked on the street and went inside. Suzy came out to meet us. She was a perky blonde in a baby blue dress suit. When we were growing up, she'd been a frequent visitor to the Wild house, so she knew both of us well.

"How are you girls?" Suzy asked. "Mirabelle, you're even bigger than the last time I saw you."

"Watch it," Mirabelle joked.

"I'm throwing a baby shower for Mirabelle," I said. "Here's the invite."

I gave her the envelope. She opened it and laughed when the baby popped out of the egg-shaped card. "Cute! Of course I'll be there. Come into my office."

Her office was very bare. No window and just a desk and a computer like all the other offices on the hall. The doors were transparent glass so we could see through them. We sat down and Mirabelle explained why we were here.

"Lena Mumson? The woman who got stabbed?"

We nodded gravely.

"We just want to know a tiny piece of information from her banking transactions," I said.

"Oh gosh. Okay. And you're investigating her murder, naturally?" Suzy gave us a wry smile.

Mirabelle pointed to me. "She is. I want very little to do with murder investigations, actually."

"Come on," I said. "You think this is as fun as I do."

"I could be kicking back with a glass of apple juice and reading baby books right now," Mirabelle joked. "But anyway, any idea what Lena would do with that money?"

Suzy did a search. "This information is confidential...but since it is to help find a murderer on the loose, why not?"

She grinned and began typing furiously on her computer. After scrolling through Lena's banking transactions, she found what we were looking for.

"She did deposit a cheque for $6840 from Sunstream Travel around this time last year, and then she made out a cheque a couple of days later for the same amount."

We both peered at the screen.

"To who?" I asked.

"Demi Williams."

"Oh my god," Mirabelle exclaimed.

"And the year before that, the same thing." Suzy said. "It was $6690 then. Also to Demi Williams."

"So every year Lena wins, but gives the winnings to Demi. But why?" Mirabelle furrowed her brows.

"They're either working together or working against each other," I said. "Blackmail?"

Just then my cell phone rang. It was Aaron.

"Let's meet," he said. "I've got some information on Cherry."

CHAPTER 10

When we drove back to the house, Aaron was already on the porch waiting for us.

"Have you had lunch?" I asked him.

"No," he said with excitement. "I haven't even thought about lunch. I've been busy all morning."

"I'm sure we have something to eat inside," I said. "Come on in."

In the kitchen, I heated up dad's curry stew from last night.

"So shoot," I said. "We have plenty to tell, but you go first."

"Well, the police weren't saying anything. They wouldn't even let me in the building. So I went to the library for a couple of hours to see what I could find on Cherry in the archived newspapers. She's pretty much perfect."

"Perfect?" I wrinkled my nose. "That sounds completely suspicious. Murderers and psychopaths often have a perfect facade. Nobody's perfect."

"Well, she's a straight-A student, always running charitable fundraisers for her high school, and she's very keen on baking. There's even a story in Hartfield High's school paper about her bake sale. Other students participated, but her pies and cakes got their own article because they were so good. She organized the bake sale to raise money for students in Pakistan to receive school supplies."

"I'm telling you," Mirabelle said to me. "Cherry's great. Plus she's super skinny even when she eats all that junk. I would hate her if I didn't like her so much."

"She is eighteen," I said. "Her metabolism is through the roof."

"Cherry said in an interview that her ambition is to ultimately get her own baking show," Aaron continued. "She sounded very ambitious in her interview. She's one of those rare kids who knows exactly what she wants to do and nobody can stop her. I thought it sounded pretty suspect as well. It's plausible that she could've lashed out at Lena from jealousy."

"Is that all you found?" I asked.

"No. I thought I'd try to go back to the station to see if there was anything more I can find out about Cherry and the case. It was impossible, because there were hoards of reporters and TV crews at the front door, but I did catch Cherry's parents sneaking out the back of the police station. At least, I recognized them from one of the pictures in the paper. Her mom had the same corkscrew hair. I followed them in my rental."

"You creep," I joked.

"Yup," Aaron said. "I followed them home and I knocked on their door and told them that I was helping you with the investigation."

"You did?"

"Sure. Like I said, you have a reputation now for detective work. People trust you. Cherry's parents did, and they were more willing to give me more information. They said that Cherry was detained as a suspect and there were no other leads. Things are not looking good because Cherry doesn't have an alibi. She walked home alone that night, and she left around the same time that Lena did."

"All the contestants pretty much left around the same time, didn't they?" Mirabelle asked.

"Yes," I said. "I thought so."

"Anyway," Aaron continued. "They said that Cherry had been upset when she lost and called home when she was packing up. Her eggbeater had malfunctioned, and she'd been stressed out. Her cake had tasted salty and she'd realized that she'd mixed up the sugar with the salt. Then she had to start from scratch, and everything was done in a hurry. Her cake wasn't as good as it could've been. She was really hard on herself."

"Hmm," I said. "Cherry doesn't sound like the type to mix up her ingredients. She's super organized, right?"

"Yes," said Aaron. "I thought the same."

"Foul play," I said. "Somebody was trying to screw up her cake."

"You think it was Lena?" Mirabelle asked.

"There is definitely a Lena-Cherry connection," I said. "After all, why would Lena have Cherry's pins in her pocket?"

"Well, Cherry's hair is so unmanageable that she probably loses them. In fact I found a few at my cafe. She must lose them all the time. It's why she uses the cheap kind. I bet she has a whole box of those pins."

"Now, what would Lena be doing with it?" I thought about it. "It could be that Cherry was the attacker, and Lena had pulled some pins out when she was defending herself...but wouldn't there be more hair in the stall where Lena was, instead of two stalls away?"

"Unless opening the door caused a breeze for the hair to move," said Aaron.

"But Sterling said it was just a couple of strands. It wasn't a clump of hair, which would fall out if they had been in a physical struggle," I said. "If he found a couple of strands, it could've just meant that she just happened to use the washroom sometime in the afternoon that day."

The ringing phone interrupted my string of thoughts. Mom and Dad were both at work, so I went to answer it. The number was unknown on the display and I almost didn't answer it because pesky telemarketers often called at this time of the day. Something compelled me to however, in case it was the police station or someone else with news.

"Hello?"

There was the sound of strong wind.

"Stay out of it," said a muffled voice. *"You and your little sidekick. Stay out of it, Emma Wild. Or off with your head."*

Click.

The caller hung up.

CHAPTER 11

"What's the matter?" Mirabelle asked with concern.

I must've had a horrified expression on my face. I told them about the phone call.

"Did it sound like a man or a woman?" asked Aaron.

"I don't know," I said. "It was muffled, like someone put a piece of cloth over the speaker to disguise their voice."

"Someone knows you're investigating," Mirabelle said. "And I wonder what they meant by little sidekick. Are they talking about me?"

"It could be me," Aaron said. "I have been doing some snooping around here and asking people a lot of questions. It's hard to be inconspicuous in this town. It's so much easier to be a reporter in a big city."

"Oh God," I said. "I hope I'm not putting you guys in danger."

"You have to call the police," Mirabelle said. "Maybe we can still trace the call."

I took a deep breath. "Right."

Even though calling Sterling was the last thing I wanted to do, I did need his help.

Sterling answered on the first ring. I explained the situation and he sighed.

"So you have been involved," he said. "Emma, this is serious. You can't be poking around with a dangerous murderer on the loose."

"I know, but I need your help in tracing this call. Can you get your guys on it? Just five minutes ago. This person called my house."

"Okay," Sterling said. "But please stop investigating."

"Sterling, doesn't this prove that the murderer is still out there? Doesn't this show that it's not Cherry?"

"Emma, I don't know. It could just be a prank. We're doing a DNA test on Cherry's knife set that she took home with her. We'll find out soon if it's her or not."

"Are you investigating other leads at least?" I asked.

"Emma, that's police business. Please just stay out of it."

Funny, he sounded like the caller.

"Just please call me back as soon as you hear where that call was made from."

"Okay," Sterling said.

I hung up. Now that I thought about it, Sterling and I didn't make a good team. He was too stubborn, never open to exploring the whole picture. He stuck to the obvious; he was more logical.

"I hope he does it," I grumbled to Mirabelle.

"Well we can't let one threat stop us," Aaron said. "Now we still have to figure out why Lena was giving Demi all this money."

"Was it a bribe?" Mirabelle wondered.

"What do we know about Demi?" Aaron asked.

Mirabelle shrugged. "She's a stay-at-home mom. Three sons, so that keeps her real busy. Her husband's a sports teacher at the high school."

"Now what would her motive be?" Aaron asked.

"Maybe she was blackmailing Lena for something," I said. "And this year, Lena didn't want to pay and they got into a struggle."

"But Demi wasn't even second place," said Aaron. "She wouldn't even have the title."

"Unless she was simply upset about losing," said Mirabelle. "But why would Lena have paid her off in the past?"

"Maybe Demi really needed the money for something and Lena wanted to help her out," I said.

"But I didn't think they liked each other," Mirabelle said. "They were a couple of years older than me in high school, but even then I was aware that they had some sort of rivalry going, starting when they fought over the same boy and when Demi got to be Valedictorian and Lena didn't."

"Where would she be now?" I asked.

"At home, probably," Mirabelle said. "Or picking up the boys, or running errands. Shall we go pay her a visit and get to the bottom of this?"

"Sure," I said. "If the three of us go, it won't be so dangerous, especially since the kids are around. She can't harm us then."

Just then, the phone rang again on the home phone. I feared it would be the mysterious caller again, but there was a familiar number on the display.

"Hello?"

"Hey, Emma." It was Sterling, calling from the office. "One of our guys traced the call."

"Oh, great! That was quick."

"It was from a phone booth on Foxmore Street, just across from the elementary school."

"Thanks," I said.

"If you run into any more problems, let me know. But please, I'm begging you, stay out of danger. I doubt you'd find much at this phone booth anyway. Do you need security? We can send some security guards."

"Oh, I'll be fine. But thanks for your concern."

"Emma..."

"Thanks Sterling, I appreciate the information."

I hung up again and told Aaron and Mirabelle this new bit of information.

"Why that street?" I asked.

"There's not a lot of phone booths in town," Mirabelle said. "At least, not a lot of working ones. They're mainly for decoration now that everyone's on cell phones."

"But is it near any of our suspects' homes?"

We took out a map and matched it with the addresses of our three suspects. Cherry lived ten blocks away. Larson lived thirteen blocks away, on the opposite side of town. Demi lived seven blocks away."

"But her sons go to that school," Mirabelle pointed out. "Maybe she was on her way to pick them up and found it convenient to make a quick phone call."

"That's plausible."

"Why don't we go check it out?" Aaron said. "Take a look, and then go question Demi."

"Okay, let's go."

When we opened the front door to go outside, there was a small box on the Welcome mat.

"What's this?" I asked.

"God, I hope it's not a bomb," said Mirabelle.

Aaron's chest puffed up. "I'll inspect it, ladies."

It was a simple small white box and a small envelope was on top. We held our breath as he lifted the lid...

"It's just a cupcake," said Aaron.

It was a red velvet cupcake with cream cheese frosting and little red sprinkles on top in the shape of hearts. The cupcake liner was pink, with little hearts printed on them to match. A heart shaped plastic sign was shoved on top that said "Be Mine" in white letters.

I took the note from Aaron's hand and began to open the envelope.

"Let's see, what it says. *Roses are red, violets are blue, Eat me quickly, and guess who?*"

"Is this a clue?" Mirabelle asked. "I mean, I can't tell if this is from a secret admirer or a death threat."

"What if the cupcake is poisoned?" Aaron asked. "We'll have to get it tested."

"It must be from this caller," I said. "He said 'off with your head', and this cupcake makes a reference to *Alice in Wonderland* too."

"Plus, it's a cupcake," said Mirabelle. "The first round of the contest involved cupcakes."

"Although none of the top four made a red velvet," said Aaron.

"It looks like the murderer is playing a sick,

twisted game with me," I said. "I'm certainly not eating it."

"Let's take it to the police," Mirabelle said.

"Fine," I said. "But please, can you do it? I don't think I can talk to Sterling again today."

Aaron looked at me the way reporters did when they thought they had a scoop. "Why? Is he an ex-boyfriend?"

"Let's just stick to the case," Mirabelle gave him a warning look. Then she turned to me. "Okay, I'll drop it off at the station and ask them to get it tested. Let's go. It's after three thirty. Demi should have picked up the kids and gone home already."

CHAPTER 12

*M*irabelle came out of the police station empty handed.

"They'll do it," she told us once she was in the car. "They'll test it for poison. That Sandra didn't look too happy to be interrupted, however. Not sure what they're doing exactly. They think this is a nuisance. She made a quip about not having time to look into the stalkers of local celebrities."

"Local celebrity?" I said. "I'm internationally famous."

"Who is Sandra?" asked Aaron. "Does she work at the station?"

"Just another useless detective," Mirabelle said.

"She's not important," I said. "Let's focus on our next task. Demi is our prime suspect right now."

We drove off in Mirabelle's Mini Cooper to

Foxmore Street to check out the phone booth first. When we got there, there was a commotion coming from the elementary school across the street.

A soccer game was taking place in the field.

"You think Demi's there?" I wondered out loud.

"Probably," Mirabelle said.

"We're in public," Aaron said. "Even better to approach her here."

"It could've been her then," I said. "She could've just slipped out from the game and made the call. It would've been so easy for her."

"True," Mirabelle said.

We looked at the phone booth. There was nothing inside, no clues, but we looked around at the neighbourhood.

"I'm not sure if anybody would have witnessed who the caller was from their windows," I said. "I suppose we can ask around. But let's talk to Demi first."

We searched for Demi in the stands. She was sitting in the middle of the three rows next to two blond boys. One was around ten and the other was around five.

Mirabelle went down the steps to where she was and spoke to her. Demi looked back at Aaron and me with a grim expression. She stood up, then leaned down to speak to her eldest boy before she followed Mirabelle up to where we were standing.

The higher stands were empty and we could talk freely.

"You wanted to talk?" Demi asked.

She looked nervous.

"Yes," I said. "We've been looking into the death of Lena."

Demi nodded. "I figured you would. Do you suspect that I did it or something?"

I looked deeply into her eyes. "Should we suspect you?"

She sighed. "I'm such an obvious suspect. Everyone knows that Lena and I were rivals. But I would never kill her."

"So, do you mind telling us why Lena was paying you the value of the vacations that she won every year at the baking contest?"

Her eyes grew wide. "You know about that?"

"Yes," I said. "Now please answer the question."

"Okay, fine. It's so embarrassing, but Lena was helping me out. Not out of the goodness of her heart, of course. The budget for my husband's sports program was getting cut. Salaries were slashed. Lena knew that if she offered me some money, I would intentionally lose just by a margin in the baking contests so that she could come out the winner."

"What?" Mirabelle exclaimed.

"Yes. She knew that I was the better baker, but she wanted the title. And she knew how desperate I was. We were even going to the food shelter at one point. Once, she saw us coming out of there with two bags of food. I mean, I have three boys. They grow so fast, and we have to pay the mortgage. Sometimes I bake cakes on the side to make money that way, but with three boys, I don't have time, so I just took her money, and lost in the contest. Besides, being second best didn't seem that bad."

"Why does she want to win so badly?" I asked.

"She wanted a book deal," Demi said. "A publisher in Toronto was interested when she approached them after her second win, but they told her they'd draw up a contract only if she won the third contest here in a row. Then that would give her a platform as a three-time baking contest winner in a cozy small town. Otherwise, she would just be a nobody. Who would give a book deal to a nobody?"

"That's all she wanted?" Mirabelle asked.

Demi nodded. "Now, I don't know who killed her, but Lena was very competitive. She did what she could to sabotage the other contestants."

"Why didn't you come forward?" I asked. "To help the police."

"I didn't know what to do. They did have evidence against Cherry, so I figured I'd just let the police do their job. Plus, I was scared. I didn't want them to think that I had something to do with her murder, with this whole money mess."

"You said she tried to sabotage the others?" I asked.

"I don't have proof of that," Demi said. "But Lena was complaining that she was afraid of Cherry overtaking her. Larson she was less scared of, because she knew his capabilities, but Cherry was young and innovative. She was a threat to Lena, so she definitely must've done something to sabotage Cherry if she came last."

"Wow," said Mirabelle.

"So that's why I thought maybe Cherry found out and they had a fight over it. Cherry stabbed Lena and ran. The police got her and I thought the case was over."

"Do you think Cherry did it?" I asked.

"I don't know," Demi said, on the verge of tears.

"But you feel guilty."

She nodded. "I know how mean and difficult Lena can be. If I'd only warned the other contestants, then maybe Lena wouldn't be so hated and dead—now."

"Honestly, we're not so sure that Cherry did it," Mirabelle said. "But Lena had her hairpins."

A thought came to me. "Maybe she picked up the pins and used them to damage Cherry's equipment. Didn't one of you say that her egg beater had malfunctioned?"

Aaron nodded. "I wonder if Lena stuck a hairpin in it to make it malfunction."

"I wouldn't put it past Lena," said Demi. "It sounds like something she would do. After all, it would be Cherry's hairpin, so it wouldn't be traced back to Lena."

"I still don't think it could be Cherry," said Mirabelle. "Once someone at the cafe accidentally spilled hot coffee on her pants, and Cherry was the one apologizing. She's not the type to snap."

"What about Larson?" I asked Demi. "What do you know about Larson?"

"Larson?" she said. "Not much. He and Lena broke up awhile ago. I think Lena complained about who got to keep the cat when they broke up, but that was about it."

"Cat?" I asked.

"Well, I think when they lived together, they kept a cat and Lena wanted to keep it."

"Did she?" I asked.

"I'm not sure."

"Do you really think it's Larson?" she asked. "I don't know him too well, but I always felt sorry for him for putting up with Lena for so long." She pressed her lips together. "Gosh, that's really mean to say, isn't it, now that she's passed away?"

"Wait, what about the phone call?" Aaron pressed. "Emma received a strange call at home today from the phone booth across the street from here."

"A phone call?" Demi asked.

"Yes, a threatening one," I said.

"I swear, it wasn't me. I was with the boys all afternoon. In fact Roddy had a field trip to the science fair and I was one of the parent chaperones. After that, I was here watching the game. I wouldn't be able to leave the boys out of my sight, even to go across the street to make a phone call."

"Fine," said Aaron. "Do you have witnesses? At around 3:30pm."

"Yes," Demi said. "The teachers can tell you that I was here with them, taking the kids back, like I told you."

Her youngest son started crying in the stands below and the older boy was becoming agitated.

"I've got to go," said Demi. "Good luck with the investigation. I'm sorry, but it was humiliating to admit that my family needed help with money. Lena really helped me out and I'm sorry that she was murdered, you know, so if I have to come forward and testify in any way, I will."

We weren't sure whether we hit a wall or we uncovered something new.

But just then, Sterling called with some new information.

CHAPTER 13

Since my cell phone was still turned off, he called Mirabelle's phone.

"So the cupcake is just a cupcake," said Sterling. "It's red velvet with cream cheese frosting."

"Really?" I asked.

"It's your favorite flavor, isn't it?" Sterling asked.

"I suppose," I said. "Who would know that?"

"Maybe you stated it in an interview once."

"Okay, but are you sure there's no poison?"

"No. Our guy said that it would've been detectable right away, but this is the perfect cupcake. Freshly baked, too."

"Sounds good," I said.

"It's probably from a die-hard fan," said Sterling. "With a crush. I'll throw the cupcake away. Do you want the note?"

I sighed. "Sure. Keep it. Maybe it'll come in handy. Did you find out anything new?"

Sterling was silent for a moment. I could tell he was contemplating whether to tell me or not.

"Not yet. Except we did get part of the autopsy report back. She'd been sliced from the stomach up to the rib cage. There *was* a knife involved. We're still waiting for Cherry's results for her knife, so hopefully we'll get an answer soon."

"Okay, thanks."

"Look, I've got to go," Sterling said.

"Go then," I said. "Thanks for the report."

He hung up. Although the cupcake clue went nowhere, the way Lena was killed with a knife stirred some suspicions in me...I had an idea who did it, but I didn't have proof.

"Hey Emma?" Mirabelle called from the living room. "I've got to go to the cafe. Cal is having trouble with the debit card machine."

"Okay," I said. "I'll just continue on with Aaron then."

"The cafe's so close and it's faster if I walk, so I'll leave you guys the car."

"Thanks."

After she left, I filled Aaron in on what Sterling had told me.

"We have to go visit Lena's boyfriend," I said. "I

heard he was gone during the bake-off on a business trip. But he's in town now."

Aaron nodded and grabbed his bag. We were off in the Mini Cooper to Lena's house. They were living together, so we knew where the house was. Lena had mentioned her boyfriend a few times during the weekend. He had lived in a nearby town, and they'd met through an online dating site. He'd moved in with her, but he traveled regularly around Canada for business.

We were just about to knock on the door when we heard voices from the inside.

Two men were yelling at each other.

"Please, put it down," one man was saying. "I promise. I won't tell anyone. You have my word."

"But is your word good enough?" growled another voice.

Just then, Aaron slipped off the porch and made a huge noise. He was holding his ankle in silence while his face expressed nothing but pain.

There was silence from the inside of the house as well. Then I heard whispering.

A man with dark hair and a fearful expression poked his face out the door.

"Can I help you?" he asked.

I was helping Aaron up, who was able to stand.

"Are you Matt?" I asked.

"Yes," he replied.

"Is everything okay? We heard yelling."

"Everything's fine," he said. "Is your friend okay?"

"It's my ankle," said Aaron. "I don't think it's broken, thank God. It's a little sprained, but I think I'll be fine."

"Can I help you with something?" Matt asked.

"Yes," I replied. "We're here to see you, but is everything is okay? We heard screaming."

"I have company over," he said. "Can you come back another time? I'm afraid I'm in the middle of something."

His face expressed nothing but fear. His voice quivered. He slammed the door shut and we heard a locking sound.

"That was weird," Aaron said.

We heard more noises, shuffling, grunting. Someone was coming out the back.

I ran around to the side of the house and saw him. Larson! He was jumping over the fence and running away.

I went inside the house from the back porch and found Matt lying on the floor with a huge gash on one of his arms.

"Oh my God!" I exclaimed. "Are you okay?"

"Call an ambulance," he said. "I feel faint."

"Yes."

I made the call and got some tea towels from the kitchen for the blood that was pouring from his arm.

"It was Larson, wasn't it? I saw him run away."

Matt nodded. "Yes, it's him."

I called Sterling next.

"Did he drive here?" I asked Matt.

"No," said Matt. "Well, I don't know, but I think he came by foot. Snuck in the house through the back."

Sterling picked up.

"Emma? What—"

"Sterling, listen, the murderer is getting away. It's Larson. He's running from the back of Lena's house. I think he's on foot, but he might have a car. You better send all your guys to arrest him right away. He tried to kill Lena's boyfriend just now."

"Wow, okay—"

I hung up and got Matt a glass of water.

"He's crazy," Matt said. "So you know he killed Lena too?"

I nodded. "Well, I suspected him, and I was just on my way here to ask you about Lena's cat. They fought over it and I thought it could've been a driving force behind this murder."

"Well, Lena's cat went missing when I came home from my business trip," Matt said. "Then I saw Larson buying cat food at the pet shop and I got suspicious. They had fought about this cat that was really Lena's pet. Larson gave it to her for her birthday or something. I thought maybe he had the cat and I'd called him to ask about it. He said he knew nothing about it. I went over there this afternoon to ask him about it again. I didn't see the cat, but he got aggressive. Too aggressive. He completely denied having the cat. I'd always thought he was a pretty decent guy. He even came over yesterday to ask me if I needed help with Lena's funeral, so it was strange to see him so worked up about a cat today."

"Maybe he realized he couldn't get out of the lie this time," I said, "because we'd been at his house this morning and we saw the cat. He probably got paranoid."

"Yes, and he came over now with the knife, threatening to kill me. I think he's a little crazy. He's just not right in the head. There was a crazy look in his eyes."

CHAPTER 14

"*H*ow did you figure out who the killer was?" Sterling asked me.

I was down at the police station, filling out a report about Larson. When they caught Larson, there was blood on his shirt. He was running towards the woods, just trying to get as far from the town as possible. He knew that we had figured it out.

He had been close to killing Matt before Aaron and I got there. When he realized that Matt couldn't be killed on the spot without killing Aaron and me too, since we were witnesses, he fled.

"When you told me about Lena's autopsy," I said. "I had this big hunch that it was Larson."

"Why?"

"Because this morning we had been at his house to give him his Chocoholic Cafe gift card for being the runner-up. He was making a cake, and he cut us each a slice. When he took out a knife from the drawer, he walked from the drawer back to the counter where we were sitting and I noticed that he had gripped it with the sharp end of the knife facing upwards. It was the natural way he held a knife. And when you said that the murderer had cut Lena upwards to her stomach, I could imagine him thrusting the knife into someone and ripping upwards."

"Okay." Sterling nodded stoically. "But why did you go to Lena's house?"

"To talk to her boyfriend," I said. "Demi said Lena and Larson used to fight over the custody of this cat that they owned when they used to live together. I saw a tabby cat at Larson's house, so I wanted to ask Matt whether it was Lena's. I wanted to see if this cat was a motive in the murder."

Sterling shook his head. "I've never seen a guy get so worked up about a cat. He has mental issues. In the interrogation room, he confessed, ranting about how Lena broke his heart, destroyed his life and kept the only other thing that he loved: his cat. He was upset that she would shove her new boyfriend in his face. He wanted to get back at her by winning the contest, but when Lena won again, he got upset. He claimed that she taunted him with taking her new boyfriend on vacation with her."

"What about his current girlfriend?" I asked.

"There is no girlfriend," he said. "He claimed to have a long-distance girlfriend, but it turned out that he was just saying that to make Lena jealous. He also thought he had a strong chance in winning the contest, but I suppose Lena knew that he didn't. Valentine's Day was their anniversary. I suppose this could also be a crime of passion. Larson couldn't stand the thought of Lena being with her new boyfriend and keeping their cat, while he was alone. He said that she was really rubbing the vacation thing in his face, telling him how happy she was that she had it all—the boyfriend, the prize, the vacation and how she was going to get a book deal."

So she was probably going to stiff Demi on her money too.

"Larson's going to plead insanity," Sterling said.

"Why did he send me the cupcake?" I asked.

"He said he didn't know anything about it. I told you, it's probably from some fan."

Before I could ask him more questions, Sandra came in, holding two cups of coffee. She passed one to Sterling with an adoring look on her face.

"Hello, Sandra," I said cheerily.

"Emma." She put on a fake smile. "Congrats on finding the murderer."

"You're welcome," I said a little too smugly. "I'm just glad an innocent person like Cherry can go free now. She could've had her life ruined for a wrongful conviction, you know."

"Well, the DNA on her knife didn't come back with anything, so we didn't have anything on her anyway," Sandra said quickly.

"But I'm sure you were just doing your jobs," I said. Even if you were doing it terribly, I wanted to add, but I bit my tongue.

"I'm sure we would've found out that it was Larson in the end," Sandra said.

"Sure," I said. "After he killed Matt, right?"

Sterling looked embarrassed. He cleared his throat. It was my cue to leave.

"If you'll excuse me, I have a baby shower to plan."

On a Sunday afternoon, Mirabelle, Suzy, Mom, and ten more of our closest female friends were competing to see who could suck beer out of the baby bottles the fastest. Mirabelle, being pregnant, stuck with apple juice. Mom won.

Mom could drink anyone under the table. I gave her the prize of a $50 gift certificate to the town's wine store and she yelped in glee.

Then we played "pin the sperm on the uterus," a game I made out of pieces of felt and Velcro. It was a hit. We had to pin each sperm blindfolded and the one pinned closest to the egg on the uterus won.

After that, we spent a good hour decorating onesies for the baby.

It was such a blast that, before I knew it, the shower was over. I had successfully pumped up the competitive spirit in everyone by giving out great prizes to fight over, like gift certificates and chocolate baskets.

The men had been banished from the Wild house. Dad got kicked out to Mirabelle's house to join her husband, and they had their own version of the shower—drinking beer and watching hockey on TV.

Mirabelle was thrilled with the shower. She told me that I should probably become some sort of party planner.

It had been a pretty eventful week.

Aaron's ankle healed. He felt stupid for slipping off the porch step, but ultimately it was for the best, because otherwise Larson would've killed Matt.

Before he left, Aaron let me read the article that would run in Rolling Stone. I loved it. It made me sound human and flawed, unlike other interviews that either glorified me or bashed me. He wrote about my small town interests, my vulnerabilities, and how I was aware of my own flaws but accepted them nonetheless. Aaron said it was his most in-depth celebrity interview, and he was proud of it, even if he didn't get to include the juicy stuff about solving a murder case together.

Cherry was released, of course, and Mirabelle split the final winnings between her and Demi. They had the option of taking the vacation...

together, but they took the money because they both needed it.

The police checked, and yes, they did find one of Cherry's pins in the blender. Cherry was shocked that Lena would stoop so low to win, but maybe it toughened her up a little. Since Cherry ultimately wanted to work in TV, I told her that this experience had probably been good preparation for the industry.

After the shower was over and all of the girls went home, including Mirabelle, Mom and I were home alone. She went into the kitchen to start on dinner when the doorbell rang.

I went to answer it. When I looked through the peephole, I was shocked. It was Nick!

I opened the door to see him holding a bouquet of roses and a cupcake.

"Surprise!" he said.

"Nick?" I grinned from ear to ear.

"I know you hate surprises, but somehow you love mysteries."

I took the cupcake that he offered, the same kind that had been left on my porch.

"It was you?" I exclaimed.

"You didn't guess that it was me?" Nick frowned.

"I thought it was from the murderer."

"What murderer?"

"Oh? You haven't heard?"

"No. There's been another murder here?"

I quickly explained.

Nick shook his head. "Geez. No. On our second date, we shared a cupcake at Serendipity, remember? I had the same cupcake shipped from New York."

"Oh my gosh." My hands went over my mouth.

"In a couple of hours, it's going to be midnight. Valentine's Day. I was wondering what you were doing on that day? Do you have a date?"

"Oh, is it tomorrow?" In the midst of all the chaos, I'd forgotten. "I'm not doing anything."

"Really? Not even with that cranky detective?"

I smiled. "Not a chance."

"Then I have a special date planned for you."

"But why didn't you call?"

Nick shrugged. "I thought it would be more fun to drop in and see you in person. Aren't you glad to see me?"

"Yes. So, you're not with Chloe Vidal?"

Nick laughed. "Why would I be? You actually believed those rumors? Chloe's become a good friend after the shoot. She's like a little sister to me. Plus she's bisexual and in a relationship with the set decorator."

"Oh." I felt stupid. "Why do I always believe the hype about you in the papers?"

I hugged him and he leaned in and gave me the sexiest kiss.

"Come on, if I believed everything I read about

you, I wouldn't sleep at night. There was one last week saying that you had been seen leaving John Mayer's apartment."

"That is such crap," I exclaimed. "You know I've been here the whole time."

"I know," Nick said. "Why are you still here? Isn't your album coming out?"

"Um, I'm still taking a hiatus."

"Sounds good. As long as we're doing it together."

"I'm just so surprised that you're here. I thought you'd moved on or something."

"I told you I wanted to marry you." Nick winked. "You should believe me by now."

I guess I couldn't. Nick Doyle to me still wasn't quite real. In fact, even seeing him in front of me, I still had the feeling that he only existed on movie screens. He was a living legend.

He was only real every time he kissed me.

And he did, again and again on the porch, to prove his existence.

CHAPTER 16

On Valentine's Day, Nick did surprise me all right. In a rental car, he drove me to the countryside where a group of huskies waited for us in the snow. After we shared a glass of champagne from the trunk of the car, we were off on a sleigh ride with the huskies!

It was the most fun Valentine's Day I'd ever had. Every year, Nick made the effort to plan something adventurous but romantic. Last year, we'd gone scuba diving in the Bahamas and had a romantic dinner for two by the sea.

I realized that although Nick did travel and work a lot, he always remembered birthdays, holidays and special occasions, and he put his all into planning special dates for us to experience together. He was a romantic and he loved me. And actions spoke louder than words.

"I hoped I'd given you enough space," he said.

"Space?"

"You know, to think about you and me. The fact that you're not with Sterling tells me that he's history. I always knew that he was a rebound."

I playfully punched him on the arm. "You're so smug. Sterling and I had a history, and I guess I thought we still had something, but coming home wasn't as easy as I thought. It's like trying to relive your youth. I'm too old for that now. Sterling and I are not compatible."

"I always knew you were only right for me." Nick hugged me close.

I pulled back. "There are still things I want, of course, like taking it easy and starting a family. Are you sure that's what you want?"

"Yes," said Nick. "You know that you're the longest relationship I've ever had? I'm so sorry that I had to lose you for a while to realize that you're the one I want to be with for the rest of my life. I'm starting to get up there too, and I do think it's time to talk about kids. I think I would make a pretty good father."

I play-punched him again. He sure was arrogant, but what did you expect from a movie star?

He pulled out a box from his coat pocket. It was

the same box with the same big diamond that I had caught a glimpse of on Christmas.

Nick bent down on one knee, in the pure white snow, in the middle of nowhere.

A cry escaped my lips. Of joy. Nick looked up at me eagerly waiting for one word.

And I gave it to him.

Yes.

RECIPE 1: LENA'S LAVENDER CUPCAKES WITH LEMON FROSTING

Makes around 12-15 cupcakes.

Ingredients:
- 1/2 cup whole milk
- 1 cup all-purpose flour
- 1 tsp baking powder
- 3 tbsp dried culinary lavender
- 3 tbsp softened unsalted butter
- 1 egg

Lemon frosting:
- 4 cups confectioner's sugar
- 1/2 cup softened butter
- 1 tsp pure lemon extract
- Finely grated zest of 1 lemon
- 4 to 5 tsp lemon juice

Combine the milk and dried lavender in a bowl with a lid on top and leave it in the fridge for 6 to 8 hours, or overnight, to infuse.

Preheat oven to 325 degrees F.

Butter, egg and infused milk need to be at room temperature. Line your cupcake pan with cupcake liners. Use a strainer to remove the dried lavender from the infused lavender milk.

In a bowl, sift together the flour, baking powder and salt. Add sugar and softened butter. Mix well (with stand mixer or handheld mixer) until texture is sandy.

With the mixer on low, slowly add the milk into the mixture. Then add the egg. Mix for 15 seconds on medium speed, then scrape the sides and bottom of the bowl to make sure everything is combined. Just don't overmix, as that will result in a dry cake.

Fill each liner 2/3 full. Bake for 20-30 minutes or when a toothpick comes out clean. Remove cupcakes and set on a wire cooling rack until completely cool.

Frosting: Mix the butter with the sugar. Add lemon extract, zest and lemon juice, beating on low speed until smooth. Increase mixer speed to medium and continue beating for around 2 minutes. Add more sugar if needed for spreading consistency.

RECIPE 2: CHERRY'S STRAWBERRY CUPCAKES WITH STRAWBERRY WHIPPED CREAM

Makes around 12-15 cupcakes.

Ingredients:

- •1 2/3 cup + 1 tbsp all-purpose flour
- •4-5 large strawberries
- •1/2 tsp baking powder
- •1/4 tsp baking soda
- •1/2 tsp salt
- •1 cup granulated sugar
- •1/2 cup unsalted butter, melted
- •1 large egg
- •1/4 cup strawberry yogurt
- •3/4 milk
- •1 tsp vanilla extract

Strawberry Whipped Cream:

- •1 1/2 cups heavy whipping cream
- •3 tbsp granulated sugar
- •1 and 1/2 tsp vanilla extract
- •1/3 cup strawberry jam

Preheat oven to 350 degrees F. Line pan with cupcake liners.

Slice strawberries. Use a food processor or blender and pulse until they are a chunky puree.

In a medium bowl, mix together flour, baking powder, baking soda and salt. Set aside

In a large microwave-safe bowl, melt butter in the microwave. Stir in sugar. Mixture will be gritty. Stir in egg, yogurt, milk and vanilla extract until all is combined.

Slowly mix dry ingredients into wet ingredients until no lumps remain. Fold in the strawberry puree. Batter will be thick! Should be enough to divide between 12 cupcake liners.

Bake for 20 minutes or when toothpick comes out clean. Transfer to wire rack; cool completely.

Strawberry Whipped Cream: In a large bowl, whip the cream, sugar and vanilla extract together on high speed until stiff peaks form, about 4-5 minutes. Add the strawberry jam and beat for another 30

seconds. Add more jam if you want a stronger flavor or a pinker color. However, the more jam you add, the thinner the whipped cream will be. Cover and store cupcakes in the fridge for up to 3 days. Serve cupcakes chilled.

RECIPE 3: LARSON'S LAZY FUDGE OREO CUPCAKES

Makes around 12-15 cupcakes.

Ingredients:

- 1 regular package Oreo cookies
- 1 package chocolate cake mix

Frosting:

- 1/2 cup butter
- 8 ounces cream cheese, room temperature
- 1 tsp vanilla extract
- 3 3/4 cups powdered sugar
- 1 package Mini Oreo cookies for decoration (optional)

Preheat oven to 350 degrees. Mix packaged cake mix according to box directions (but do not bake). Line cupcake pan with liners. Place a regular Oreo at the bottom of each liner. Take half of the remaining cookies to chop coarsely and add to the cake mixture. Fill the cupcake liners. Bake for 15 minutes (or time on box directions).

Frosting: Cream butter and cream cheese together. Add vanilla, then powdered sugar slowly until blended well. Chop remaining regular sized Oreos finely (or put them in the food processor) and add to frosting.

When the cupcakes have cooled, frost and decorate with Mini Oreos.

RECIPE 4: DEMI'S CLASSIC VANILLA CUPCAKES WITH BUTTERCREAM FROSTING

Makes around 12-15 cupcakes.

Ingredients:
- 1/2 cup all-purpose flour
- 1 cup sugar
- 3 large eggs
- 3/4 cup milk
- 1 tsp baking powder
- 1/2 tsp salt
- 8 tbsp (1 stick) unsalted butter, room temperature
- 1 1/2 tsp pure vanilla extract

Frosting:
- 1 cup unsalted butter, room temperature
- 2 1/2 cups powdered sugar

•1 tbsp vanilla extract

Preheat the oven to 350 degrees F.

Line your cupcake pan with paper liners.

In a bowl, sift together the flour, baking powder and salt.

In another bowl, cream together the butter and sugar until light and fluffy. Add eggs, one at a time, and then beat in vanilla. Alternate adding the flour mixture and milk, beginning and ending with the flour mixture.

Fill each liner 3/4 full. Bake until golden, around 20 minutes, rotating the pan once if needed. Transfer to wire rack; cool completely.

Frosting: Whip the butter on medium-high speed for 5 minutes, stopping to scrape the bowl once or twice.

On low speed now, slowly add the powdered sugar. Then increase the speed to medium-high and add vanilla. Whip until light and fluffy, about 2 minutes, scraping the bowl as needed.

You can store any unused frosting in the fridge in an airtight container. Take it out when needed and let sit until it's at room temperature, and then give it a quick whip before using.

RECIPE 5: SURPRISE RED VELVET CUPCAKES

Makes around 12-15 cupcakes.

Ingredients:

- 1 cup flour
- 3 1/2 tbsp pure cocoa powder
- 1/2 tsp baking soda
- 1/4 tsp salt
- 1/3 cup and 1 tbsp butter, softened
- 3/4 cup + 2 tsp sugar
- 1.5 eggs
- 1/3 cup + 1 tbsp sour cream
- 3 tbsp + 1/2 tsp milk
- 1 ounce red food coloring
- 3/4 tsp pure vanilla extract

Vanilla Cream Cheese Frosting:

- •3/8 (8 ounce) package cream cheese, softened
- •1 tbsp and 1 3/4 tsp butter, softened
- •2 1/2 tsp sour cream
- •3/4 tsp pure vanilla extract
- •3/8 (16 ounce) box confectioners' sugar

Preheat oven to 350 degrees F. Mix flour, baking soda and cocoa powder in a medium bowl.

In a large bowl, beat butter and sugar with electric mixer on medium speed for 5 minutes or until light and fluffy. Beat in eggs. Mix in sour cream, milk, food color and vanilla. Gradually beat in flour mixture on low speed until blended. Do not overbeat. Fill cupcake liners 2/3 full.

Bake for 20 minutes or until toothpick comes out clean. Cool completely.

Frosting: Beat cream cheese, butter, sour cream and vanilla until light and fluffy. Gradually beat in sugar until smooth. Frost cupcake.

ABOUT THE AUTHOR

Harper Lin is a *USA TODAY* bestselling cozy mystery author.

When she's not reading or writing, she loves hiking, doing yoga, and hanging out with her family and friends.

For a complete list of her books by series, visit her website.

www.HarperLin.com

13711774R00263

Printed in Great Britain
by Amazon